SHOULDER SEASON

A Lake Michigan Lodge Story

Kathy Fawcett

Prologue

There are two major problems with owning a family business my parents didn't anticipate. The first is when there's no family. The second is when there's no business.

My parents left big shoes for me to fill when they passed away. In fact, they left me everything. Except any clue as to how to run the business that they built, or reasons to keep trying in the face of utter ruin.

I'd like to say I've been doing my best. But that wouldn't be entirely true, because I haven't had to do much of anything. My parents created a well-oiled machine.

But all machines and daughters fall apart sometime, don't they?

1

Nobody in my family calls me Kay.

I've been Kaker since I first tried to say Kay Kerby as a toddler.

But sadly, the people who call me Kaker are an endangered species. I don't even need an entire hand to count them—there's my aunt, my uncle, and my brother Tad.

Dr. Theodore Kerby, Tad, has been away from our Lake Michigan home since he graduated from high school. A busy orthopedic surgeon in Georgia, he still calls me when he can. His wife Selby calls, but will not call me Kaker. She says in her honeyed Atlanta drawl that it's too *familyah*, and insists that their girls call me Aunt Kay.

Family cannot be too *familyah*. I believe a nickname is a term of love and endearment—of claiming one's own. That's why it sounded so sweet hearing Aunt June call me Kaker on this beautiful Tuesday morning, the day after Labor Day. On what could be, should be, her very last day at the lodge.

Sitting on the big rock by the shore, drinking my coffee from a chipped Kerby Lodge mug from long ago, I watched the waves tumble over the Petoskey stones. There is a peace and quiet that comes when the last summer guests slam their car doors and drive up the hill towards home. It's an absence of all noise, except the loons and the water.

And the snapping of twigs behind me.

Looking up and over my shoulder, I could see June coming my way, traversing the rocky, uneven terrain.

"I used to love this day," I called up to her, "waiting for the school bus." I felt a catch in my voice, and turned back towards the lake. "It feels so lonely now, June."

A cool breeze snuck up on me, reminding me that summer was over.

June laughed from a distance. "Kaker, you sound like you're ten years old."

As I watched her carefully making her way down the bluff, holding something soft and yellow in her hands, it broke my heart to think she wouldn't be coming back. She and Uncle Zeke had been at Kerby Lodge every summer of my life—and even before Tad and I were born.

They had wanted to discuss their retirement since they arrived three months ago, I was sure, but I couldn't bring myself to have that conversation this summer. They were the last thread of family I had at this supposed family-run business, and I was finding it hard to let go.

Now, though, I felt deeply ashamed. I suspected my aunt and uncle had been watching for signs that I was ready to stand on my own, as the owner and operator of Kerby Lodge. I was certain I'd let them down.

Zeke and June signed on for the great adventure forty years ago, as soon as Mum and Dad decided to turn their new home into a resort. My dad, Fitz, had been away for twenty years with the Army Corp of Engineers, and Zeke, his younger brother, had missed him.

Still a young man at the time, my uncle thought it would be almost bearable to be an accountant in Florida if he and June could escape the sweltering heat and humidity each summer. A few months of swimming and sailing in the cool Lake Michigan waters could be just the ticket, he concluded—in exchange for helping out and keeping the books, of course.

"I got a place on the lake, and no property taxes," he liked to say, and laugh. A joke I never understood until I inherited the inn, and taxes and I became dance partners.

There was always a room waiting for Zeke and June at the house up the hill. The house Dad had built for his and Zeke's mum, Gram Kerby. Since Gram passed away, my aunt and uncle stay there alone. But like Gram, they have become frail. And in the midst of my own troubles, I hadn't noticed. Until now.

The past few years have been rough for Kerby Lodge, and Uncle Zeke's gloom-and-doom spreadsheets—the ones I look at anyway—tell a sobering story. All because the guests are no longer showing up for me the way they showed up for my parents, Fitz and Raya.

There used to be so many devoted families that came to Kerby Lodge, summer after summer. We provided an *Unforgettable Family Vacation*, as promised in the brochure. In return, they provided our family's ample income.

And repeat.

But with the recession, these same families have been cancelling in droves. They're either vacationing elsewhere or staying home. Some may be losing their homes.

Uncle Zeke tried to talk to me about the future of Kerby Lodge several times this summer, and I brushed him off. "Let's wait until peak season is over," I had said. I was trying on a phrase my mum would use when she was busy, but how lame it must have sounded coming out of my mouth. My peak guests were a laughable fraction of hers.

Now, my aunt and uncle were leaving with important things left unsaid.

June reached me, and draped a thin, buttery soft sweater over the goosebumps on my arms. "Shoulder season," we whispered in unison, and I couldn't help but smile. The shoulder seasons are what innkeepers call the months on either side of summer, when rates are cheaper, and the air is cooler.

Labor Day is the start of a shoulder season, and Zeke and June always left the day after to make their way back home. It didn't make me sad when I was young, because I had adventures to look forward to. But those days were long gone.

"Kaker!" June startled me from my thoughts. "Hang a sign on the door and hop in the car with us. Come stay for a few weeks or months. Stay for the winter."

I watched her sweet earnest face as she spoke.

"We can introduce you to all the single men at the golf club," she said, excitedly. "You're so tall and pretty, your dance card will be full in no time!"

"Those lucky, lucky guys," I joked, as I pointed down at my faded, ripped jeans and unpedicured toes.

She ignored my attempt at humor and sat down next to me on the big rock. Wistfully, she looked up at the great clapboard lodge, with its peaks and gables, and faded green roof. "Fitz and Raya sure adored each other, Kaker, didn't they?"

I nodded at her words.

She nestled in and patted my knee. "Now, they were a great team. I know they would not want you striving to run Kerby Lodge alone," she said. "It's too much!"

If I had married years ago, I wouldn't be alone. I'd have a partner. There were plenty of local guys who I went to the restaurants and the movies with in high school. Guys who were also tied to their family businesses—the charter boats, restaurants, sand dune tours, and souvenir stores. But no one was special to me.

I see many of them in town now with their young families, and we all nod and smile. Our lives and livelihoods, our successes and troubles, are all intertwined.

"Zeke and I worry you have isolated yourself from the world—and from other possibilities for your life," June said, as if to cushion what was coming next. "Because very soon, it might be time to consider other… possibilities."

Tears pricked my eyes as I thought of Mum and Dad, gone twelve years now. The sadness of their passing seemed fresh, and that sadness slammed into the melancholy of Zeke and June driving away for the last time—along with the guilt and shame I felt at the epic mess I was making of everything.

I buried my head in June's arms.

My lovely aunt stroked my hair as I cried, until I regained my composure enough to speak. "I don't know where that came from."

"Don't you?" she asked kindly, and I saw that her eyes were moist. I often failed to remember that others were hurting, too, from the void Fitz and Raya left behind. After all, they were probably Zeke and June's closest friends, as well as family.

With the waves splashing in the background, we reminisced a little about Mum and Dad, Tad and Gram, and the fun we'd had over many summers at this rustic resort.

It was a sprawling home when Mum and Dad purchased it in 1971. They changed very little when they moved in, and little has changed in the 40 years since.

Raya loved the stone fireplace that sits in the massive great room. It reminded her of the homes she once knew in Scotland, along the North Sea, and how the owners would gather 'roond the fire against the wind and storms. Fitz fell in love with the imposing screened-in front porch, where a dozen people could sit and watch the sun set every evening.

On one side of the great room is a wing of guest rooms, with shared and private baths. On the other side, my parents carved out an apartment for our family, with three cozy bedrooms, a small sitting area, and the lodge's large kitchen—where we spent a lot of our time.

Upstairs sit two summer apartments, sans heat registers, in what was once the attic. Legend has it the original owners designed the mirror-image living spaces for their two mothers, who were invited to visit for July and August. And who were highly sensitive to any preferential treatment detected towards the other.

The original property also featured a few guest cabins as well as a carriage house.

4

The main house, what we call the lodge, is an old Cape Cod perched on a bluff facing the lake. It's close enough that guests can reach the beach in several long strides. And far enough back that a smattering of oak and pine trees along the shoreline provide afternoon shade.

And the price my parents paid? Let's say it was less than I pay each year for property taxes. Uncle Zeke never gets tired of mentioning this.

"Life has seasons," June said, gently pulling me back from my thoughts, "and we've had good ones. But Kaker," she continued, "Zeke and I have overstayed our welcome in the season we've been in. It's time for us to slow down."

I smiled and nodded, for she deserved far better from me than I'd given her this summer—this sweet woman who'd done her best to be Raya's surrogate. Just then, we heard a car horn, and June moved to walk back up the bluff. I jumped up to walk with her, taking her arm. I would be more aware of her needs, I resolved.

"But you—you are still young!" she exclaimed as she paused to check her footing.

I shrugged, feeling much older than my 35 years.

"It was unfair. You had to make such big decisions when your parents died," June said. As she walked, I helped her navigate over way too many twigs.

"Here you were, about to embark on your own life, away from Kerby Lodge," June said, stopping to look me in the eye, "then you put your plans on hold so everyone could have their vacations that first summer!" She shook her head. "And just… kept it going."

I didn't think it was possible to capture twelve full years in one statement, but my aunt had done just that.

"That pretty much sums up my entire adult life, Aunt June," I said.

Although in June's version, I come off as being a lot more selfless than I am. I didn't care about anyone else's plans that summer after my parents died—it was easier to keep things going. But it wasn't heroic.

It was deep, dark, mind-numbing grief.

We reached Zeke as he was parking the massive Cadillac in front of the lodge, all loaded with their suitcases. "The house up the hill is closed, and ready for winter," he stated. "Cleared out the pantry. Turned off the water lines so they won't freeze."

I held his gaze as he spoke.

For a silent moment, we sized each other up to determine which of us was the most fragile—the elderly accountant in plaid shorts and black knee socks, or the orphaned and floundering business owner, sporting torn jeans and a blotchy face.

Sadly, I think I took the prize.

"You been crying!" he said, unfolding himself out of the car for a proper goodbye. "Save your tears for when you get your tax bill. Mail it to me. I'll look it over before you have to send them your arm and your leg."

At that, I smiled and sniffed, and we hugged.

"You know," he said, "your parents bought the place for less than your tax bill!"

"Is that so?" I said.

"Yes it is," he said with authority.

I nodded as if I was hearing this for the first time.

June went on to say how much they hated to leave, but needed to put some miles behind them before the sun went down. I knew their accounting business could no longer wait. Indeed, since they started bringing their laptops with them the past few summers, the line between work and vacation had become blurred, as they received a steady flow of client emails.

Not so long ago, these emails energized Zeke and June, and they couldn't wait to get back to the business of business. But now that I was looking, I could see how tired they were.

These two were ready to retire—as they'd been threatening to do for a few years—from their business, and from the lodge. They rarely went golfing or sailing anymore. And not once this hot summer did they venture down the uneven path to the cool lake.

"You two get along and don't worry about me," I said, finding my voice. "Worry about finding a motel before dark, and call me when you do." I waved my cell phone as a visual reminder.

I loaded a bag of my own into their back seat with sandwiches and cold drinks from the Rusty Nail, a nearby market that sold gourmet meats and cheeses. They also sold expensive bottled waters, all sorts of crackers and spreads, and in-season fruit and vegetables from nearby hobby farms.

"Hydrate!" I said, pointing to the picnic bag I had packed. "And eat!"

As they got into their car after giving me last bear hugs, both Zeke and June restated their invitation for me to come with them.

"Aw, I would, but there's only two sandwiches," I said, feigning regret.

They smiled and nodded, as if this were a valid reason.

"Come for Thanksgiving!" they said.

I smiled and nodded. We all knew I wouldn't.

"And the next time we speak, let's discuss the pros and cons of selling the lodge, versus keeping it running at its current capacity," Uncle Zeke said. "I left you a spreadsheet."

"Won't that be a fun chat," I said.

He gave me a stern look, over the top of his glasses. Before he could scold me, I said "Okay, I hear you loud and clear. I'll put on my big girl long johns and call you soon," causing them to laugh a little.

"And when I call," I said, digging deep to find a tone of confidence, "you two can tell me where in the world you're going next summer after you retire."

"But how will you manage without us?" Zeke seemed genuinely alarmed, though we both knew it's what he wanted.

"I'm not sure, Zeke," I said with a lump in my throat. "But it's time I learned."

"Besides," I continued, "I need accountants with more experience. And a bigger car."

Before they could tell me this wasn't the time for jokes, I said "We will talk on the phone this winter—a lot. And next summer, you'll send me a postcard from anywhere except Kerby Lodge, okay?"

The relief on their faces was evident. Now they could drive away with lighter hearts and make plans for their future. I'll bet that felt nice.

"We'll talk soon," we all said over one another. Suddenly though, Aunt June leaned out her window and shouted "Don't forget Kaker, you have a lodger way over in the A-Frame. I checked him in yesterday."

Good grief. That had completely slipped my mind.

And if I had jumped in the getaway car—what then? How far down the road would the three of us have gone before they'd be dropping me off at a bus station?

I was, quite possibly, the worst innkeeper in the history of the world.

2

Rain, rain, go away
Our soggy family wants to play
-KERBY LODGE GUEST BOOK-

I lied about the sandwiches.

There was a ham and aged cheddar on brioche from the Rusty Nail waiting for me in the great room—along with an oatmeal cookie. I just needed to grab an iced tea from the kitchen, and I could celebrate the beginning of the shoulder season. Completely alone.

Setting my lunch on a side table, I plopped down in one of the old, oversized guest chairs. *Whoa!* I sank down much further than I had expected.

Most of the great room furniture was old—many pieces were even original to the place. But new furniture was not in the budget, that was for sure. I supposed the worn-out furnishings were part of the authentic charm of the lodge. I would be over forty myself in a handful of years, and hoped to lean more towards authentic charm than worn out.

Taking a huge bite, I remembered I had missed breakfast and I was famished.

I forced myself to slow down so I wouldn't choke, which was the single girl's secret nemesis. I was the only one here now. Just me and the mystery man in the lodge's most remote cabin. Who may or may not know the Heimlich Maneuver. I pictured him coming into the lodge for clean towels, to find me slumped over in my chair. Telltale crusts in my lap.

Looking over, I noticed a lodge brochure sitting on the table next to my glass. I picked it up and flipped it over as I tried to eat smaller bites and sip, not gulp, my tea. And there it was. Even after twelve years, it surprised me to see my name:

Kay Kerby, Owner and Proprietor of Kerby Lodge.

The spring after completing graduate school I came home to mull over teaching and administrative positions, and to decide which to accept. And yes, I did have multiple job offers. I like to flatter myself remembering this—especially on days when I have to chase mice from the cabins, or plunge a clogged toilet.

I had hoped to discuss the pros and cons of each offer with Mum and Dad. But the severe pneumonia that plagued them both that winter, and kept them from coming to my graduation, overtook them just days apart. Very soon after I arrived.

Of course I knew they had been ill, but they would not hear of me coming home. My aunt and uncle had arrived early, and friends from town were helping as needed. So I fully expected to see them *on the mend*, as my family would say; weakened, but recovering.

But when I saw Tad's face, I knew their condition was worse than anyone had let on. They had all kept me in the dark, allowing me to stay focused on my final thesis. Never suspecting the worst outcome.

For a few years, I stewed in anger over their decision, but the bitterness was eating me alive. There was nothing to do but to forgive—if there was anything to forgive.

"We all thought they'd recover Kaker," Tad told me, looking more helpless and miserable than I'd ever seen him look. Before or since.

The fact that Tad was there at all when I got home told me more than words could say. Recently added to the roster at a sports medicine facility in Atlanta, I knew that only the gravest family emergency would allow him a leave of absence.

So, there it was.

Together, over a few weeks' time, he and I journeyed back and forth from the lodge to County Hospital. Then we traveled back and forth—and back and forth—to the funeral home.

Finally, we traveled together to the office of our parents' estate attorney.

"What?"

I had shouted at the lawyer, forgetting to mirror his somber tones. My brother took my hand. I was flat out shocked when our attorney told us both that I was sole heir of the lodge and surrounding twelve acres—owner of the main building, cabins, cottages, house, and 1,200 feet of prime Lake Michigan shoreline.

All these assets were valued at nearly 5 million dollars at the time. And they were mine, not ours, as I had expected.

If Tad was surprised or disappointed, he hid it well. He seemed almost relieved, truth be told. Maybe because he had made it clear when he left for school that he wanted nothing more to do with the resort. He would not, he said, be coming home to work during his breaks. He planned on taking summer courses and expediting his undergraduate degree.

"*See you never*," I said through teenage tears to the back of his car, as he drove away all those years ago. I remember being so hurt at his leaving, and his lack of family loyalty. But my parents were proud and happy. After all, he'd always had his eye on medical school and warmer climates, and made no bones about it. They'd helped him in every way they could.

They would miss him terribly, they said. But they loved Tad and wanted him to follow his dreams—just as they did.

The truth was, Tad's nature was to make the best of every situation at any given time. He poured his heart and soul into 18 summers on Lake Michigan, and would equally pour all his energy into school, then medical school. And then into a life he loved.

I always wished I could be more like him, instead of the brooding and miserable kid—and sometimes adult—that I was, especially when it came to the business end of the lodge.

But this made the inheritance even more of a mystery.

Why me?

One thing I do know, if they'd left Kerby Lodge to both Tad and I, we'd have sold it in a heartbeat, and split the proceeds. By giving it to me alone, they must have known there was a chance I would keep and run the resort.

Was that their real wish?

"The other lakefront property will go solely to Tad." I snapped back to attention as the attorney continued.

The other property?

It seemed that while I was absorbed in applying to graduate schools, my parents inherited several acres of inland lakefront property, 10 miles from the lodge.

This property was from Gram Kerby—one of her investments after she moved to Lake Michigan. She also held a valuable parcel of undeveloped Florida property, which she left to Zeke and June.

"But who'd want to own land in a salty swamp?" I asked my dad.

"Who indeed," he had answered, looking out at the freshwater horizon.

The inland lakefront property flew under my radar. My parents never spoke about developing it or selling it. Later that night, though, going through papers, Tad and I discovered offer letters from developers and private buyers, and the numbers were staggering. It seemed Lake Michigan was not the only valuable shoreline in the county.

Though smaller, the inland property rivaled mine in value for a few reasons. First, it was undeveloped, and without the liabilities of the lodge and older buildings that sat on Lake Michigan. And the shoreline didn't suffer from erosion, as many Great Lakes coastlines did.

Also, the inland lake was a very desirable all-sports lake, conducive to boating—and therefore, to a coveted dock and boathouse. More so than the often volatile Lake Michigan.

Last but not least, the properties on either side were being developed into summer compounds by two wealthy business rivals from Detroit, who both wanted the Kerby land—now Tad's land—as their own. At any price.

With our respective heads reeling after the attorney's revelations, and the weeks leading up to them, it was time for Tad to say his goodbye's.

We were both drained, heartbroken, and overwhelmed on every possible level. Selfishly, I wanted him to stay and help me sort out the responsibilities our parents left on my shoulders, but we were not children anymore. He had a family who needed him, and patients who were waiting.

The night before he flew home, the two of us went to dinner at Mitch's restaurant—a favorite of both locals and summer people. We captured a quiet table with a waterfront view because it was early in the season. The tourists had not fully descended on the area.

"May I express my deepest, heartfelt sorrow!" Mitch himself came to our table, sad at the loss of our parents. They had been much more than customers, he had told us, they were good friends. Tad and I both found ourselves blinking hard. Mitch told us that it would be his privilege to pick up our tab that night.

Together we celebrated Mum and Dad, and their full life, well lived. And reminisced for hours about growing up at Kerby Lodge. It was good to be with my brother again. With our backs to the dining room, we talked, laughed, cried, and ate. I felt I could get through the dark days to come with Tad by my side, and dreaded him leaving.

"Kaker," he said gently, "I know your heart is broken—mine is too—but you are not alone in this world," he said with real feeling. A sharp knife turned in my heart as he said this. I had missed Tad more than I realized.

"You are not without family or resources," he said. "Sell the lodge—that dinosaur—for the millions it's worth, and start a new life near me, Selby, and the girls. Be part of our family."

I was too overcome to speak.

"I'm not coming back here," he went on, "and I want you there. We want you there."

Picking at my cheesecake, I knew I wasn't ready to make any big decisions—especially when it came to leaving my home, and turning my back on all that our parents had built.

Tad, on the other hand, had no qualms about making such decisions.

I'd barely had time to daydream about Tad and his wife and young daughters building a vacation spot nearby before the dream was dashed. After dividing the land into three parcels, he sold the center lot to an area builder, and the two bookend lots to the business rivals for a maximum return.

Soon after, Tad sent me an email with photos of their new vacation condo in Savannah, Georgia, and news of their membership at an exclusive golf club on nearby Skidaway Island. The subject line of the email read "Come and see us Kaker!"

I crafted a reply: "Really Tad? Leave the world's most beautiful lake to have nightmares about your spooky moss trees—or get eaten alive by your invisible bugs? I don't think so."

Then I changed it to "will do" and hit the send button.

3

*Our home away from home is a
knotty pine cabin at the Kerby.*
-KERBY LODGE GUEST BOOK-

We all had our own jobs to do at the lodge on Lake Michigan, all those years ago. When our family was at its fullest. And our business at its busiest.

My father, Fitzwilliam Kerby, was the visionary by nature, and the handyman by necessity. Every morning before the sun came up, he'd put on his army issued boots, then crunch the pine needles of the forest floor making sure everything about the inn—old and new—was in good repair. Scanning the hills, the trees, and the sandy shoreline with blueprint precision, he'd calculate his plans to tuck new cottages into the woods as money allowed.

Also the self-appointed marketing director for the new venture, Fitz jumped on the most cutting-edge media available to our small coastal town forty years ago—paper restaurant placemats. My parents framed one, and it hangs on a wall with Dad's slogan:

Bring your entire family to Kerby Lodge this summer!

"It's no detergent jingle," he liked to say, "but it did the trick."

And it did. There was a high demand for vacation lodging around the Great Lakes in the early 1970s. One that was escalating like crazy.

All these nice, big families, Mum would explain in her Scottish brogue, were driving '*roond and 'roond,* looking for somewhere to stay after a day at the lake. Eager to unpack their station wagons, they would invariably go eat at one of the diners by the water and debate, should they stuff their group into a too-small motel room, or pitch a tent at the state park? Then someone would spot the Kerby Lodge ad, sitting right under their pancakes.

Mum lost count of how many people dialed our number from phone booths outside the diners. Or came into the lodge carrying a placemat with the coffee rings still wet, as if it were a ticket for admission. My parents were at capacity within a few years, and had no trouble booking new cabins and cottages as they were built.

Mum knew all about inns and guests. She had firsthand knowledge of the gears that had to turn to make the trains run and the clocks chime. As Raya Stewart, she had been the manager of the Roost Inn outside of Inverness, Scotland, long before my dad and his fellow engineers checked in for their stay in the late 1960s.

Gob smacked, Dad was, when he laid eyes on the red-haired Raya.

As for herself, she was equally smitten with the tall, quiet fellow who came in from the cold, and they were married two months later. He, a bachelor at 35. She, an *auld maid* at 32.

For the next few years, Fitz and his "Raya sunshine" travelled together across several continents as his assignments dictated. Until one hot summer day, they found themselves in the United States, on the golden beaches of Lake Michigan. They'd only heard about this water, one of the world's largest freshwater lakes, but in the time it took my dad to say "Well, Raya, will you look at that," their lives were changed.

Lake Michigan was, Mum had said about their first sighting, as vast as the sky, and as majestic as the ocean. It was so unlike the frightening waves of the North Sea she had grown up fearing, or the alligator infested swamps that Dad stayed clear of as a boy in Florida.

It took her breath away.

They had been driving on a curvy road, between dunes and forest— Raya with her nose in a map. Suddenly, they came around a bend, and there it was. They both gasped.

The blue water was so close, Raya felt she could reach out the car window and scoop it up with her cupped hand. They pulled over and ran to the shore.

Mum told me how the white sand beach was like soft, hot sugar on her bare feet. And how the water itself, after the initial cool shock, felt like velvet against her skin. "Kaker, it was clear as crystal," she had said with wonder in her voice, "I could see all the way *doon* to the tiniest pebbles."

As for Fitz, he once told me that while the water was stunning, it was Raya he couldn't take his eyes off of. She was beautiful with the glow of excitement shining on her face as she ran to the water, wearing her sunny yellow bathing suit. Standing waist deep in the lake, gentle swells rising and falling around them, Raya lifted her smiling face to the sky, and a constellation of freckles burst forth on her tanned skin like fireworks.

14

Fitz Kerby had saved his money for twenty years, and was prepared to retire from the army. He was ready to put down roots, it was only a matter of where. On that day, standing with Raya in the unsalted water of Lake Michigan—looking up at the white cliffs of sand, and over at a tall brick lighthouse surrounded by white pines—he knew the answer.

They purchased the sprawling Cape Cod on twelve lakefront acres, and they were home.

Turning the property into a resort was accidental. Soon after offering their extra rooms to a nearby inn for their overflow guests, they were receiving steady calls for availability.

So, the big house became a lodge. And the few guest cabins that were on the property became ideal for families who simply wanted an unassuming place to flip their own pancakes, before walking to the beach.

As quickly as my dad could get new cabins built, my mum was right behind him, getting them dressed and ready for company—and ready to turn a profit. He liked to call her the heart and soul of the resort, and she indulged him.

But what I saw was a cunning red fox.

Raya Kerby ingeniously fostered, coaxed, and invented an environment where families would bond with each other—over card games, gin and tonics, sunsets, skinned knees, teenage romance, and macaroni casseroles. And then, these same families would insist on doing it all over again the following summer.

"Same week, same cabin!" became the mantra.

And subsequently, the Kerby Lodge business model.

Mum would catch guests early in the week, before people were sluggish from eating too many potato chips, and sleeping on creaky iron beds that weren't their own. Before they began missing their central air conditioning and country club dances. And she'd offer them the same cabin and time the following summer, for a not-refundable deposit.

"You must come back. We're coming back!" guests would encourage each other.

"We will if you will!"

And for many years, they all did—bringing with them their expanding broods.

When my older brother Tad came of age, he was put in charge of the carriage house. Built for summer buggies and winter sleighs, it became home to the dozens of bikes, trikes, and wagons that were a huge treat for the visiting children. For they all knew better than to go into the water before their parents were good and awake.

Every morning, Tad was larger than life to the small kids waiting to race for their favorite toy. Slowly unlocking the great hinged doors, Tad built up excitement to a feverish pitch—causing kids to clamor and trip over each other when he gave the nod.

Tad also helped arriving families unload their cars, and stack their firewood. It wasn't his job, but they tipped him well. He'd smile and make small talk with the guests, and offer his services throughout the week as a golf caddy, or fishing guide, or swim instructor—for even more money and tips.

Tad discovered that the mums and dads were happy to pay him to carry in grocery boxes and stacks of beach towels, while they ran off to say *yoo-hoos* at neighboring cabins.

My aunt and uncle were hard workers too—helping wherever needed. Of course, the day Zeke and June arrived every summer was cause for celebration, and a family reunion cookout. Gram would glow with happiness at having her entire clan in one place.

Gram Kerby had her own jobs, and took them seriously while she was alive. She patrolled the perimeter in her electric golf cart like a general, Dad would say. He made certain that Gram had beefed-up tires to navigate the uneven terrain—the rocks, dirt, sand, and the pine cones that lay on the bed of the forest.

She kept an eagle's eye out for anything amiss during the three-ring circus that was summer at Kerby Lodge: beach towels carelessly thrown on tree limbs; little sailboats left unanchored and bobbing in the waves; paper plates blown into the tall grass; teenagers venturing too far into the thick of the woods, thinking they would be invisible—or invincible.

Gram's most important job, in my eyes, was to cook a big breakfast for us on Sunday mornings after church, before the new batch of guests arrived. At her house up the hill.

Dad had the year-round home built for Gram, when she indicated she wanted to move up from Florida. He also thought a family house by the main road might prove useful during the harsh Lake Michigan winters, from which Fitz and Raya did not intend to turn tail and run.

I had after-school and weekend jobs too—my parents saw to that—in spite of the great show of brooding I staged every spring.

"That's winter fun," Mum would say if I tried to stay inside and watch cartoons. And if I bristled at coming outdoors, she might allow me to stay in if I agreed to take phone messages. A harsh punishment.

Our old brown answering machine could barely contain all the calls that came to Kerby Lodge while everybody was outside doing spring clean-up. This one wanted to change their week, or their cabin. That one wondered if there was finally a cancellation they could slide into this summer—after all, hadn't they'd been trying for years? Another person would want to know if they could cancel "just this once" without losing their yearly reservation.

I frantically scrawled notes on a legal pad, and we were all left trying to decipher my schoolgirl handwriting at the end of the day.

It was enough to drive me outside to twig duty, where I'd pick up the endless branches that fell during the winter storms. Dad built a child-sized wheelbarrow so I could cart the twigs to the fire pit, and Mum painted *wee lass* on the side. Which was adorable when I was five, I'm sure, but a great embarrassment as a tall and gangly twelve-year-old.

Wheeling the little cart full of twigs past the carriage house, I'd be sure to sigh and roll my eyes at Tad—trying to get him to commiserate. As if to say, "Can you believe our rotten life?" But of course, it was not a rotten life. I loved the lodge. It's the only home I've ever known. But I can't say I ever loved the business that came with it. Or the lack of access I had to Mum and Dad between Memorial Day and Labor Day.

"Can it wait for the shoulder season, Kaker?" Mum used to say, whenever she had a lot on her mind. "Unless there's a broken bone, or *bleedin' from a major art'ry*," Mum would say, her brogue getting more pronounced as guests were about to arrive for the week, "let's get through peak and we'll talk about it then." And after a strong hug and a kiss to my forehead, Raya would be off to welcome one of a dozen or so families.

Endless shoulder seasons and never-ending winters. That's what I used to wish for when I was growing up. Rather than the busy summer months at Kerby Lodge, where I tried to become invisible—only to be summoned outside to *say hullo* to so-and-so. Or to run extra blankets to a cabin. Or to help someone pull the little sailboats into the water. Without ever getting a tip.

I still do my best to be invisible during the summers at Kerby Lodge, but since I own and run it now, that's a challenge. Running the resort was easy at first. Fitz and Raya had done the hard work. What was there to do but keep every detail the same? The way guests have always expected Kerby Lodge to be.

But over time, I found that things change, regardless. Why, the trees alone—hundreds of them—are continually changing and growing. I've watched their roots push up and ruin the nice things that Fitz constructed, like driveways and foundations. And the limbs! I can never predict when they're going to fall onto the roofs of cabins or cars from decay and wind.

The cottages in the dense woods are gathering moss, and the moss, it seems, rots everything. The old swing sets are rusting. The canvas sails on the little boats are tearing. Meanwhile, my insurance payments keep rising. And a few years ago, a recession slammed into Kerby Lodge like a tidal wave—pulling me down and out like a strong Lake Michigan undertow.

I'm not alone, but there's no comfort in knowing that. Businesses are closing right and left. People I've known my entire life are moving away to find jobs. Properties and homes are being foreclosed faster than I can keep up with.

My regular guests are suffering too, I know. And I'm sorry for what they must be going through. Many can't afford vacations right now, but I can't afford for them not to come.

I'm just one *wee lass*, trying to keep my head above water.

4

See you next July for s'more fun
-KERBY LODGE GUEST BOOK-

Should I have listened to Tad when he told me to sell the inn twelve years ago?

He had called it a dinosaur. But back then, it was a multi-million-dollar dinosaur that would have helped me start a new life. In this economy, it's just a dinosaur.

So am I, I realized. If I can't get enough business to pay my property taxes, Kerby Lodge, and my home could become extinct.

Taking the last bite of my oatmeal cookie, I gazed through the quiet and empty sun porch, enjoying the lake breeze through the opened French doors.

"Couldn't the lodge be my home, and not my business?" I'd asked Zeke, more than once. But the answer was always no.

"Kaker, the only people with twelve acres on Lake Michigan are you and the multi-millionaire business owners," he told me. "Big, big, business owners," he clarified, holding his arms out wide.

Without the income from the guests, I couldn't afford the taxes—I'd have to be independently wealthy. And I would only be wealthy if I had sold Kerby Lodge years ago.

Poor little rich girl.

Some days, some years, I feel trapped. But I keep this to myself because nobody in their right mind would feel sorry for me—spending my summers swimming in blue, pristine waters, and enjoying nightly sunsets while walking along the white sand beach. My private beach.

I wouldn't feel sorry for me, either.

Beautiful bright sailboats gliding along in the distance—that's the first thing I see every morning when I open my eyes, through a filter of fluttering golden birch leaves. With the first deep breath of the morning, my lungs and soul fill up with the scent of clean unsalted water, and fresh fragrant pines.

Every starry night, I fall asleep to water lapping over the rocks on the shore.

Owls sing me to sleep.

Owls.

It's magical, really, this life I live. Yet, hadn't I been chomping at the bit to leave it a dozen years ago, in order to teach?

From the time I was a child, standing and waiting for the school bus, teaching is what I wanted to do. It's what I went to school for. It was about to become my reality when my parents passed away. And then I lost my confidence. My certainty.

I often wondered what Mum and Dad saw in me that I didn't see in myself when they deeded me the inn. I'd barely shown any interest in being the daughter of innkeepers, let alone becoming an innkeeper myself.

And what didn't they see in me—did they doubt my ability to be a teacher? Were they saving me from sure failure? I'll never really know. "Joke's on you, Mum and Dad," I said to the great room walls. "You kept me from failing as a teacher, so I could fail at running your lodge."

I picked up my dishes and made my way to the kitchen to check out the ledger that June, no doubt, had left out for me. It was likely next to the spreadsheet from Zeke—but that could wait for now. I needed to see when the next guests were arriving, and how long my current guest was staying. I didn't want to be caught unprepared. In early September, I generally had a few weeks' reprieve from guests until the fall color peepers descended.

As I looked around at the paneled walls of the apartment and the vintage furnishings I'd known all my life, everything felt very sad, and lonelier than usual. Yet I wasn't alone, was I? Someone else was on the premises, a man I hadn't met or even seen. A single man at that, which was unusual. Kerby Lodgers were almost always families, or couples.

I thought about Raya, minding her own business all those years ago at the Roost Inn when she was swept off her feet by my dad. And I wondered what it would be like when this stranger and I met.

Then I caught my rumpled reflection in a window. The only sweeping taking place, I surmised, would be me, deep cleaning the cabins.

The lodger was a Daniel Mayne from Chicago, according to June's records. He was staying in the farthest cottage from the lodge—the red painted A-Frame. It had a hand-scraped log staircase that my dad had crafted himself. The staircase led to a roomy sleeping loft, suspended above an airy living room and open kitchen.

The sofa and easy chairs encircled an old iron wood stove, which could heat the cottage most handily in cooler weather. All the furnishings, though worn and faded, faced a picture window that looked out over Lake Michigan.

The A-Frame was one of my favorites. It had been unoccupied most of the summer, and I had been meaning to repair or replace the chairs that sat around the dining table. The wooden legs had dried out, and were too loose and rickety for guests. I made a mental note to swap them out for some sturdier chairs stored in the carriage house.

But how did Daniel Mayne end up there? It was protocol to first put guests in the cottages on the other side of the lodge, along the road to the entrance. These cottages were easier for the cleaning crew to reach than the more remote cabins—and June knew this system as much as anyone. Heck, she probably invented it.

Looking back at the ledger, June had recorded his license plate number and wrote *Silver BMW* next to that. Pretty, pretty car, I thought. Quite a departure from the stuffed-to-the-rafters station wagons, SUVs, and vans that brought family after family to Kerby Lodge.

According to the note, my one lodger only needed clean bedding and towels delivered each Saturday. June also wrote that he had paid in full through the end of November.

"November?" I heard myself shout in surprise. Now I recalled the conversation about Daniel Mayne—I really had been flighty this summer. I should have paid closer attention to many things.

My lodger had insisted on renting the A-Frame—it had to be the A-Frame—for three full months, even though June tried her best to tell him that it was very isolated. Even more so towards the end of autumn, as other guests would be long gone.

But to appease her, he said he required very little from the lodge's housekeeping amenities, which was pretty much me this time of year. He would keep to himself, he said. And since he agreed to the peak rates she quoted him, June accepted.

Just then, hearing the sound of an engine outside, I looked out of the small kitchen window that overlooked the circle driveway in time to see a silver BMW drive past, towards the road and up the hill. The driver was hunched down, so that all I could make out were dark curls and shadows surrounding his face, and gloved hands on the steering wheel.

"Who are you, mister pretty car," I said out loud, to no one. "And why are you hiding out at my lodge?"

5

*Raya, I lost a green Tupperware salad bowl
at the pot luck. Send if you find! - Maeve*
-KERBY LODGE GUEST BOOK-

At some point, my parents began booking families to arrive on Sundays for their week-long summer stay, to leave the next Saturday morning. If anyone objected to losing out on a day's vacation, they never complained. Every guest knew there was a long wait list of others ready to take their place.

For a few hours on peak season Saturdays, it was all hands on deck to re-make the beds, run the vacuums, and clean the small baths in all the guestrooms, cabins and cottages.

But after this flurry of activity, Saturday nights and Sunday mornings would find the Kerby family free to run into town for dinner, and have our stretch of the beach mostly to ourselves for a little while. We could even nap in our hammocks on Sunday before welcoming the next wave of mums, dads, grams, dogs and kids.

Summer income was all my parents seemed to need to live a rich and full life year-round. And by rich, I mean we had a boat to enjoy during the peak season, and new boots and coats every winter to help weather the cold.

In addition to the funds for repairs and expansion, Mum and Dad had money to pay the bills long after the guests went home, and food in the pantry to eat like kings until spring.

My parents welcomed a few guests for the fall colors, but it was never a warm welcome. Fall visitors were tolerated more than encouraged.

No, Fitz and Raya's bread and butter were the summer Kerby Lodgers—families, with kids. Families that adhered to a strict Midwest school calendar. Back when everyone knew that decent families didn't travel in the fall—not when they ought to be occupied with homecoming dances, football games and trick-or-treat parties.

By the time the inn became mine, however, patterns and attitudes had shifted. Tired of vying for the same flights to Florida each spring as every other family, school boards began staggering vacation dates. Thereby widening travel seasons.

Homeschool families started coming out of hiding, and booking vacations during the shoulder seasons for better rates and availability. The empty nesters do the same.

Girlfriend weekends became a thing—busloads of women from Chicago, Detroit, and South Bend now come every fall, with the same itinerary. A hearty breakfast of free wine tastings, then shopping and lunch in our little towns. After that, the buses stop at more wine tastings on the way to the outlet stores.

Somehow, the girlfriends are impervious to the weak economy. They throw money around like confetti, and are treated like celebrities wherever they go.

And couples have made Autumn a second, smaller peak season, for inns in the Midwest.

So it's not surprising that while my summer numbers are way down, I seem to be holding my own for the fall colors. These weekends have been giving the inn a financial kick in the pants that I can desperately use.

The local tourism councils are getting more active, thank you everyone, and trying to boost travel between Labor Day and Thanksgiving. Festivals of all types are drawing big crowds.

Last October, a prominent vineyard organized an antiques festival in their large open barn. A food truck was on-site, owned by James Mauer, a local chef and friend of mine, who served cider-braised pork sliders with apple slaw, and cinnamon apple donuts.

My guests went wild over the affair and booked ahead for this year's event.

The screened-in porch and shoreline of Kerby Lodge are popular destinations for fall colors, as moody autumn skies contribute to the most stunning sunsets of the year.

As guests check in, I show them where they can find corkscrews, paper plates, and napkins in the lodge cupboards. They settle in, and nosh on crackers and cheese with grapes, and sandwiches from the Rusty Nail.

And while the great outdoors is the main attraction of summer, it's the great room that's a magnet in the fall. It's almost always full of people quietly reading, playing board games, or gazing at the lake. Brave guests will bundle up and enjoy the screened-in porch on chilly days and evenings. Or sit outside around the fire pit.

I can overhear many guests introducing themselves to one another, and sharing information about where to get the best take-out pizza in town. Others keep to themselves. My mother could never resist drawing out the loners, but I let them be. I'll never be as gregarious as the young and beautiful Raya was in her summer heyday—or as intuitive. The few times I've tried to imitate her enthusiasm, I fell flat.

Even the red tones and waves of my hair pale in comparison to hers.

As a result, I've never played cruise director, or tried to connect people, as my mother had been so adept at. Raya *saw* people, and made them feel noticed. It's one reason she was loved. And probably why people came back, year after year, as much as for Lake Michigan.

More and more, I realize how much I am like Fitz. Tall and gangly, for starters. Comfortable in my own company, or in small groups. And happy to stay in the background.

Both drawn, inexplicably, to the very early mornings of Kerby Lodge. He, to walk in the forest among the other easily startled woodland creatures. Me, to tiptoe across the great room and porch, gathering glasses, napkins and crumbs from the night before. To tidy the magazines on the big log table. Then, as quiet as a mouse, to clear the ashes from the cold fireplace and lay new starter logs.

The fall guests are the most appreciative of the fires that cut through the chilly air and dampness of the autumn mist and rain. The hissing and crackling of the damp logs act as an alarm clock to my lodge guests—as one by one, they stagger in their flannel robes towards the large electric percolator that once belonged to the Methodist Church.

Thanks to my great find at their *Our Blessings* sale a few years ago, I can, brew so-so coffee in great abundance.

Then, like Fitz, I skitter back behind the scenes.

6

*"Into the woods I go, to lose my mind
and find my soul." -anonymous*
-KERBY LODGE GUEST BOOK-

"No new buildings, I see," Bob Rike, the tax assessor said, "on this side anyway."

We had been walking the property between the lodge and the entrance—where the small cottages and larger cabins are, and the carriage house.

"Nope, same as last year, and the year before that," I said, inhaling the crisp early October air, hoping to calm my pounding heart. "As I mentioned, there hasn't been any building going on here for twelve years, at least."

I tried to keep the panic out of my voice, but couldn't keep the knot out of my stomach. His yearly visits always played into my insecurities, and my belief that I was inadequate in knowing the intricacies of the lodge.

I remember as a child, watching my father walk the land with a much younger Bob, and they would be talking and laughing as respected colleagues. Yet, since taking ownership, I have not been able to progress beyond seeming wary and evasive with him.

On a rational level, I realize that there is nothing new to add to my already hefty property assessment. But irrationally, I fear Bob will find something I didn't know about. A little cluster of hidden cottages in the woods, perhaps, tucked behind a thick wall of ivy. A secret hideaway that would push my tax bill into foreclosure.

He began walking to the other side of the vast property, toward the more remote cabins and the A-Frame, while checking the notes on his clipboard. I continued to follow along.

As we got closer, I could see my tall, dark, and brooding lodger outside stacking wood between two trees in the yard. Daniel has been here for over

a month—five weeks, I believe—and we still haven't met. He has never been in on Saturday mornings when I drop a clean pile of towels and sheets onto the deck chair—the one that sits under a protected eave.

I have never been in when he's dropped off a linen laundry bag by my apartment door. Or when he throws trash into the dumpster. Or when he fills up the flat wheelbarrow full of split wood from the large pile by the driveway—until today, that is.

Does he wait until I'm gone to do these things? I wondered now, alarmed and uneasy at the thought. It seemed strange but likely, since I was home more than away. It made me uncomfortable to think he'd been watching my comings and goings.

As we got closer, I lifted an arm in a tentative wave—sure that I had caught his eye. After all, Bob was crunching the dry leaves like a champ as he stomped around in his big boots.

Daniel Mayne stopped stacking long enough to give me a terse nod in return.

"This is it," I said under my breath, "It's time to meet my lodger."

I started to break off from Bob to walk over and say hello, but then Daniel Mayne, seeing that I was coming his way, completely turned his back to me. He went into the A-Frame and shut the door. Tight.

Stunned by his rude behavior, I froze. Then I turned and walked stiffly back towards the lodge—my cheeks burning with embarrassment and anger.

"What do you suppose he's hiding, June?" I said on the phone later that evening as the sun was setting, and the trees in the forest cast long, dark shadows.

I was trying to tamp down the growing nervousness I felt. It was the middle of the week, and we were currently the only two people on the lodge property—and often for days at a time, in between guests. I'd never felt this level of trepidation before at my familiar habits—such as not locking the main lodge doors, as guests were invited to come and go from their cabins to the coffee pot and book shelves at all hours.

It dawned on me that Daniel hadn't been inside the lodge for either of those things, which also seemed suspicious. What kind of person could resist an entire wall filled with books? Or a large urn filled with mediocre coffee? Or even just the company of others after so much solitude—which seemed excessive, even by my own standards.

"He seemed nice when I checked him in," June responded. "A bit downcast, but I didn't peg him as dangerous. Maybe he wants to be left alone."

I wondered how much stock I could put in my aunt's intuition that he wasn't dangerous. June was a bookkeeper, not a psychologist. But I wanted her to be right.

"Okay," I said reluctantly, "I'll email his information to Tad, just in case."

"Just in case *what*, Kaker?" June asked. It was a question I wasn't prepared for. And her tone was a little too glib for my taste—it was easy for her to poke holes in my anxiety from down there in her gated community.

"Well, I don't know," I said. "I prefer not to think about *what*, Aunt June. But if *what* happens, at least Tad will have some idea of *who* might be responsible."

I said a polite, if a bit cool, farewell.

During the daytime, calmer heads prevailed.

Daniel Mayne obviously wasn't hiding from the authorities, because he came and went in broad daylight. I even saw his car in town, near the post office and police station, as well as at the grocery and hardware stores.

There was also that one time at the steakhouse by the marina, when I was meeting friends for dinner, that I saw him eating by himself. I briefly considered inviting him to join our group but then he looked up at me and I swear, he glowered.

His payment for the cabin, though hefty, went through without a hitch. And I had a photo copy of his driver's license. So did Tad—who, after a few days responded with "You're losing it Kerby."

Still, it was strange that a man the age of Daniel Mayne—44, according to his identification—would have the luxury of a three-month stay in a cabin on Lake Michigan.

It was off-season, so he wasn't a teacher on break. He was too young to be retired. Working remotely, maybe? Not with our unreliable internet reception.

Maybe he was a method actor, studying for a role as an unpleasant loner that didn't have any friends, and liked to eat steak alone.

But by the end of October, I'd almost forgotten Daniel Mayne was there at all. Our interactions were perfunctory and virtually anonymous. I dropped off clean linens. He drove off to the stores. He was harmless, apparently, and I was busy with my other guests and the sheer magnitude of their activity.

People checked in—bringing with them a rush of cold wind each time the door opened. Along with rain and wet oak leaves from the parking pad.

In and out. In and out. Wind, and leaves, and suitcases coming in. Suitcases going out, and more wind coming in. Doors opening and closing.

The coffee urn was omnipresent. In the great room, the fireplace and its stone hearth were frequented each morning by the early risers, and each evening by the night owls—and all day in between by the readers.

Thankfully, most men on fall color trips, I discovered, had an innate need to coax a fire—so it rarely went untended. I almost didn't need the sign on the mantle:

The fire is for your enjoyment, so keep it going.
And grab a bundle of wood on your way in!

Daniel Mayne certainly was not afraid to grab great bundles of wood from my pile—he was stacking logs between trees like it was his full-time job. Like he was staying through the winter. It's no wonder though, after the first taste of cold winds that were blowing off the lake.

I needed to order more split logs, I realized—never having a guest stay this long past summer before. Especially one who devoured wood like it was Halloween candy, and he was a kid who didn't eat his dinner.

I wondered how this would affect my budget, and thought of calling Uncle Zeke. But that would open the window for *the talk*—discussing selling or keeping the inn—and I wasn't ready for that. Besides, I could hear Zeke saying: "you won't read my spreadsheets about tax structures and asset management, but you want my advice on a pile of dead trees?" and he'd be right. Another reason not to call him.

Surely my lodger had been thinking ahead to November, which was fast approaching. A time when the storms and gales could push the lake's waves as high as twenty feet—when no one in their right mind would be anywhere near Lake Michigan.

Just us die-hard Kerby's. Or rather, Kerby. *Singular.*

I worried about having enough wood to last through the winter for my own fireplace. The A-Frame, of course, didn't have a furnace, and would depend on wood for heat through the always cold November. So Daniel's fires were a necessity.

I however have a furnace keeping the lodge warm in the winter, so my fires were luxuries. Unless the power went out, which was a regular occurrence. Each outage lasted for a few hours or a few days, and I had to be ready for anything.

My backup generator kept my fridge and freezer operating, my toilets flushing, and a few lights on—but not the heat. The big old furnace drew too much power. In a winter power outage, I would move into the great room, and rely on space heaters and the stone fireplace for warmth. But with my firewood diminishing, it seems I had not planned well.

Thankfully, time was passing quickly. In another five weeks, my guest would be driving his pretty silver car up the hill, and far, far away.

Good riddance! It couldn't be soon enough.

I had not fully counted the cost of Daniel Mayne's stay at Kerby Lodge. A realization I would return to many times before winter was through.

7

Holy muskies! The fish were biting
this summer, eh Fitz?
-KERBY LODGE GUEST BOOK-

"I think it's time we met," I spoke to the man lying in the hospital bed—thinking how this was a meeting and location neither of us expected.

Wired to monitors that were beeping, and a blood pressure cuff that was puffing and exhaling, Daniel Mayne slowly rolled his heavily bandaged head towards the sound of my voice. His face was scratched, with shiny patches of ointment covering several areas. He kept his eyes closed, and every movement looked like a great effort.

He was highly medicated, and in a lot of pain.

Daniel eventually opened his eyes and nodded slightly before closing them again, sinking back into his pillow. I assumed he knew who I was, even though we had never spoken.

Two days earlier, I took a stack of clean linens and towels to my one lodger. It was the middle of November, and I wasn't expecting any other guests until spring. My fall guests had all gone home to get ready for their holidays, and things were quiet at the lodge—maybe a little too quiet at the A-Frame.

When I arrived in my four-wheel-drive Jeep, I saw the BMW parked by the deck, which was unusual. Daniel had always been away—purposely, I had assumed—when I came by on my regular Saturday morning rounds.

I also noted with increasing alarm that the door to the A-Frame was ajar, and the wood smoke that I'd seen and smelled for the past two months had ceased.

"Hello! *Hullo*, is anyone home?" I yelled louder than I would have if I didn't have a river of adrenaline coursing through my guts. I could hear the panic in my own voice, and a touch of Raya's brogue, which always made an appearance in times of great stress.

No answer.

I pushed the door open until I could see inside.

Taking my cell phone out of my coat pocket, I dialed 911 immediately upon seeing Daniel Mayne laying on the floor of the cabin. He was perfectly still, next to a broken chair and tipped-over table.

Why hadn't I replaced these old pieces?

His face was pale, and a quick touch told me that his hands were ice cold. Thankfully, the cell reception at that moment was clear and uninterrupted. An ambulance was on the way, I was assured.

My mind and heart raced.

How long he'd been there, I had no idea. But I guessed—and hoped—it was hours rather than days. I was scrambling to remember when I saw him last.

"I'm pretty sure he's going to be fine, Kay." Patrick, one of the town's paramedics reassured me twenty minutes later. "Looks like he knocked himself out—I think he fell off the chair changing a light bulb."

One look at the old chandelier, and the splintered chair below, led me to the same uncomfortable conclusion. On the floor I saw pieces of thin coated glass from the shattered bulb glinting among the wood. My stomach twisted into a knot, knowing that I caused this fall.

Patrick's partner was Jennifer Jansen, a high school classmate and friend of mine. They loaded my lodger onto a stretcher and then into the ambulance. Before leaving, they asked me to find his identification and insurance card, if he had one, and meet them at the emergency entrance of the hospital.

"Take a minute and calm down before you get behind the wheel, Kay," Jennifer said with a quick, reassuring hug. "You've had a bit of a shock yourself."

I nodded.

Once they drove off, I took a minute to survey the cabin—I hadn't been in it for months. I recognized a wooden bowl from the cupboards. It sat on the counter holding two apples and a still-green banana. A loaf of bread sat next to that. The refrigerator held a modest selection of lunch meats and cheeses, and a half empty gallon of milk.

On a hook by the door hung a flannel-lined canvas jacket. There I found Daniel's wallet and keys tucked in an inside pocket, and put them both in my own coat pocket. As I did, I couldn't help but notice how soft the well-worn fabric felt to my touch. I breathed in the not unpleasant aroma of aftershave and wood smoke.

As I turned to go, I saw a stack of magazines on the coffee table by the sofa, and walked back to the living room to take a closer look. There were several issues of *Clean Design, Architecture Handbook,* and other design-centered publications. These surprised me, though I wasn't sure why.

Taking Jennifer's advice, I sat down on the sofa for a minute to collect myself. I hadn't realized that I'd been holding my breath, and my stomach was starting to ache. Exhaling, and leaning my head back against the sofa cushions, I looked over and saw a laptop computer, closed and tucked neatly on a side table.

What was upstairs—his suitcase? I wondered if I should go take a peek. But then recognized the distracted rabbit hole I was starting to go down, and the lines of privacy I was about to step over.

"Get going, snoop!" I scolded myself then, knowing the ambulance was likely at the hospital by now, and people were waiting to know who they were admitting.

I wanted to know, too.

8

The sunsets were right on time, every night.
How do you guys do that?
-KERBY LODGE GUEST BOOK-

"This is Luke Mayne. Who's this?"

I was surprised to hear my phone ring as I sat on a chair next to a sleeping Daniel Mayne, flipping through an outdated gossip magazine. It felt awkward to have the chair meant for anyone but me, sitting with a man who actively avoided me and would not talk to me.

But someone should be at the hospital with him, in the absence of family. Though the sights, and smells, and sounds brought back painful memories.

"Hang on," I said in a hushed tone. I got up and walked to the visitor's lounge, and was relieved to find it empty.

"Luke Mayne," I repeated. "You must be related to Daniel."

"His brother. I got a call from Daniel's insurance company. He had me listed as his emergency contact," he went on. "They told me he was admitted, and gave me this phone number—you brought him in, apparently."

I remained silent as I followed along with what Luke was saying.

"And you are...?" he asked.

"Oh, right," I stammered. "I'm Kay. Kerby. Kay Kerby." *Och, get it together, lass.* "Your brother has been at my inn for three months, in one of the more remote cabins on the property. He took a fall."

I wasn't sure why I felt the need to say it was a remote cabin, except to squash the growing guilt I felt about not finding Daniel sooner—about my inability to keep my one and only lodger safe and sound.

But truth be told, my guilt was mixed with a little anger over the carelessness of Daniel Mayne—who would recover, while my struggling business might be ruined.

While looking at the gossip magazine headlines, I could picture my own scandal unfolding in the press. *Inn Crumbles! Guest Tumbles!* With photos of a bandaged and limping Daniel.

Although, where this ruinous article would be published, I didn't know. The *Shop and Save,* maybe? You never knew what could happen on a slow news day. And every day around here was a slow news day.

"I haven't spoken with my brother in months," Luke interrupted my thoughts. "He hasn't returned my calls lately, and I stopped bugging him. Can you tell me what's going on?"

"Sure," I said, organizing my words. "He fell two days ago. Probably off a chair."

I cringed as I said this last part.

"I found him," I continued, "but we're not sure how long he'd been lying there."

Luke groaned on the other end of the line.

"He's been in and out of consciousness, but the doctor said the concussion is mild—he suspects Daniel is recovering from exhaustion. He's in a deep rest, aided by the painkillers." I spilled out the story. "Oh, and he fractured his ankle when he landed."

"Okay, wow," Luke said, taking it all in.

"It sounds bad," I continued, "but the nurse said he's doing better than he looks. They'll most likely release him in a day or two—that's where I'm guessing you come in."

Luke was silent on the other end.

"He'll be on crutches for several weeks," I said. "And someone needs to make sure he doesn't slip into a deep sleep."

When Luke still didn't volunteer a solution, I added "I'm... only the innkeeper."

"Right. Right," he said, "I'm thinking this through. I figured he was still in Chicago. Not on vacation, or sabbatical, or whatever it is that he's been doing."

"He's kept to himself," I said. The understatement of the year.

"I live on the other side of the country, you see, in California—I'm getting ready to guide a class full of students through mid-term tests. The timing could not be worse. I know that sounds lame, Mrs. Kerby, but I'm being honest with you."

"Miss... Kerby. Just Kay."

"Kay."

I tried to remain silent. This situation and solution were on Luke, not on me. But then I cracked. "Is there anyone else—parents, sister, girlfriend?"

"Man, a *sister* would be great, right? I'm sure she'd be more helpful than I am," he said, and I couldn't help but smile. "Our parents are on an Alaska cruise," Luke continued, "I *bon voyaged* them myself a few days ago. They've been planning this for years."

"And they won't want to abandon ship because their grown son fell off a chair?" I said out loud—before I could stop myself. Which I probably should have.

To my relief, Luke laughed. "I wasn't going to go there, but right?"

"That means our only hope is a girlfriend," I said, suddenly wondering if I wanted Daniel to have a girlfriend or not. Was I still hanging on to the thinnest strand of hope, in spite of our rocky, nonexistent beginning?

"I've heard rumors of a girlfriend, but I'm guessing that if Dan's been hiding away for three months, she's out of the picture. Unless she's a saint—or has the patience of one."

"We could all use a saint right about now," I said.

And before I could repeat that my only connection with Daniel Mayne is that mine was the inn from which he was removed on a stretcher, Luke said "I guess I'm it."

I covered the mouthpiece so he could not hear me exhale from relief.

Luke gave me his contact information and asked for the hospital address. He would get back to me after he made reservations. "Give me a day or two please. I'll do my best."

He sounded sincere, but could Luke Mayne's best compete with winter's worst?

Snow was coming—and it was coming fast!

9

One week at the lake
Gets us through the other 51
-KERBY LODGE GUEST BOOK-

"Whatever you do, Kaker, don't say the words *I'm sorry.*"

It was the following day, three days after Daniel Mayne's fall. I signed in at the visitor desk and was about to go back into his hospital room. The nurse called me this morning to tell me he was awake.

I found I was actually feeling nervous about speaking with him in person—after nearly three months of him rudely avoiding me, and the horrible circumstances in which I found him. Which wasn't the kind of *meet cute* you want to tell your grandkids about down the line.

When I first saw grandpa, he looked dead as a doorknob!

I stopped walking—checking my thoughts. What was the matter with me? June was right. I had isolated myself for much too long.

It was time to stop harboring romantic thoughts towards this cold and aloof man. At no time did my lodger indicate that he wanted anything to do with me. I was nothing more than his towel delivery system; the anonymous girl who drove around in a golf cart, wearing her dad's oversized flannel shirts.

Daniel Mayne had obviously found me quite *resistible.*

Walking much slower now towards the wing that Daniel's room was in, I felt my phone vibrate, and saw an incoming call from my brother, Tad. Grateful for the diversion, I ducked into the lounge for privacy—and to re-center myself.

The television was on silent, but was tuned to the weather. Looking up at the screen, I saw illustrated blue and white snowflakes, being mercilessly shoved towards Lake Michigan by aggressive red arrows. The animated bully arrows were poking those poor flakes across the water, and right to my lodge.

"I see you got my message," I said into the phone, trying to process my brother's comment. I had called earlier, telling his answering service what had happened.

Tad skipped the pleasantries.

"Whatever you do, don't say *I'm sorry* or in any way imply responsibility for the lodger's accident," he said. "That dude will get an attorney and eat you alive—as it is, he's probably planning on suing the inn and taking everything."

I let that sink in for a minute.

"Tad," I said, "he's barely awake. And you're a doctor, not a lawyer."

"I play handball with lawyers," he responded, "and this is their advice."

"You think he'd sue me," I asked, "when he's the idiot who stood on that rickety chair?"

He groaned. "Let's make that the very last time you say *rickety chair!*"

I let out an exasperated sigh.

"Believe me, Kaker," he said with great seriousness, "a guy with a BMW, who took a slip and fall on your property, is exploring all of his financial options. I guarantee you—suing the lodge is one of his options."

And just like that, it no longer sounded that crazy.

A few minutes after hanging up, and promising my brother I'd guard my words, I made my way into the private hospital room where Daniel Mayne was sitting up. He was eating what looked like a school cafeteria lunch, segmented into pink plastic containers.

"Can I come in?" I asked, cautiously, half in and half out of the room.

"Sure," he responded with a dry voice—as someone who hadn't spoken much in a few days. He was about to put his spoon into green jiggling dessert cubes but set it down instead.

Daniel wiped his mouth on a napkin and set it on the tray. He looked at me intently—as if he were trying to recall who I was. Or trying to clear his vision after the fall he'd taken.

"I'm glad to see you awake," I ventured. "I'm Kay. Kay Kerby. The owner of the lodge. Kerby Lodge." I heard myself ramble on, and willed myself to stop. These Mayne brothers were really tripping me up.

Daniel was staring at me, frowning, as if he couldn't understand my words. And maybe he couldn't. Perhaps his head injury was worse than the doctor thought.

I was starting to feel sick to my stomach, as I pictured a judge pounding his gavel in a courtroom, and handing my inn and property to Daniel Mayne.

"You... called the ambulance?" he asked, in a dry voice.

"Yes," I answered, "as soon as I found you on the floor."

"The floor. Right." Daniel was watching me closely. And then his eyes narrowed as he levelled his raspy blow. "Because your chair smashed into a million pieces."

My mouth dropped open. He found me out.

"I'm sor..." *Don't do it, Kaker! Don't say you're sorry.*

Tad's words gripped me as I started to apologize, stopping me in my tracks. But then, the irritation I felt towards Daniel got the best of me, and I blurted out possibly a worse thing.

"I'm sorry... that you didn't use a ladder. They're made for that, you know."

We locked eyes, staring without speaking, or even blinking. As I held his gaze, he smirked. And then, with a smug and self-satisfied look on his face, he leaned back against his pillow and closed his eyes. Our *meet cute* was over, and it was an epic fail.

With his eyes now shut, I took a close look at Daniel Mayne. His hair was a mess of deep brown curls that stuck out from the top and bottom of the white gauze bandage wrapped several times around his head.

He was probably taller than I was, and I was above average height. They say that the bigger you are, the harder you fall, so he must have fallen pretty hard. I shuddered at the thought.

Overall, Daniel Mayne looked older than 44. Maybe it was the scratches on his cheekbone. Or maybe the unshaven beard. But I thought it more likely that it was his forehead. He seemed to wear cares and worries there, even sadness, in the deep lines.

Aunt June said he didn't seem happy with his life. I probably have the same look, I thought just then, and lifted my hand to smooth the worry lines from my own brow.

Why am I here, anyway? I don't owe this man my time. But as I got up to leave, I remembered the good news I came to deliver.

"Oh, your brother!" I said. "Luke is on his way here. Tonight."

I figured this news would be reassuring to him—I know it made me pretty happy. But it had the opposite effect. The deep shadow that crossed Daniel's face when he opened his eyes and looked my way made me wish I hadn't said anything.

"What? Luke is coming... *here?*" Daniel had found his voice, and it sounded surprisingly harsh. The way he enunciated the word "here" told me everything. That in spite of choosing to stay at Kerby Lodge, he truly believed that the hospital, the town, and even my resort were all inferior locations—worthy of his disdain.

I was speechless.

"Why would you trouble my brother, asking him to fly all the way from California?" he continued, practically growling. "Do I look like someone who needs to be *rescued*?"

10

"I did not call your brother," I said in a calm, professional voice that would have made my own brother proud. I went on to tell a very red-in-the-face Daniel Mayne that Luke had been the one to phone me, after being called by the insurance company.

"But, *why?*" He yelled. For some reason, his brother's involvement was a red-hot button that was pushed, and I couldn't un-push it.

"I don't know," I responded, evenly at first, as if to a small child. "I suppose it's a crazy hospital policy that when somebody is laying on the ground, unresponsive, looking half dead with a head injury," my voice was escalating at this point, "that a family member is notified!"

I was talking too loud for a hospital room, or even a hockey game, for that matter, and I took a few deep breaths to calm myself down.

Daniel turned away from me. Just like he turned away from me at the wood pile. Just like he turned away from me in the steakhouse. His hands were clenched into fists on his abdomen. One hand had a gauze bandage wrapped around the knuckles—probably the hand that had been holding the now-broken lightbulb. The other hand was connected to the IV tubes at his wrist.

Clenching his eyes closed in anger, he threw his head back into his pillow. Silently dismissing me, once again.

Even though he was no longer watching me, I nodded before exiting. I would have to be careful going forward. And not so eager to be the jolly goodwill ambassador.

All that mattered now, more than ever, was that Luke Mayne was on his way. And when he arrived, he could take over! He could have the keys to the pretty car—already moved into the covered garage to protect it from storms and tree limbs.

He could have the family chair in his brother's hospital room. He could have Daniel's possessions—the magazines, the laptop, and the banana. I would go home and pack up his things myself, and then deliver them in the morning. Because, according to the cartoon arrows, the snow was arriving with a bang the next afternoon.

"Kay, it's Luke," said the message on my phone, when I checked it upon leaving the patient wing to head home. "I'm at the airport."

Hooray! My spirit soared to think he was at the nearby airport, and would be here shortly. But then he continued, "I'm in California."

"My flight has been delayed because of the weather in Denver. The airline thinks we will board in a couple of hours," he went on. "I will keep you posted."

Yes, you keep me posted, Luke Mayne.

"Kay, I'm glad I caught you." Doctor Petersen stopped me by the elevator. I was shoving my hands in my coat sleeves, a little harder than I needed to. Good thing my hat and gloves were still in the pockets from the last time I'd worn this coat. I could see outside the window that the winds were picking up.

"Daniel Mayne is your lodger…" the doctor said.

"Was," I interrupted.

"…okay, he *was* your lodger when he fell," he said.

"But it wasn't my fault, or the lodge's fault," I said, too defensively.

"Well, no—of course not." Doctor Petersen seemed confused by my response, but went on, trying to regain control of the conversation.

"It's just that, we will be discharging him tomorrow morning, hopefully before the snow storm hits. I wondered who would be driving him home," he said. "He's stable and out of the woods, but won't be able to drive for a few months with that injured ankle."

I hadn't realized until now it was his accelerator foot that was injured.

"And he should have someone staying with him to help with meals, and to watch his sleep patterns. To make sure he doesn't slip into a coma—at least for a few days. And to dispense his pain medication, in case he loses track of the schedule. It's easy to do when you're medicated," Doctor Petersen smiled, and seemed to think this last bit was funny. He had no way of knowing how unfunny I was feeling.

"Also, to bring him to follow-up appointments," he finished.

I looked blankly at Doctor Petersen, who I had known for most of my lifetime. "And he's being discharged?"

"Yep," he said. "Hospitals like to get people home. Away from germs, infections, and liabilities." He grinned at me again, "And you worry that your lodge is going to be sued—imagine how paranoid we get around here."

I wasn't ready to joke just yet about lawsuits or snow storms, or discuss the care and feeding of Daniel Mayne.

And I certainly didn't want to tell him that while the hospital had an entire legal team—my team was a couple of sweaty handball players down in Georgia.

"Don't worry," I said, "His brother is coming. Tonight." And I walked away.

11

Hospitals like to get people home, that's what Doctor Petersen said. But where is home for Daniel Mayne? His parents are in Alaska. His brother lives in California. His driver's license has a Chicago address, but he's nowhere near that city.

We could have had a civil conversation about this at the hospital, if he hadn't erupted into volcanic anger over his brother being contacted.

Since I hadn't heard from Luke regarding any more delays, my assumption was that he had landed safely at the airport, and was at a hotel, or in a rental car and on his way.

Whatever the case, it was no longer my concern.

I was drinking my coffee in the dark, wee hours of morning, the day after my unpleasant encounter with my former lodger. Pondering how good it would feel to be rid of the Mayne boys and all their drama. There was enough drama happening in my own back yard with the impending snow storm—local news could talk of little else.

The snow hadn't started falling yet, but this first storm of the season would be a doozy, it was predicted. They were talking of the accumulation in feet, rather than inches. It was forecast to begin around noon, and the snow could last for days.

With the buffer of trees between the lodge and the main road now mostly bare, I could hear the cars whizzing by. People were either heading inland, away from the lake-effect winds, or on their way to the grocery and hardware stores for bottled water, loaves of bread, fire wood, and batteries for flashlights.

Oh, and because people tend to romanticize snow storms, cans of tomato soup and cheese slices. They think of how much fun it would be to eat grilled cheese sandwiches with soup by the fire, while playing cards.

Fun, that is, until pipes freeze and burst. And older roofs cave in from the weight of the snow. And frozen tree limbs start breaking off in the wind and plummeting onto cars and through windows. Fun until there's an emergency, and nobody can reach you except on snowmobile—but only after the storm dies down and there's some semblance of visibility.

I spend a good deal of every Autumn getting ready for the winter and the inevitable storms. I turned a spare room into storage for drinking water, non-perishable pantry items, batteries and lanterns, blankets, and extra snow gear.

My generators are at the ready, and I am prepared to hunker down. Thankfully, my kitchen stovetop is gas, so even in an outage I can light the burners and cook my meals—which yes, will feature plenty of grilled cheese sandwiches and bowls of tomato soup.

But first things first.

My plan was to go to the A-Frame after finishing my breakfast, pack up my lodger's belongings, and then deliver them to the hospital first thing. That way, there would be no reason for Luke to bring Daniel here after his discharge. I had also planned on refunding the entire month of November to Daniel Mayne—since there was more than a week left, and he obviously wasn't coming back.

The BMW was another matter. I considered driving it to the hospital and parking it there, but that seemed risky on many levels. I would let Daniel and Luke know that the pretty silver car could remain in my covered garage for the time being, but not so long that it would raise my property insurance rates.

The BMW, I calculated, was worth more than all the other vehicles at Kerby Lodge—combined.

Two hours later, I was getting ready to head to the hospital. Daniel's belongings, including his magazines and computer, were packed in a large duffel bag in the lodge foyer, ready for me to grab. Laying on top of the duffel bag was his flannel-lined coat, with the car keys zipped safely in the inside pocket.

While at the A-Frame, I bagged up all the food items from the refrigerator, counter, and pantry to toss into the dumpster. I grabbed the linens, closed the curtains, and shut off the water lines so the pipes would not freeze.

The cabin was now locked up tight for the winter. These chores took a little longer than I had expected, but I was glad I had taken the time.

Eventually, I'd go to the cabin and bring the firewood back that Daniel had been putting aside for himself. I never did order more.

It was still mid-morning when I was ready to head to town, but the sky was a dark, steely gray, and the wind had changed. It was blustery, and snow was visible in the swirling gusts already—hours earlier than expected. I would have to move fast to get on the road, or risk getting caught in dangerous white-out conditions.

But when I got outside to warm up my Jeep, I looked up to see a car making its way down my steep road, heading right to the lodge.

"You've got to be kidding me!" I exclaimed to the snowy heavens.

I had no idea who it was, but felt irritated that my errand would now be further delayed. I wanted to make it to the hospital and back before the roads became treacherous.

In the car's headlights, I could see that I had missed my opportunity to avoid the storm, and my heart sank. Snow was coming down hard.

As if to confirm this, the oncoming car fishtailed on the ice and snow as it made the turn into the circle driveway—sliding to a slippery stop.

It was then I noticed that the completely snow-covered car was a taxi. The driver got out and nodded silently to me. Before I could ask him his business, he ducked to open the back door, offering a hand to his passenger—Daniel Mayne.

No! No! No!

Daniel was wearing only jeans and a flannel shirt, the same clothes he wore to the hospital. He must have been freezing cold without his coat. He had no gloves on his hands; both of them were bandaged. His crutches were slipping in the new, icy snow. He held tight to a plastic bag with the County Hospital logo on it—I assumed it contained his medications.

The tight circles of his dark curls, still warm from the cab and sticking up above the tightly wrapped gauze, were catching every snowflake that came his way, quickly covering his head. He gave it a light shake, but managed to shake loose only some of the heavy snow.

Shocked to see him standing in front of my lodge, and watching for his brother to get out of the cab, I almost didn't hear the taxi driver shut his door, and accelerate the engine. Before I could protest, the driver was heading the other way as fast as he could go, trying to build up enough speed to make it up the snowy, slippery hill.

Daniel and I stood mesmerized, watching the taxi driver as he sped, slipped, and fishtailed his way back up the lodge road, revving his engine dramatically the entire time. Miraculously, he made it up the steep incline, leaving deep tracks in the fresh snow.

I could no longer see him after the road curved around the tall pines, but could still hear his engine revving as he made it up to the tennis courts and out onto the main road. At least I assumed he made it, otherwise his car would have slid back down the driveway like a toboggan on Christmas Day.

In the silence created by the departure of the taxi, Daniel and I both turned and glared at each other. Neither spoke as the snow continued to blow, piling up on our heads, shoulders, and boots.

"Wow," Daniel eventually said, talking into the wind, "there's a guy who *really* didn't want to be snowed in at Kerby Lodge."

Amazing. Even covered in snow and ice, he was as mean as a hornet.

"A guy who really wanted you out of his car, you mean," I shot back. But out of the corner of my eye, I saw the crutches sliding apart from each other and instinctively reached out to grab Daniel's arm before he could fall—almost falling myself onto the icy driveway. That's the last thing either one of us needed!

There was no other option but to help him get inside the lodge, and then find out what in the blazes was going on.

After guiding Daniel to an oversized wing chair next to the roaring fire, I wordlessly, and angrily, kicked an ottoman over with my snowy boots, then gave a sharp nod in the direction of his bandaged ankle. He obediently put both feet up on the stool and leaned back into one side of the chair.

When he closed his eyes—tuning me out in my own home—I had to bite my lip.

"Like he owned the place," was a phrase that eerily kept going through my mind. I hoped it wouldn't turn out to be a prophecy.

Not trusting myself to speak, I left the room and went back to the apartment to remove my snow-covered boots, coat, gloves and hat.

What was he doing here, anyway—did he not know there was a full-fledged blizzard going on? He can't drive his car out of here, that's for sure. Even if the roads were clear! He came for his stuff, but then what was his plan? And where was his brother? All I knew was that my head was spinning from the unanswered questions.

Exhausted from my morning's activities, and from standing in the snow and wind, I dropped my weary head into my still cold hands.

A half hour later, I came back into the great room carrying two mugs of hot chocolate, and saw that Daniel Mayne was in a deep sleep, and not about to wake anytime soon. After covering him with a thick wool Pendleton blanket, I sat back in the matching wing chair and drank my cocoa.

Then I drank his.

12

Perspective is often missing during a Lake Michigan snowstorm. There's so much bluster, so much white on white—so much snow on snow—that you can't always tell where it starts or stops, or how deep it is. You have to measure it against something.

As I looked outside, the lake told me nothing. But the red Adirondack chairs on the front lawn told me the snow was already up to the high side of the seat—that meant we'd gotten eight to 10 inches of snow in just three hours, with no sign of it slowing down.

I turned back to look at a sleeping Daniel, and tried to broaden my perspective. I weighed and measured what I wanted, which was for him to not exist, against the reality of the situation. He wasn't going anywhere in this weather. Even after the snow stopped, he might be here for days.

The cab driver wasn't coming back—maybe ever again. He was probably sitting at home thanking his lucky stars for the bullet he dodged. I wondered what he thought would be worse: getting snowed in here with the two of us, or having to bring Daniel Mayne home with him to ride out the storm.

Then there was no-show Luke Mayne. He was supposed to be my hero, but was more problem than solution at the moment. He was either stuck in California, stuck in an airport, or stuck in a snow bank. While I was stuck with his brother.

No, Daniel wasn't going anywhere for the foreseeable future. The two of us would have to make the best of things.

On the bright side, I was not worried for my safety. I was sure I was more than a match for hospital-weakened crutch wielding Daniel Mayne. For the time being, he was more wounded animal than imminent danger.

But there would be ground rules and conditions. I wanted to know more than his name and address—I wanted answers. I wanted to know his story. And if anything doesn't smell authentic, I decided, I would strap him on the back of the snowmobile and haul him to the hospital, or to a hotel, or even to the dog pound.

Then someone else could sort him out.

"He's *WHERE?*"

Tad's phone message sounded surprised, protective, and slightly crazed. Try as I might, there was no easy way to tell my brother that the man who was plotting to steal my inn, Tad was sure—the man I wasn't supposed to speak to—was snowed in at Kerby Lodge. So I took the cowards way out and left a message with his answering service. I just couldn't deal with another conversation with my brother at the moment.

For now, he would have to trust that everything would be okay.

That would make one of us.

"Wakey wakey" I sing-songed to my visitor, while placing a mug of piping hot chicken soup next to the chair where Daniel had been sleeping for hours. I gave him a few minutes to open his eyes, and to remember where he was.

He gave a start, as if he were going to get up and bolt. But then his body must have reminded him of how much pain he was in, and he settled back and looked around.

"While the soup cools down," I said at last, catching his eye, "let me show you where you can freshen up, and sleep tonight. It will be more comfortable than that chair. Though you've been sleeping in it for nearly five hours."

Slowly, he got up and positioned his crutches, then followed me just a few steps off of the great room to the wing where I had six guestrooms. Luckily for him, the first room on the right had an attached bathroom and shower he could maneuver. The other five rooms shared a larger bath, but it was a longer walk, at the far end of the hall.

I showed him the room and the bed—it was on the smaller side, but it was warm and cozy. I had opened the heat register and added extra quilts, and turned on the bedside lamp.

Looking around, he could see that I had unpacked his medications from the plastic hospital bag, and placed them in the room, along with a glass and pitcher of water.

Daniel's coat and a few clean flannel shirts from his duffel bag now hung on wall pegs, with the rest of his clothing tucked away in the small dresser. On top of the dresser was a neat stack of his magazines, sitting next to his computer.

If I had expected gratitude, I would have been disappointed. Daniel Mayne matter-of-factly took in all my efforts and merely nodded. No appreciation registered in his pained eyes—no thank you was spoken from his dry, parched lips.

A short while later, we ate our soup to the sounds of the wind blowing and waves crashing, and thankfully, to the fireplace crackling. The snow was midway up the back of the Adirondack chair at this point.

"I was going to have the taxi drop me off at the A-Frame cabin this morning," Daniel broke the silence between us. His voice was gruff, but measured, "but it took so long to get released from the hospital that the snow had already begun. I was lucky to find any taxi willing to take me anywhere."

I kept eating, bracing myself against his next verbal attack. He was trying to be civil—but clearly it was a barely contained effort.

He continued, "it was my plan not to bother you any more than I have already."

I nodded at his slight concession to my inconvenience—which I felt to be significant.

"That driver wasn't willing to take you all the way to the cabin?" I asked, facetiously.

Daniel shook his head. "I'm lucky he didn't make me tuck and roll onto the driveway, while he tossed my crutches out the window."

I couldn't help but smile a little at that image. But the other image of Daniel Mayne in the A-Frame during a blizzard, with a fractured leg and a concussion, sobered me up.

"The A-Frame isn't insulated—it would have been freezing cold," I said. "That little wood stove is cute, and good for the shoulder seasons, but not full-on winter."

He nodded, frowning, taking it all in.

Then I said, "and having you freeze to death at my lodge would be really bad for business. It's bad enough as it is."

I immediately regretted exposing my vulnerability, and wished I could take back my words.

After the warm soup, and a spell of exhausted silence on both sides, I brought out a plate of cookies I picked up at the town bakery, and two glasses of milk. A serious snack for the serious turn our conversation was going to take.

I threw a few more logs on the fire, and sat back down. A sudden gust drew both of our eyes towards the horizon, as the wind rattled the big windows and shook the lodge. The lake was barely visible now against the darkening skies and heavy snow.

"When I was growing up here," I said, as I positioned a blanket on my chilled lap, "I used to hide from the endless turnover of families and kids every summer."

Daniel watched me as I spoke.

"My parents were anxious for me, I guess you could say. They wanted me to make friends every week, just like they did. But I couldn't," I went on. "A week wasn't enough time for me."

I stopped to eat half of a cookie as Daniel turned to stare at the fire.

"So, I spent a lot of time watching other kids play," I said. "From the apartment, from the porch, from trees where I sat in the branches. I needed to watch to see how they interacted with others—to know whether someone was a cheater, or played fair."

I hated letting my guard down, but it was the only shortcut I knew to hearing what I wanted to hear. I took a drink of milk and went on.

"I guess what I'm trying to say is that old habits die hard. I should have introduced myself to you after you checked in—whether you wanted to meet me or not," I said.

Daniel frowned and nodded slightly, maybe just to show he was listening.

"This is my lodge and my job, and you were a guest." I purposely used the past tense. The guest ship had sailed. He was now an intruder.

"I should have taken responsibility," I continued. "Instead, I tried to sum you up by observing. And I made assumptions that may have been wrong," I said, finally.

I looked at Daniel, worn out and pale by the fire. He was leaning into the side of the chair as if he had no strength left. Just a few days ago, he had been healthy and robust, and I had been counting the days until he would return the key, and drive off into the brisk November air.

"But here you are. My worst nightmare." I gestured to the room that we were sitting in together, and to the storm raging outside. Strong winds pelted snow against the lakefront windows, and each of us held our wool blankets a little tighter.

"We are stuck together, maybe for a week. Probably longer," I said.

The wind rattled the windows again.

"And you don't know me," Daniel said, after we'd turned our attention back to each other. "You don't trust me."

I stopped myself before saying "and I sure as heck don't like you," but hoped that was understood.

"You've put me in an uncomfortable position," I said, which made Daniel's frown deepen. "I have to make sure you don't slip into a coma, or take too many pain meds. If you do either of those things," I said, indicating the raging storm outside, "we're both in big trouble."

Daniel turned towards the fire, avoiding eye contact with me.

"This has gotten real personal, real fast," I said, quieter than before.

He nodded.

"So in return, I want to know everything," I stated, with little doubt as to my seriousness. "Who are you, Daniel Mayne? And why have you been hiding at my lodge for three months?"

After a time, Daniel answered. "You want to know if I'm a cheater, or if I play fair."

"For starters," I said.

After what seemed like a long pause, Daniel spoke.

"That hospital bed was brutal," he said, "and those quilts are calling me."

I was about to protest, when he continued.

"Can you please make a big pot of coffee in the morning?"

"Yes," I said. "It's pretty bad. But there's plenty of it."

"Perfect," he said. "I'll see you then, and I'll tell you everything."

I watched as a very weak and weary Daniel Mayne slowly got up from the chair, leaned on his crutches, and made his way from the great room to the guest room. After he disappeared I turned to listen to the wind as it continued to drift snow against the windows. I hoped the power wouldn't go out in the night—that's the only way things could get worse.

It had been a long day, and my own warm quilts were calling me.

13

*I think we're taking half your beach home
in our shoes, towels, and car.*
-KERBY LODGE GUEST BOOK-

I woke much too early the next morning, but kept my eyes closed and listened to the storm rage outside. The gentle clanging of the old furnace, and the distant rumbling of the refrigerator motor coming from the kitchen, let me know that our power had not gone out. I wasn't eager to climb out from the warmth of my bed and face the snow, or my intruder. I tried to doze a little longer.

Why was I so eager for summer to end every year, when these storms were waiting to pounce?

When I was a child, I couldn't wait for that feeling of freedom I felt the day after Labor Day—my favorite day of the year. After an entire season of watching family after family enjoying their getaways at our lodge, I longed to get away too. Even if it was to school.

Our bus stop was way up at the main road, by the lodge entrance, and Gram's house. Where I would happily wait for the school bus to take me away.

Tad and I were the only students within miles who were picked up from a home on Lake Michigan. That's because most of the homes along the coast were summer cottages. The kids from those cottages, who we heard screaming and laughing on boats all summer, would be standing at their own bus stops this morning in Chicago, Detroit, or Minneapolis.

I sometimes wondered what they thought happened to us after the summer was over. Did they think entire coastal towns full of restaurants, gift shops, art galleries, and carry-out pizza all closed up because they were gone—like game pieces going back in a box?

The truth was, I realized when I got older, those kids didn't give us any thought at all. But that didn't matter. The summer tourists faded away for us, too.

Winter was our time—still is. The peak social season for us locals. It's when locals eat in the restaurants we work in during the summer. It's when we frequent the pubs and bars—driving our snowmobiles through heavy drifts and across icy fields—just to eat, dance, and gossip. Winter is when we have our weddings and our deferred birthday and anniversary parties. It's when we can stop being "on" and truly relax. Be ourselves.

The uniforms of a Lake Michigan summer—the pink and green polo shirts, oxford button downs in faded blues and yellows, and khaki shorts and skirts—are replaced with our stretched-out sweaters and thick flannel shirts, layered over long-johns and blue jeans.

No slip-on deck shoes for us. We stomp the snow off our heavy boots wherever we go—being careful not to slip and slide on ancient slat floors.

The deep winter will find about half of the local business owners gone south or west, to ride out the worst of the snow and ice. But just as many of us stay put.

When they were alive, my parents longed for nothing more than to enjoy long winter days by their big stone fireplace—reclaiming, for a season, the massive great room they turned over to guests during the summer.

Kerby Lodge could host around 100 guests at any one time, and my parents hit capacity for nearly 13 summer weeks every year. But during the dead of winter, our family lived in the lodge like happy mice.

We stockpiled firewood just outside the front door, half blocking the lodge's summer entrance. We dragged warm quilts and throws onto the sofa and chair cushions our guests had worn to pancakes over the years.

We played endless board games, ate meals from the well-stocked pantry and freezer, and watched movie after movie as the wind raged outside, while log upon log was tossed on the fire to keep it blazing hot.

Dad called it "hunkering down season" and exclaimed, proudly, that we were experts.

Anyone who has ever lived along one of the Great Lakes in winter understands why coastal dwellers pack up and run inland by Labor Day. The weather changes quickly, and relentlessly. What starts out as a lovely "nip in the air" can turn into rain, then freezing rain, and finally snow and ice—sometimes in mere days.

"Why, we were just swimming in that lake a few weeks ago," is a common sentiment shared by locals as they stock up on supplies at the hardware and grocery stores. This, while steel-gray skies become deeper and darker. And the winds begin.

To say that we listened to the wind makes it seem as though we had a choice. Instead, we endured the wind and the crashing waves it produced. We couldn't tune it out or turn it down. Wind fiercely pushing at the lodge was the background noise to every puzzle we assembled, every game we played, and every meal we ate. No matter how many logs we added to the fire, the frigid sound of wind and waves always lurked in the background.

"Every night sounds like a tragic shipwreck," I exclaimed once to my parents and brother years ago, as we sat in the lodge with the winter wind howling outside. The exterior storm windows that Dad and Tad put up in October would rattle along the length of the old lodge, while old-growth trees would bend and sway like they were about to snap in two.

Even though the nautical flag pole between the lodge and the shoreline was stripped of flags, the pulleys, ropes and metal hooks whipped, twanged, and vibrated as the wind violently tried to set them free.

Our savin' grace is th' cove, Mum would note. It was true. We sat on a strip of land in a coved semi-circle—the shoreline reaching out well past Kerby Lodge like strong arms holding back the bigger lake. Those arms protected the lodge from the worst of the lake winds from November through February.

In the summer, when the water was blue and quiet, it was a pleasure to look out and see the lighthouse jutting out on the land's end to the left, and a sand dune cliff on the land's end to the right. But not in the winter, when the waves thundered against the shore. As the waves pounded I sometimes felt just a little jealous of the summer kids, safe and sound in their quiet cities and suburbs, far from the crashing surf.

Now, with the hazy daylight peeking through my curtains, and a stranger recovering on the other side of the lodge, it would be days before the snow stopped falling—and more days before anyone could plow the Kerby Lodge driveway.

As I tried to work up the courage to get out from under my toasty blankets, what moved me was my responsibility for my accidental lodger. I needed to check on Daniel to make sure he wasn't sleeping too deeply for his head injury.

And I could do with a hot meal and a warm fire.

Dressed in double-thick leggings and wool socks, and one of my dad's long flannel shirts, I grabbed my phone, which was plugged into its charger, and noticed a message.

"Kay, it's Luke." He sounded tired and defeated.

"Got half way to Denver, and the plane turned around and brought us back. Couldn't land in the storm. I guess you're getting quite the storm, too." He continued, "Just know I tried, and call me when you can. Please let me know if you've heard from my brother. The hospital said he was discharged, but that's all I know."

Well, hats off to you, Luke Mayne, for trying to be my hero, anyway.

14

*We thought it wasn't supposed to
rain at Kerby Lodge? Oh well.*
-KERBY LODGE GUEST BOOK-

As I passed through the dining room towards the great room, I plugged in the Methodist Church coffee urn, which I'd set the night before.

And then I heard the fireplace crackling.

"This room hasn't changed in 32 years," Daniel said from the winged chair as I entered. He was wearing a clean flannel shirt, and looked as though he shaved—as much as he could shave around the scratches on his face, that is. Between the attempt at grooming and the sheer quantity of sleep he'd gotten, his face looked more relaxed, and slightly less threatening.

He had a great fire going.

"Of course," I responded, "you've been to Kerby Lodge before."

"The summer when I was twelve, and my brother was about eight, our family spent two weeks here, in the A-Frame," he went on, staring into the fire. "I think that cabin was pretty new then—we might have been the first family to stay in it."

"That sounds about right," I replied.

When I was a toddler, Dad built the red A-Frame for Mum, thinking they might want their own getaway spot, away from the lodge. But when they realized how much income it could generate, they rented it out instead. The same story could be told about most of the buildings my parents constructed.

But I remember Mum packing me a little picnic basket filled with snacks and toys, and holding Dad's hand as we ventured to the A-Frame building spot. It seemed so far from the lodge! There, I would spend hours happily playing, and napping, on a sun-warmed blanket while Dad painted the walls, and crafted the log stairs.

"My folks slept up in the loft," Daniel continued, "and while there was plenty of room up there, Luke and I slept in sleeping bags on the living room floor. Every morning we'd get up early and slip out without waking our parents. We just slept in our clothes every night," he said, "so when we woke up we could go exploring for hours and hours."

I silently set a mug of coffee on the table next to Daniel, and sat down with my own.

"We would walk through the woods and climb the trees. We'd take a canoe out on the water and paddle along the shoreline. We would sneak into the side door of the carriage house and pull out a few bikes without your brother knowing—and we'd ride up and down the hill until we were winded."

"Then we'd head back to the A-Frame where Mom would have pancakes, eggs, and bacon waiting for us to devour! Afterwards," he said, "we'd all get on our swim suits and spend the afternoon on the beach and in the lake; swimming, sailing, and eating ham salad sandwiches with chips and lemonade."

Daniel looked into the fire. "It was the best summer of my life."

If my parents were still alive, they would be touched to tears hearing these happy memories of Kerby Lodge. It's what they hoped to achieve—and they were a success, by Daniels' account. But it was his mention of Tad and the carriage house that hit home for me as he spoke.

Each spring, I could always find Tad in the carriage house, using wrenches, oil cans, and air compressors to get dozens of bikes, trikes, and wagons in tip-top shape for the crush of summer kids—who would often repay his efforts by recklessly riding the toys too hard into the woods or onto the sand. In ways they wouldn't dare treat their own toys.

Some of the older boys would crash the bikes into trees like bumper cars.

They'd abandon the toys in the middle of the driveway, or out in the rain to rust as they ran into their cabins for dinner, leaving Tad to gather them all up at the end of each day and return them to shelter.

Sadly, I haven't opened the carriage house doors in years, and haven't tried to maintain the bikes and toys on my own. Now, the rusty metal fenders and petrified chains seem more liability than asset to the lodge.

"Daniel," I said, pulling us both back from our memories, "grab your crutches and come into the kitchen. You can sit at the table while I cook us breakfast."

I was sure I had everything to whip up pancakes, eggs, and bacon.

"But your family never came back?" I asked later, as I drove my last piece of toast around the egg and syrup on my plate. "That's what most families did. Once they stayed here, they could reserve the same week for the following summer. It was a huge draw."

"I begged them to come back," he said, sipping his coffee. "But they wanted us to have different experiences every year—and I shouldn't complain. We went everywhere."

Daniel frowned into space while listing all his travels, in a tone that made them sound like childhood illnesses instead of the privileges that they were. "Amusement parks, rafting in the Grand Canyon, a dude ranch in Montana, a villa in Italy, the beaches of Jamaica."

"Wow. Just wow."

"Like I said," he repeated, though a little sharply, "I shouldn't complain."

"And of all the places you traveled," I said, treading lightly, "you came to the A-Frame at Kerby Lodge when…"

I was about to infer that Kerby Lodge was Daniel's *happy place*, but I let that comment go unsaid. To think that such an unpleasant man had a happy childhood, or a happy place, seemed impossible.

Was this miserable person raised by wolves? His wild dark curls and scratches could support the theory. But I doubted that wolf parents took cruises to Alaska.

"Let's go back by the fire," Daniel said, "I'll add a few logs."

"And you should put your leg up," I said, hoping he wasn't stalling.

We both turned to look out the window. It hardly seemed possible, but the wind had increased, piling the white snow drifts deeper and deeper.

15

What a great week—best weather ever.
See you at Jim Junior's grad party!
-KERBY LODGE GUEST BOOK-

"I worked for a large advertising agency in Chicago these past 19 years." Daniel was back in his wing chair. He had a quilt on his lap and his bandaged foot elevated, and was staring into the fire. His scowl was back. He held his hand on his forehead, as if he were battling a headache.

"I started in the mat room," he said.

I shrugged to indicate I had no idea what the mat room was.

"The mat room was filled with recent design school graduates, all trying to stand out and break into the business. We were the ones who pulled all-nighters, eating pizza while putting together presentations for the creative teams to show their clients."

"Paying your dues?" I asked.

"Yes, and paying attention—at least for my part. The mat room was a chance to get a first-hand look at the creative ideas that were making it in front of the clients," he explained. "It was a great post-art-school education, if you kept that perspective."

I nodded. I had zero knowledge of real-world jobs, or what it took to get ahead. I suppose picking up twigs was my mat room, and my big break was... I didn't want to finish that thought.

"After a year, I got my opportunity. A group of designers, copywriters, and producers had an opening for a junior-level designer and they gave me a chance. I ran full speed, working long days and late nights to prove myself worthy."

After a pause, Daniel continued. "Eventually, I worked my way up to senior designer, then to associate creative director, and finally to the position I held for the last five years: senior creative director and vice president."

"*The* vice president of the company," I said, impressed.

"No," he corrected me, "one of many. It's just a perk some people got in lieu of a raise. Looks great on your business card."

I listened to Daniel, trying to take it all in.

"The next step in my career would have been the biggest one of all—a promotion to executive creative director. The head of the agency's entire creative department. I had every reason to believe that job and title would be mine. People treated me as if I were the 'heir apparent' to the current person in that role, who was about to retire. So..."

Daniel seemed to have something caught in his throat. I got up and refilled our coffee mugs, and then gave him a few minutes to continue.

Finally, Daniel turned and looked right at me. "Every morning when I walked in, people would take notice. They'd been waiting for me. They'd hand me urgent messages as I walked through the hallway. They'd tell me what meetings were on my calendar that day—everyone wanted me in their meetings."

"My assistant would ask me what I wanted to order for lunch," he said.

I tried to visualize this frenetic work environment, where my wounded and heavily bandaged lodger was the king of the hill.

"Teams of people would be standing outside my office when I arrived, waiting to pitch ideas and get my input," he went on. "I'm the one who approved ideas—or killed them."

That got my attention.

"Sure, I was tough on people, that was my job," Daniel said, as if to ward off criticism. "That's how I got people to push themselves and do their best work."

"Trust me," he said, "creative people don't need a best friend for a boss. They need to be provoked. Prodded. Challenged. Iron sharpening iron. And then," he paused before finishing his thought, "and only then would they take truly great work into a presentation, and sell it like they believed in it."

"Our agency was great," he said, "because our work was great. And our work was great because..." And here Daniel seemed at a loss for words. "I still can't believe they..."

Daniel took a moment to gaze outside before he went on.

"The current lead creative director was a huge talent; an industry legend. But she became so busy planning her retirement and vacations—well, as the saying goes, she had one foot out the door."

"And you had one foot in the corner office?" I ventured.

Daniel nodded, as he turned to glare into the fire.

I was spellbound, wondering what could possibly have gone sideways for Daniel.

Finally, he went on.

"This past August, early in the month," Daniel sighed. "I walked in on a normal Wednesday, and the air seemed charged. Key people were missing, like it was a ghost town. Nobody met me in the hall or took my lunch order. There was nobody waiting outside my office. It was surreal."

"When I logged into my computer there was just one morning meeting on my calendar, and it said MANDATORY in the subject line. It was located in a conference room off the main floor lobby that I wasn't familiar with. I assumed it must be about a new business presentation, but I couldn't scare anybody up to ask."

"I was surprised to see one lone person sitting in the conference room when I got there, with a stack of papers and folders in front of her. She told me she was from the Human Resources department, and said that my services were no longer required at the agency. Effective immediately."

"They were letting me go." Daniel swallowed hard. "I knew it must be a mistake!"

He paused for a minute before continuing.

"The blood must have drained from my head, because it was spinning. But the HR lady just kept talking and talking, regardless. She walked me through exit paperwork—the severance pay they were giving me, my health insurance options going forward—things like that."

"All I could think was *where's my team?* I was sure they would flip when they heard the news, and would demand to have me back. But I found out later from a friend that, not only did they know, but they were already moving on," Daniel said.

"Turns out, the entire agency was packed in the auditorium, being introduced to the new executive creative director—the position I thought would be mine."

"He was a so-called 'creative genius' they'd lured from the UK—full of the *fresh energy* and *global perspectives* that I, apparently, was lacking."

"That's terrible," I couldn't help say.

"This genius was talking to everyone in the auditorium, and wowing them with his accent, and by saying *brilliant*, and *rubbish*, and then *brilliant* again," Daniel said. "And of course, everyone was so eager to be liked by the new boss, that they were laughing and applauding every word that came out of his mouth."

"Meanwhile, I wasn't even allowed—trusted—to go to my office and gather my things. Without a hint of human feeling she handed me my car keys, and said they would mail the rest of my belongings. She actually told me 'security has been notified' and told me I would no longer be allowed in the building."

He took a deep breath and closed his eyes for a few minutes.

"Two security officers walked me out," he said at last, with eyes still closed.

I was gripping the hem of my flannel shirt.

"I was in shock. I was embarrassed and humiliated," he said, quietly. "I felt like a complete fool—for walking into work that day, thinking I was on top. Then for discovering that all the people who worked with me, and worked for me, were being told that my work was stale. That the agency would be better off without me. After nearly twenty years."

We let silence fall between us for a time while I threw a few logs on the fire.

"And you came here to figure out next steps?" I asked, after a few minutes.

He nodded.

"At first, I figured I'd have another position in days," he said. "In the past, other agencies tried to lure me away. For more money, even. But I stayed loyal." He shook his head at this.

Daniel told me that colleagues from other agencies who had once been beating down his door, stopped calling—and wouldn't even return his calls.

"Apparently I was no longer a hot commodity," he said, "once I was actually available."

I listened in disbelief.

"So, I sublet my downtown apartment, put my severance check in the bank, and came to Kerby Lodge to stare at Lake Michigan and put my life back together," he said.

Daniel went on to say that in his three months at Kerby Lodge, he'd gone through all the classic stages of grief: shock and denial, bargaining with God, reflection and loneliness—all while avoiding me, and postponing contact with family and friends.

Now his behavior towards me was beginning to make sense.

"And then, in the middle of November," he said, "I was sick of being with myself. I'd had enough introspection to last a lifetime. I was ready to turn things around. I was determined to pick myself up, and work towards a better life."

"But then you fell off a chair," I said, continuing the story where I came in.

Daniel nodded, ruefully, "adding injury to insult."

16

Teens will be teens, won't they?
Someday we'll laugh at this summer.
-KERBY LODGE GUEST BOOK-

I insisted we stop, so Daniel could take his pain medication and go lay down for a rest. He was drained from retelling such a heartbreaking and personal story. I was drained from hearing it.

The snow continued its steady fall, silently piling deeper, beginning to obscure the view from some of the windows. When I put dinner in the slow cooker I would also have to take a few things out of the freezer for future meals—we were not going anywhere anytime soon.

It occurred to me that Thanksgiving was just days away.

I always attended the community feast, even if I had to arrive by snowmobile through the deep drifts. We locals couldn't let a little snow scare us off from important social engagements. But Daniel wouldn't be able to ride in his condition, and it wouldn't be right to leave him here alone.

I had ingredients on hand to cook a small Thanksgiving dinner for two, just in case the driveway wasn't clear and we had to stay in.

Later that afternoon, while Daniel continued sleeping, I bundled up and ventured outside. The first order of business was unearthing the snow shovel that sat by the front entrance, and clearing the area. Along Lake Michigan, the term "snowed in" could be very literal when tall drifts blocked entryways.

I shoveled the snow away from the door and landing, and then started loading split logs onto a rolling carrier to bring inside by the fireplace. I had also planned on making my way to a few of the outbuildings to check on things, but I quickly abandoned that idea. The snow was too deep, and visibility was nonexistent.

The wind was whipping icy snow onto my exposed face and eyes—I should have put on my ski goggles before coming outside. My warm breath was turning the snow into icicles on the scarf I had wrapped around my neck and cheeks, making this layer of protection feel cold and scratchy. Time to go inside.

After hanging up my parka and snow pants, I put on dry socks and a fresh flannel shirt. Then I ran warm water on my cold face and hands, and liberally applied face cream and hand lotion to counteract the harsh winter elements.

Making my way into the kitchen, I heated up the soup from the day before and brought two mugs and a platter of crusty bread into the great room.

Daniel was up and adding logs to the fire, while leaning heavily on his crutches.

"How does your brother figure into this story, Daniel?" I asked as I set the warm mug next to his chair. I could hardly wait to sit down by the fire and warm my chilled feet and legs. "Luke sounds like a nice guy, who's worried about your well-being."

I continued to tell Daniel about our conversations, and about Luke's concerns.

Daniel scowled at me, and then down at his bandaged foot, "I wish he could have been kept out of this—all of this," he said. "Until after I figure everything out. The job, the injuries—then it would just be a funny story to tell Luke someday."

I frowned at Daniel. "I don't know what passes for humor in Chicago, but no part of this story is funny," I said.

He sat back down, taking his time to elevate his injured foot once again. The pain on his face was evident—but I doubted it was all from the accident.

"Kay, did anyone ever call you a *show off* when you were a kid?"

"No," I snapped back.

Daniel looked up sharply.

"What I mean is," I said, softening my tone, "I was not that kid." I turned my thoughts to all the adolescent boys over the years who tried to get my attention by diving into the lake off the tire swing, or riding the bikes too fast down the hill.

"Yeah, well I was," Daniel said. "I feel as though I've been showing off to my brother all these years. When he had a break from teaching, I'd invite him to come with me when we filmed commercials for our biggest clients."

"We always went to great locations and stayed in nice hotels," he continued. "I was the client of the production company, and they bent over backwards to entertain me—and Luke, when he was my guest. We ate in the best restaurants, went to shows, went shopping—I sat next to the director during the actual filming."

I nodded slightly, thinking again how little I knew of his world.

"And now, I'm a nobody," he finished.

"You're being hard on yourself," I said. "It sounds to me like you were just sharing your experiences with your brother, not showing off," I said. "I don't imagine that Luke, as a teacher, would have the same travel opportunities you've had."

"Maybe," Daniel frowned.

"Our families love us for who we are, not what we do," I said. "They know us at our best and at our worst, and at our best again—and none of it matters."

Daniel looked at me intently.

If I didn't believe what I just said was true, I'd be miserable. I know that I loved my brother apart from his distinction as a successful doctor. Just as I counted on his love and acceptance, even though I wasn't anything I set out to be. Even though I may single-handedly lose our family home.

"So, Luke doesn't know about your… career change?" I asked.

Daniel shook his head.

"The little brother who idolized you. Followed you around while you climbed trees and canoed the shoreline—scammed bikes from the carriage house with you—tried to fly here in a snowstorm because you needed help—*he's* the one you're shutting out?" I persisted.

"It sounds bad when you put it like that," Daniel said, uncomfortably.

"Well, from what you've told me," I said, "you've had a lot of people in your life who were drawn to your importance. Who won't return your calls now."

Daniel groaned.

"You have one person who never cared how important you were—only that you were happy and doing what you loved," I continued. "And you're not returning his calls."

Daniel frowned at me and was about to protest, but I cut him off.

"More soup?" I smiled, and walked towards the kitchen.

17

If we gotta wake,
Let's wake at the lake!
-KERBY LODGE GUEST BOOK-

"Happy Thanksgiving," I said to Daniel a few days later, as we entered the great room from different areas of the lodge. I was in a long flannel shirt, leggings, and wool socks, and he was on his crutches. My greeting was a small olive branch. I was finding that maintaining anger took a lot more energy than I had.

He nodded, and offered me his usual frown.

The snowfall and winds had tapered off, and the sun was shining, making a beautiful, peaceful scene as we drank our coffee and looked out over the lake. It was too early for ice floes to begin forming, and without a wind, there were no whitecapped waves—only gentle swells of water rising and falling to the horizon.

I couldn't help but smile. The turkey was in the oven, with the smell of sage stuffing beginning to waft through the air. I found I was happy not to be by myself on this day, even if my companion was the gruff and injured Daniel Mayne. Who was looking a bit stronger and healthier, by the way. The scratches on his face had lost their redness. I could see that the sleep he was getting in the chilly guest room, under a pile of quilts, was restorative.

"I spoke with Luke last night," Daniel broke the silence.

Finally. I hoped there was more to the story.

"He was sympathetic—about the job and the fall," he said. "I apologized to him for not calling sooner, and he said he understood."

"Of course he did," I said. "My brother will always be there for me."

I resolved to give Tad a call that day, and catch up with him while Selby cooked their feast in Atlanta. Also, it occurred to me, while talking with Daniel about Luke, that I've been a hypocrite—there are important things

67

I need to tell my own brother that I've been avoiding. Today might not be the day, but I would have to come clean, and soon.

I would also call Aunt June and Uncle Zeke in Florida, and give them an update on all things regarding life and lodger.

Later that afternoon, after large helpings of turkey and cranberries, potatoes, stuffing, and baked green beans with crispy onions, Daniel was dozing in the wing chair by the fire, while I was napping away my own turkey coma on one of the great room sofas. The fire felt warm and inviting, and lulled me into a deep sleep.

It wasn't long before I was dreaming about being a child again, during a Lake Michigan winter. In my dream, I was riding on the back of my dad's snowmobile, trying to get to the bus stop in time. It seemed so real. I could almost hear the revving and whining of the two-stroke engine. It was getting louder and louder—until I woke with a start, realizing an actual snowmobile was approaching the lodge.

Daniel heard it too, because his eyes were open as he tried to orient himself.

"Sounds like someone's here!" I exclaimed.

"Happy Thanksgiving, Kay!" Patrick and Jennifer, our personal EMT team, were standing in the entrance of the lodge minutes later, covered in snow and snow gear.

They were holding a boxed-up pumpkin pie and a larger cardboard box, which I took from them so they could peel the snowy layers off in the warm foyer of the lodge.

"I missed you at the community feast," Jennifer said as she shucked out of her winter gear, "you always come!"

"I know," I hugged my friend, who now looked like herself in sweater and jeans.

Patrick chimed in, "we thought we'd check on you two."

"You *two*?" Daniel said, standing on his crutches in the background. "How did anyone know I was here?"

Patrick and Jennifer laughed.

"It's a small village," Jennifer said.

"Especially in winter," Patrick added.

As it turned out, the taxi driver was sitting across from Patrick at the community Thanksgiving dinner, and entertained everyone with his harrowing story of dropping Daniel off at the lodge, then barely making it up the hill as the snow storm began.

"He had us all laughing, but he was exaggerating, right?" Jennifer said. Daniel and I exchanged glances.

"When I mentioned to Patrick that we should go check in on you," she continued, "Gretel from the post office, also at our table, believe it or not, said she had a package for a Daniel Mayne, and asked if we could deliver it. She thought it might be important."

"So here you are, sir," Patrick said as he pointed to the box on the coffee table.

Daniel nodded his thanks.

"And when Mitch heard we were coming to see you, he insisted we bring one of the extra pumpkin pies—he made them all himself," said Jennifer. "We'll gladly share this one with you, if you have a cup of that awful coffee you make so well."

I laughed out loud and threw my arms out to hug her again. And Patrick.

"Afterwards, we will check and re-dress your bandages," Patrick said to Daniel, "on order from Doc Petersen."

"Don't tell me," Daniel said, flashing the first genuine smile I'd ever seen from him, "he was also at your table, sitting between the taxi driver and Gretel."

The four of us laughed and talked over each other as we pulled our chairs closer to the fire, and ate large pieces of pumpkin pie with whipped cream. Patrick and Jennifer filled me in on the gossip and news from town, while Daniel tried his best to keep up with who was doing what and where.

I noticed that while he spoke, Patrick reached over for Jennifer's hand more than once, and she turned and smiled at him in return. They hadn't mentioned *this* little bit of gossip.

After clearing the coffee mugs and pie plates, I took them to the apartment kitchen on my favorite vintage metal tray, featuring an image of Santa Clause drinking a bottle of soda. Patrick and Jennifer, meanwhile, helped Daniel to one of the sofas. They used the medical kit they carried in a backpack to check his blood pressure and temperature, and the dilation of his pupils.

They removed the large bandage from around Daniel's head, and replaced it with a small square bandage, adhered to his wound at the hairline. The new bandage made Daniel look more like he was on the mend and less like a Civil War reenactor.

They unwound the bandage that wrapped around his ankle, and gently manipulated his foot in every direction to test its flexibility.

"Swelling has gone down a bit," Jennifer said, "but try to elevate it more often."

"Don't walk on it, it's too soon," Patrick added. "And don't let Kay talk you into chopping firewood or shoveling snow just yet," he joked, in a loud voice that I'm sure he meant for me to hear from the next room.

"No problem there," I said quietly, to myself. The *laird o' the manor*, as Mum would say, is fully accustomed to being coddled and waited upon by now.

"When you get back to the hospital for a follow-up, Doctor Petersen may be able to give you a walking cast," Jennifer added while talking to Daniel.

They checked his prescriptions, and they both seemed pleased with his progress.

"Overall," Patrick was saying, as I walked back into the great room, "you look a thousand times better than the last time we saw you—laying on the floor of the A-Frame!"

Daniel surprised me by turning my way. "Thanks to the innkeeper," he said.

At the door, saying our goodbyes, there were hugs and kisses all around. Just one couple, saying goodbye to another couple. And it occurred to me that it wouldn't be terrible to be part of a couple. I just wished that my other half wasn't the often irritable, sometimes charming, Daniel Mayne.

I would gladly trade a little less of his unreliable charm for a lot less of his brooding—I had that character trait covered all by myself, thank you very much.

"Next time, we'll play cards," I heard Daniel say to Patrick and Jennifer, which they readily agreed to, as they went through the front door to get back onto their snowmobile and drive away on top of the deep drifts—waving to us as they went.

"Kay?" It was Luke on the phone. I was just about to turn the light off next to my bed, and curl up under the warm blankets.

"Am I calling you too late—I sometimes forget the time difference between California and your neck of the woods—hope I didn't wake you." He sounded a bit sheepish.

"No Luke," I said, "it's late, but I was still up. Happy Thanksgiving," I added.

"Same to you," he answered. "I wanted to catch you and thank you for taking care of my brother. I know this is going above and beyond your innkeeper duties," he continued. "I filled my parents in when they called from the ship. We are all indebted to you, Kay."

"It's a first for sure," I laughed a little, "but it's okay."

I thought for a minute about how, in past years, I'd come home on Thanksgiving night from the community feast by myself, to a dark and cold lodge, and how nice the day turned out just by having another person there—even if it was Daniel Mayne.

And the unexpected visit with Patrick and Jennifer was the icing on the cake—or rather, the whipped cream on the pie at the end of the day.

"Did you have dinner today with family and friends?" I asked, realizing I knew very little about Luke Mayne.

"Just us lonely co-workers," he replied.

Luke went on to tell me about the charter school where he taught, and how he, and many of the teachers, were there for a two-year commitment. The ones that were single and away from home pooled their talents for a group dinner.

"It was an eclectic feast," Luke said. "We had turkey, and also paella, tacos, and stir fry."

I couldn't help but laugh. Why couldn't it have been Luke Mayne who was snowed in at Kerby Lodge, instead of his unpleasant older brother? I might have enjoyed someone with a sense of humor.

He went on, "I get a little sentimental for tradition this time of year. I'd kill for a leftover turkey sandwich tomorrow, with cranberry sauce and stuffing piled high."

"Hmm, that's on our menu for tomorrow," I said, stifling a yawn.

Luke pretended to groan.

"Good night Luke."

18

Drink coffee. Swim in the lake. Grill burgers.
Repeat. Repeat. Repeat.
-KERBY LODGE GUEST BOOK-

"Kay, are you asleep?" I heard Daniel whisper. I was awake, but not fully.

"Mmm," I managed.

"Were you serious when you said your business was failing?" He was still speaking softly, probably in case I was asleep—it was too dark to see.

But I was awake now, thanks to the topic that kept me awake most nights. I opened my eyes. "Serious as a heart attack," I managed.

It was late one night, during the second week of December. We were tucked into sleeping bags, trying to rest on the two massive great room sofas—the formidable log coffee table between us.

The power had gone out in the lodge, likely from the heaviness of new snow on the power lines, and my generator could not run the massive furnace. But between the fireplace and space heaters, the great room would stay comfortable, even on the coldest days. And hopefully, nights.

"I'm sure I will be fine in my guestroom," Daniel protested at first, in his grumpy, gravelly voice when I told him of the arrangements for the night. But when he opened the door to his room, he realized just how cold the shut-off wing became once the furnace stopped blowing warm air.

"The property taxes are sky high," I continued, wondering if Daniel had fallen asleep waiting for me to talk. "And my guests have really dwindled these past few summers. I guess people are finding other things to do, and other places to go with this recession."

"I'm barely bringing in enough to cover taxes and expenses," I said. "There's a new assessment coming any time now, and I'm dreading it."

There was no point in pretending to be too proud to admit these things—although I hadn't admitted them to anybody else. Maybe to

Jennifer, the last time we'd had lunch in town. It must have been the intimacy of the fire crackling in the darkness that made me all chatty about my business failings.

"All it will take is one time. If I am unable to pay my tax bill, I might as well hand the entire lodge and acreage to the government—because I won't recover from a tax lien, with its compounding interest and penalties," I said. "At this rate that time is not so far off."

I might as well paint an accurate picture of the financial realities of Kerby Lodge—if Daniel does want to sue me and take the property, at least he'll know what he's getting into.

"You don't want to sell it?" He surprised me by asking. I guess he was awake.

"I suppose I'd rather sell it than lose it. But not to one of the carpetbaggers prowling around right now, practically stealing homes and properties from hard-working people who are temporarily down on their luck."

I was determined to not give the lodge away. If I could find a way to get more guests to stay here next summer, then maybe I could hang on to it for a few years until the value started increasing again. There were signs that values could be on the way back up, after sitting on the bottom for way too long.

"I don't want to sell it for pennies on the dollar. The economy will recover soon and this amazing land, this shoreline, is my family's heritage."

"There's no place like it," he said, after a pause.

I lay there wide awake, long after Daniel had fallen back to sleep.

Daniel and I had been snowed in for three full weeks now.

After Thanksgiving, a second storm had put a new blanket of snow on top of the one that was just getting cleared throughout town. But in spite of the current power outage, my long sloping driveway, deferred several times, was finally going to be plowed during the night by Chip DeWolf. He's been working overtime plowing the parking lots of the hospital, schools, and police station.

I checked my phone for a text from Chip telling me that he had pushed my driveway to the back burner once again, but there was no such bad news.

"Thank you, Chip," I whispered before rolling over in my sleeping bag on the hard sofa cushions.

Chip was one of the guys I dated briefly in high school. But a year after graduating, he married Sue Spondike—eldest daughter and heiress to the many Spondike souvenir stores dotting lakeshore towns within a hundred miles. An industrious couple, Sue has managed to keep most of her stores open in the face of the recession, while other store owners have closed their doors.

As for Chip, his main income is earned during the summer, providing landscape services to wealthy cottage owners. In the winter, he plows driveways and parking lots for the county. As well as for cash-strapped innkeepers such as myself. He doesn't charge me very much, thankfully, but in return, I have to sit on the bottom of the list.

It's okay though. I know he'll get to Kerby lodge when he can—usually in the wee hours of a night like this one. But in the morning, I can finally drive into town, and run my lodger to the hospital for a check-up.

"Well, *Hop-Along*, let's take a look." Doctor Petersen was kind to fit Daniel into his schedule, once he heard that I was able to get my Jeep up the slippery driveway of the lodge, and into town. He followed Daniel, who was moving slowly on his crutches, to the examination room. I was sorry that I had been so disagreeable with the doctor at our last meeting.

Sitting in the waiting room of the hospital, I began scratching a list on a subscription card from one of the magazines. There were a few perishable items I wanted to remember at the village grocery store while we were out and about.

"Hey stranger!" I heard Jennifer's voice as she came into the waiting room, wearing her EMT uniform. "I saw your Jeep in the parking lot."

She sat down and we caught up on what had been going on since Thanksgiving.

For her, holiday-themed dates with her new boyfriend, Patrick, and helping the sick and injured in the county. For me, zero dates and zero holiday-themed anything, unless you counted the endless Christmas movies on TV about big city executives who had sworn off Christmas—only to find themselves stranded in a town where they find the true meaning of, yes, Christmas.

That, and helping one sick and injured person, who wasn't recovering fast enough for me, I told my friend.

"I like Daniel Mayne," Jennifer said. "He's nice, and he's smart. Patrick liked him too."

"He's okay in small doses," I conceded, and this made Jennifer laugh.

"Isn't he grateful for all you've been doing for him, Kay?"

Was he grateful? Or did he feel entitled? Was he settling in to what he considered to be his home now? His legal conquest?

Then she asked, "isn't he some sort of marketing guy? Why don't you pick his brain about the lodge while he's there? Put him to work."

Jennifer smiled and got up to leave, but promised she and Patrick would block out an evening for cards and pizza at Kerby Lodge in the next week. I told her our schedule was pretty wide open. We shared a quick hug goodbye.

I sat back down in the waiting room, quietly chewing over what Jennifer said.

Over the past three weeks, Daniel and I had fallen into a comfortable routine. I would cook our meals and bring in great armfuls of fire wood. Weather permitting, I made the rounds to a few cabins to check for natural disasters or animal intruders. Like the small black bear years ago who thought he would hibernate in the chalet on the hill. I called my ranger friend at the DNR, who coaxed him back into the forest to find another location.

After checking for animal squatters, I'd curl up and read by the fireplace, or watch old movies. Daniel would sometimes watch the movies with me, but more often he would be flipping through his endless design magazines—in fact, that's what filled the heavy box Patrick delivered to him on Thanksgiving night.

In between his naps, he tended the fire. When the ashes became thick, he'd let the fire die down so he could clean the old coals out, and start over. I appreciated that every task he did was much harder while balancing on crutches, and tending the fire was important during this exceptionally cold and snowy Lake Michigan winter.

Though he moved slow and rested often, Daniel seemed to feel better and stronger. We talked, but mostly small talk. He was interested in the history of the inn, but neither of us continued the conversation about losing the lodge—the one Daniel started when we were sleeping in the great room.

"Don't think I'm going to get up in the morning and follow you around the woods like Luke did," I had jokingly remarked, after unearthing the cold flannel sleeping bags from the storage closet, and burrowing in.

We were like an old married couple, only without the friendship, affection, or good memories that keep people warm on cold winter nights. But why hadn't I talked with Daniel about growing my shrinking business, or asked for suggestions or insight? Jennifer seemed to think I should, and I trusted her intuition.

I shook my head.

Could it be that this gruff and grumbly wounded lion—dropped at my doorstep—just might have the answers I'd been trying to find on my own?

Answers that could help me save my home and Kerby Lodge?

19

Our two boys "left only footprints" on every inch of this beautiful property these past 2 weeks.
-KERBY LODGE GUEST BOOK-

After weeks of being tied to the inn by the weather, and Daniel's injury, our first trip into town felt a little like a prison break. Of course if it were just me, I would have driven my snowmobile back and forth to town a half dozen times since the middle of November. But it wasn't just me.

Following the trip to see the doctor, the two of us were giddy with newfound power and freedom. The handful of storefronts and restaurants that remained open through December looked like shining palaces to us, glistening with sparkling holiday decorations and powdery snow, and beckoning us to come in.

Before long, my Jeep was loaded with heavy packages from the post office for Daniel—more magazines?—and bags of groceries. We had a few dozen cookies from the little bakery tucked in the back. And I bought a box of Christmas cards at Spondike's.

We stopped to pick up a carry-out pizza to take home and reheat for dinner. We even ducked into an art gallery—the only one open—to browse the nature photography and oil painted canvases of the shoreline, woods, and wildlife.

We ooh-ed and ahh-ed over every piece we saw, with exaggerated appreciation. It just felt so good to rest our eyes on anything more colorful and vibrant than the gray skies, white snow, and the earth tones of the lodge's great room.

Daniel now had the additional mobility of a walking cast. He still needed to rely on the crutches, the doctor said, except for an hour or two each day—which he was currently using up on our many ins-and-outs. I hoped he wasn't overdoing it, but I understood how he must feel at being set free, because I felt it myself.

"Why do they call it a walking cast when I still have to use the crutches?" he grumbled, frustrated with his limitations. I had no answer. Doctor Petersen also removed the hairline bandage completely, which was an improvement.

But he still had a long way to go.

I parked the Jeep in front of the Village Diner for a late afternoon lunch. As we were getting out, Daniel spotted a barber shop on the corner that was open. He wanted to run in and get a haircut before we ate. There was no new snow expected today, so we were safe.

I told him I would grab a booth, and wait for him inside while I, myself, enjoyed a little people watching out the diner's street side window. After settling in, I signaled the waiter for a cup of coffee with cream, and sat back to take in the view—a much different view than the one I'd had for days. Weeks. Years, even.

Bundled up, people in goose down parkas, heavy scarves, and snow boots were walking single file along the narrowly shoveled sidewalks, and in and out of the stores. Only a few had bags in their hands. I hoped, for the sake of the store owners, that they weren't all just window shopping.

Standing out from the crowd, one man caught my eye because of the smile on his face. It was my wounded lodger, walking across the street from the barber shop.

After our lunch was half eaten, Daniel said "I feel like a kid in a candy store, just enjoying the little things in life again. Buying groceries. Ordering a sandwich for lunch."

I agreed.

Still mulling over my brief conversation with Jennifer, I was wondering if this slightly more approachable Daniel was someone I could have a personal discussion with. Or would he prove himself to be as self-centered as the day we met? I was about to try, when Daniel spoke.

"Great little shops," he declared, gazing out the window. "Not overly perfect though, which I like. They're not *cookie cutter* perfect like in the more exclusive coastal towns."

"What are you saying, Daniel?" I asked, suspecting that his compliments were actually insults. My feelings of good will and happiness were starting to deflate.

"Just that… the stores seem very real," he said. "The awnings are just the right level of, what's the word, *tattered*—and the paint colors on the storefronts are worn and authentic."

I stopped in my tracks.

"Daniel, are you… are you *art directing* my home town?"

He started to speak, but closed his mouth. Just as I suspected.

"Did you want to suggest a wardrobe change for our waiter? Or the barber?" I asked.

Still no answer.

"This isn't a movie set, Daniel," I pointed out. "Real people live here and work here—at least the ones who haven't lost their homes or businesses to foreclosure."

Daniel's shoulders dropped and his expression softened. I had probably made my point already, but he'd hit a nerve, so I continued.

"I'm glad you approve of the tastefully tattered awnings. The shop owners are working hard to keep everything as nice as possible in this economy. They have to scrape together their rent and utility payments every month," I said, "even though the tourists haven't been coming. And the ones that do come, aren't spending a whole lot."

Daniel, with a potato chip in one hand, held his other hand up in a universal gesture of *please stop*.

Our waiter came just then to refresh our coffees, and asked if we needed anything. When he walked away, Daniel said "For the record, I wouldn't change a thing about our waiter." We both conceded a small smile as we went on with our lunch. For my part, I smiled because Daniel was in a good mood, under his arrogance, and it was contagious.

And I realized I wanted him as an ally. Warts and all.

I also felt a bit guilty. I'd been hoping for more conversation from my one lodger, and what happens when he does open his mouth to speak? I attack.

"I shouldn't have jumped on you like that," I said.

"Oh, you absolutely should have," he said, good naturedly.

I looked across the booth at Daniel, who looked years younger, handsome even, with his shorter hair, and shaved beard. He was savoring his sandwich and chips, and was without his perpetual frown as he gazed out the window. I wondered if he'd been in touch with the rumored love interest back in Chicago.

I also realized that he was tough, either by nature or by profession—in spite of the injuries that had weakened him for a time. I was pretty hard on him, just now, yet he was unfazed. I liked this about him.

There! I found something I liked about the unlikeable Daniel Mayne. I would have to tell Jennifer the next time I saw her.

"Daniel," I said, not sure myself what words were going to follow.

"Hmm?" He looked up at me.

"Maybe it's the haircut, or my good cooking, but you look as though you're doing well," I said, "all things considered."

Daniel's eyes narrowed, and he put down his sandwich. "You want me to leave the lodge, don't you? That's understandable. I've imposed on you enough."

"Just the opposite," I said, choosing my words. "Stay through the winter, and recover. Get your strength back. I think our arrangement is... okay, for both of us."

"Well, that's a surprise," he said.

"Actually, I would like your help."

I definitely had his attention at that statement.

"Look," I said. "I need to make big decisions within the year about the lodge, and until now, all of my wise counsel has been my own family—people who are too close to the history and the memories of this lodge to be objective."

Daniel didn't answer, just stared at me as I spoke.

"I need to talk about the future of Kerby Lodge with someone who is objective," I went on, "and detached from the situation."

"And I'm the most detached person you know," Daniel said, finishing my sentence.

If the snow shoe fits, I thought.

"Kay, what exactly are your expectations?" Daniel's glower was back.

We were on our third cup of coffee, and had both ordered a piece of the diner's homemade pecan pie—because it looked amazing and, I suspect, to prolong our outing.

"You're an idea person, Daniel, and I need ideas." I stated.

"What kind of ideas?" he asked. "Stale ones? I specialize in those."

I stared back in response to the self-pity from my lodger. If only he knew how much was at stake for me.

"Okay," he said, holding up his hands to stop me from speaking. "That was pathetic, and I'm sorry I went there. This is about you, and I am indebted to you."

It was good to hear him verbalize his gratitude, even though I'm the one who felt guilty, still, at leaving unsound chairs in the A-Frame for Daniel to fall off of. I softened my posture and expression, and he softened his tone in response.

"It's just that... I don't know if I have what it takes to fix your problems before it's too late, Kay." Daniel looked uncomfortable as he continued. "Helping you save your inn is a far cry from designing a magazine ad for toothpaste, or branding a new micro-brewery."

The door of the diner jingled as a large group of customers walked out into the snowy streets. I was glad we were sitting away from the open door, and the cold draft.

Daniel stirred his coffee.

"Even if I were at the top of my game, and not limping around and napping all day, the way I am," he said with real frustration in his voice, "that's a lot of responsibility. The hospitality industry is very competitive, I know that much—but that's pretty much all I know."

I didn't respond, and instead, waited for him to continue. My hope was that by talking it out, he would eventually run out of excuses and agree to be my knight in shining armor. So far, the Mayne brothers were full of good intentions, but light on action.

"At the agency," he went on, "I had entire research teams and account executives to give me background information and reports—here, it's just me."

Daniel raised both of his empty hands, as if to show how little he had to work with.

I wasn't ready to give up. There was too much to lose.

"My offer to stay through the winter is sincere, whether or not you agree to help me—but I think you could help me, Daniel," I said.

"Look at me Kay, I'm a mess," Daniel said, gesturing with his hands. "I can barely help myself right now. I can't cook. I can't drive. I'm out of work," he said. "I'm just a washed up marketing guy."

Stirring more cream into my coffee, I let Daniel's comments sink in for a few minutes. He had to realize that the afflictions on this laundry list were all temporary.

"At least you're not an insurance salesman," I said, trying to lighten the mood. "Then I'd have to ask you to leave."

Daniel half smiled at that.

"You *are* out of work, I'll give you that." I said. "But washed up? That's a choice."

He looked at me, and I saw a small glimmer of pain and confusion. Then I was angry—angry at the agency that had thrown him out like an old shoe, without any regard for his tenure or his loyalty. They tossed money at him, sure, but that only served to finance a period of depression, while he struggled to work his way back to ground zero—to finding his bearings once again.

"Daniel," I said, "please stop giving that agency power over you. You left with more than just your wallet and keys—you took your creativity and your experience. And your ability to portray something in its best light. These are real things," I said.

He seemed to hear me, and nodded.

"These are things I need," I said, more quietly.

We were silent for a time, each calculating the road ahead for our individual quandaries.

"I'm not asking for more than you can deliver," I said at last. "I don't even know how much can be accomplished with my limited funds, or if it's too late. But," I was trying to remain professional, "this next summer needs to be lucrative for the lodge. I need to make the phones ring, as you marketing guys say, and I have no idea how to do that."

Daniel frowned into the bottom of his coffee cup before he answered me.

"I'm afraid I'd let you down," he said.

"I'm already down," I shot back.

"You won't like the things I have to say," he said, with more confidence.

"I won't *like* losing my property," I retorted.

In fact, there were a lot of things I desperately would not like, and foreclosure was just one of them. There was no longer living on Lake Michigan. Or showing up penniless at my brother's doorstep. Or having to get a job down at the fishing docks, fileting perch for the tourists. I couldn't imagine that Daniel Mayne's words had more power to hurt me than these potential realities.

"Try me!" I mustered my inner strength and met his gaze.

"All right," he said, matching my stare. "Remember when I told you that your lodge hasn't changed in over 30 years?"

I did remember!

"That was not a compliment," he stated.

20

What good luck to stumble upon Kerby Lodge.
Can't wait to come back for more of the same.
-KERBY LODGE GUEST BOOK-

When I walked into the great room the next morning, the air felt still, and cold, even though Daniel had the fire blazing. I didn't see him at first— he wasn't in his usual wing chair by the hearth. Instead, he was perched on one of the large sofas, absorbed in reading a magazine. His injured leg stretched out in front of him.

I brought my lodger a cup of coffee, partly as a peace offering, but also because he could not carry the mug while maneuvering his crutches. Not without sloshing the hot bitter liquid all over the rug.

"Thanks," he said simply, without looking up.

We didn't talk on our ride back from town yesterday. It seemed that I'd spoiled the fun day we had. And now, I fully expected us to revert to our first days together, when words were terse and few.

But Daniel surprised me.

"Kay, there's something I'd like you to see," he said.

And without waiting for my response, he motioned to the big log coffee table, and with a sweep of his hand, to the stacks and stacks of magazines he'd placed there.

"Which one?" I asked, surprised at how much his collection had grown since we picked up another heavy box from the post office yesterday.

"All of them," he said, now looking me in the eye.

And before I could protest, Daniel patted the sofa next to where he had settled in, in front of the big coffee table, and gave me a command.

"Sit."

After sleeping fitfully, I woke up this morning with a painful knot in my stomach that I knew was situational rather than viral—I was out of options. And I had probably been unfair yesterday in my expectations of Daniel.

Maybe I'd been watching too many "happily ever after" movies in the past few weeks and they had skewed my judgment. But I was fairly certain there was not going to be a town benefit on Christmas Eve to *Save Kerby Lodge*. Daniel and I were not going to kiss under the mistletoe at midnight. My troubles would not be wrapped up in a neat bow in 90 minutes, with commercials.

Unhappy endings were all too real in my world.

As I lay in bed, I began cataloguing them. The short sales, the foreclosures, the heartbreaking estate sales at the most prominent homes and lodges in the area.

There was the old Sunset Lodge up the road, one of the few lodges that predated my own. No sooner had they installed a new well, and brand-new lodge and cabin siding, when they had their entire property repossessed for defaulting on a loan.

And then there was Candy French, friend and business rival of Sue Spondike. Candy took over her parents' tee shirt business when they retired. But when times became tight, she had to forego drawing a salary—and lost her new dream house on Lake Michigan. She was stretched too thin when the economy crashed.

Sue, of course, had the ever-frugal Chip to help sustain their own finances.

They have been able to weather the financial storm through Chip's penchant for squirrelling away money for a rainy day. Sue used to make fun of Chip for this, referring to him as "The Chipmunk," in other words a cheapskate, on girl's nights out. But she stopped doing so after seeing her friend lose her home.

The elder French's wanted to help Candy, but their own retirement funds had taken a major hit with the recession. All they could offer was her old bedroom—after they figured out what to do with the home gym equipment they had installed there.

There were dozens of such stories along Lake Michigan.

But so far, I had hung on.

Of course I kept the lodge the same! Even if I had money to make changes, I wouldn't dream of having it any other way, the way my parents found to be successful.

In spite of what Daniel seemed to be insinuating at the diner, maintaining the integrity of the lodge is the least I could do, for whatever time I have left here. Won't the faithful few abandon Kerby Lodge altogether if I start changing it up?

Yesterday, I was so angry at Daniel's insult—saying it wasn't a compliment that the inn had stayed the same—that I stormed out of the diner. Proving to be the nightmare client I had all but promised not to be.

So before even getting out of bed, I vowed to keep my cool today, no matter what Daniel said. After all, he hadn't rejected my proposal. But I needed to expect more from myself, and keep an open mind.

But... *sit*?

Spend a day looking at design magazines?

What a waste of time.

"Your parents were brilliant Kay," Daniel broke the silence.

We had been sitting side by side, flipping through magazines for hours. I would occasionally get us fresh coffee, and maybe a cookie or a sandwich. Daniel silently accepted each mug or snack, and continued his perusing.

At first, it felt like a chore. Like I was a kid again, being told to pick up twigs. But after an hour or two, when I realized Daniel was absorbed in his own reading and not monitoring me, I began to relax and actually enjoy reading the publications.

How different these books were—the smooth, glossy covers were so unlike the stacks of worn out magazines that had been sitting on the bottom shelf of the lodge bookcases for years and years. Or the outdated and crumpled magazines in the waiting room of the hospital, filled with the latest diet crazes.

These issues were pricey, and heavy, and felt good in my hands. They depicted life and design and the way people were living right now. A life I'd lost touch with, if I had ever been connected to it at all.

Architecture, paint colors, clothing and fabrics, furniture, home restorations, watches, cars, modern farmhouses—everything from lakeshore cottages to city apartments were documented and brought to life on these pages. I had no idea why Daniel wanted me to browse these with him, but in spite of my own stubborn resistance, I was getting lost in this eye-opening experience.

"Hmm? My parents?" I asked.

I had to pull my concentration away from an article about a couple in Connecticut who turned a grain silo into a guest house. The custom cabinetry was stunning, and perfectly fit the curves of the round walls. I wondered how Kerby Lodge would look with cylindrical grain silos dotting the forest instead of cabins.

"Your parents were ahead of their time," he continued. "They built a community; a captive loyal audience for their product." He spoke with real admiration in his voice. "What they achieved by sheer instinct forty some years ago, marketers today spend millions of dollars trying to replicate."

This got my attention, and I had to rest the magazine I was reading on my lap.

"An audience for their product?" I challenged. "This lodge was their life and passion, not a product."

"I guarantee that you're wrong," he said.

"You never knew my parents." I could hear the combative tone in my own voice.

"True," Daniel said evenly. "But I see what they built—a product, and an audience. You said so yourself Kay, people would come once and keep coming back."

"Yes, but this was their home," I insisted.

"The apartment is your home; should be your home," he said, though not unkindly. "Everything else—every cottage and cabin and the A-Frame, the beach and woods, even this room we're in, except during the winter, of course—is the money. Until you can come to terms with that, your livelihood will continue to… deteriorate."

We were silent after this. He was aggravatingly matter of fact about topics that were so close to my heart—but was this true?

It was Daniel who spoke first. His tone was kind, but the words cut deep. "Kay, it's my fear that you're trying to preserve your parents," he said, "by not changing anything they built or touched. From the rugs and books—to your dad's shirts."

Ouch. That felt like a sucker punch, but Daniel, oblivious, kept talking.

"You're the proprietor, or so it says in your brochure," he went on, "but there's nothing of you here. You are young and beautiful, and smart, and this lodge should reflect these qualities. Instead, you're like a… a caretaker of the past. Of a cluttered gramma's attic. Of a dark and musty museum."

I held my hand up to indicate that I got his point.

"This is why I can't help you," he finished.

Every word hurt to hear. I threw down the issue I was reading like a spoiled child and hugged my arms tight around my waist—around my dad's flannel shirt—as if to protect its very existence.

21

Following our heated afternoon exchange, my lodger gave me time to collect my thoughts before we continued my assignment of flipping, flipping, and more flipping through his publications. Eventually I resurfaced, coming out of the kitchen with a large mug of black bean chili for each of us, complete with corn bread squares. He nodded and picked up the conversation where he left off.

"Design is renewal, Kay; it's never ending," Daniel said to me as I sat down. He put his chili on the coffee table, next to a magazine titled *Cottage Reborn.*

"As designers, if we're lucky," he went on, "we get to create something fresh and new. But more often, we find ourselves executing and expanding on ideas, or trends, that are one step ahead of us—and we just scramble to keep up."

Daniel picked up his chili and took a few bites.

"Trends are like lightning in a bottle." Daniel gestured to the log coffee table with his spoon, pointing to the collection we'd been leafing through the entire day. "And though you wouldn't think that the economy could play a role in design trends, there is a movement of simplicity that has its roots in this recession."

He had my full attention—not just from his words, but the authority and cadence of his voice. I could see why his former coworkers wanted Daniel Mayne in their meetings.

"You and I have seen the devastation. Friends and neighbors losing their jobs, their businesses, and their homes," he said.

I nodded in silence.

"We've passed the heartless evictions—a lifetime of furniture, toys, and clothes carelessly tossed onto a front yard." Daniel spoke with real emotion, and I knew how he felt.

"Kay, this economic crisis has inspired massive change," he said. "Resale shops, thrift stores, and charity clearance centers are popping up out of nowhere. Because people are downsizing from big homes to small homes, from small homes to apartments, and from apartments to their parents' basements."

Poor Candy French.

"People that aren't moving are affected too," Daniel said. "Everyone's looking inside themselves and discovering their own false sense of economic security. They've been buying too much stuff and too many things. Now they want to have less, and fewer reminders of their excess."

"The resulting design trends are gaining momentum—and I don't see an end. The words *repurpose* and *reuse* and *upcycle* have become mantras. People are now painting their grandmother's old furniture to create something new—instead of buying new."

"Small and simple has become the new luxury. People crave cleaner lines. Less clutter."

While he was talking, Jennifer came to mind. She had been collecting and repainting furniture castoffs for the past few years, in hopes of opening a shop in town.

"What I'm trying to get at, Kay," Daniel looked right at me, "is that you have a new generation of people to appeal to—and they have different sensibilities and expectations."

"But Daniel," I interrupted, trying to be just as conversational, "the people that come to Kerby Lodge want the nostalgia that the inn provides."

"No doubt they do."

I was surprised to hear Daniel agree with me.

"But nostalgia won't pay your bills," he said. "The generation of people nostalgic for Kerby Lodge is on the way out, and you haven't replaced them. You're too busy looking back, instead of looking ahead."

I stared into the fire, wrestling with what Daniel was saying. I was keeping things the same for the good of the lodge. But I also knew, deep down, how quickly the present can become the past.

Was I living in the past? Was I afraid of change?

Just then, a gust of wind off the lake shook loose a memory from my university days. A Chinese proverb on a bookstore poster that went something like:

When the winds of change blow, some build walls, and others build windmills.

Later that night, I got up out of bed and padded to the sofa, and to the design magazines. I had gone to bed early, emotionally spent and headachy from my day of being challenged, and contradicted, and educated.

Everything I'd held near and dear, from my vintage books to my dad's shirts, felt under attack and vulnerable. In my heart, I had pushed back vehemently—though I tried to keep an objective façade.

Somewhere in our painful conversation, I heard the words *young, beautiful,* and *smart* being said about me. I know that to Daniel, the words were just part of a well-constructed insult about the lodge, but secretly, they felt wonderful to hear. Like a splash of cool water to my parched heart and soul.

I picked up an issue that I had returned to several times. It featured before and after photos of several cottages and farmhouses that had streamlined their décor.

Oak trim and walnut paneling painted white? I thought it was sacrilegious to paint wood, especially when the grain was so beautiful in its natural state. But I had to admit, it made the rooms look lighter, and more inviting.

Setting the issue on my lap, I looked around the great room, imagining that I was seeing it for the first time.

The entire wall stuffed with books was impressive. But the spines and covers, I now saw, were dark and muted. They all blended together into one dark muddy blob of color. Nothing popped out as a book I'd want to grab and look at.

That wasn't always true—my family used to spend our winters devouring the summer reading. The brand-new books that guests brought with them to read while lying on the beach, and left behind in their cottages or guestrooms. I remember when we cracked the books open months later, grains of Lake Michigan summer sand would fall onto our quilt-covered laps.

But I hadn't read these books in years. Had any of my guests?

The paneled walls were pretty—or were they? Not nearly as nice as the solid walnut paneling someone dared to paint over in one of the cottages in *Cottage Reborn*.

My ceiling was dark wood with rustic beams, and the walls were dark. The floors—gosh, they were dark too. But my parents used to talk about the golden heart pine flooring underneath the ancient wine-colored carpet, and how one day they'd unearth them.

In the meantime, my parents threw area rugs and runners on top of the carpet traffic patterns. Making it a patchwork of matted down fibers that had been dripped on, spilled on, walked on with sandy shoes and icy snow boots for decades.

I recall Tad and his buddies running through the great room one summer carrying poorly sealed containers of fishing bait, and Mum shouting *child, th' worms are drippin!*

Looking down at my lap, I could see that my dad's blue and brown flannel shirt, the one I often threw on as a bathrobe, was nearly the same pattern as the 40-year-old plaid sofa cushions I now sat on—and it hit me.

"Kerby Lodge *is* old and dated," I said to myself, in genuine despair, "and I am too."

22

Came here when I was a kid.
Now bringing my kids. Full circle at the Kerby.
-KERBY LODGE GUEST BOOK-

"*The Tortoise and The Hare,*" I said, over the phone.

On a whim, I called Luke Mayne to touch base, and give him an update on his brother. It was the third week of December, and we hadn't spoken in a few days. He sounded glad to hear from me, apart from getting an update on Daniel's health.

I mentioned a childhood story that reminded me of the Mayne brothers, and their chosen professions.

"I can see that," Luke said. "While Daniel has been rising to meteoric success in his design career, I've been plodding along. Turtling. I mean, teaching."

I laughed at that, and was glad Luke didn't take offense, because none was meant.

"It didn't turn out well for the rabbit in the story, though, did it?" I asked.

Luke laughed. "Not at first, but I think the rabbit should be doing okay," he said. "The rabbit probably made more money in a year than the turtle makes in five years."

"Really?" I said, genuinely surprised.

"If the rabbit was smart," Luke said, "he'd have a nice nest egg to keep him warm while he figures out his next race."

And before he hung up, Luke reminded me that while his brother drives a sleek silver Beemer, "the turtle putts along in a pre-owned domestic sedan."

23

"You said that you don't see me in this lodge?" I stated as much as asked while walking into the great room with a tray of steaming coffee mugs and bowls of warm oatmeal.

Daniel was leaning on his crutches, staring at the steel-gray morning skies and lake through the closed-up porch. The snow was only lightly falling, but the wind had picked up, and the deep snow was blowing and drifting outside as if it were a new blizzard.

My driveway would not be clear for much longer, as all the snow that Chip pushed to the sides with his plow would be finding its way back.

We had been reading design magazines by the warm fire for a few days now, progressing from petulant—me—and arrogant—him—to a more harmonious pair. When we found something interesting, we would most often share it with each other, and then nod in appreciation. I was beginning to understand why Daniel wanted to show me the world I'd lost track of while hunkering down. First in my grief, and then in my... what, apathy?

Whatever the label, it had gone on far too long.

As a kid, I learned how to swim in Lake Michigan, with its swells and currents. Dad would stay close to me as I gulped and paddled to stay above water. But when a wave crashed over me, I would struggle to fight my way back up. That's how I felt now—as if I were fighting to swim to the surface after being under water without air in my lungs for a very long time.

"You don't see you here," he answered, turning to make his way to the wing chair for our breakfast, "from what you've told me, I don't think you ever have."

Sadly, this was probably true.

I was just passing through Kerby Lodge, I realized, on my way to my own life. And I got stuck—good and stuck, like when I was a kid riding bikes, and my flared jeans would get caught in the greasy chain. No matter how hard we pulled, Tad would have to get the garden shears from the carriage house and cut a length of the hem off to set me free.

"I never wanted it," I said at last, surprising even myself by this admission. "I figured I could dabble at being an innkeeper, stay as long as I wanted in my family home, and then sell it at any time. Take my millions of dollars and walk away," I said. The former value of the property was a safety net—a chicken exit I could take if I wasn't successful.

"Before the recession hit, I was considering a pretty generous offer." I never told anyone this before. "But things went south and my buyer went bankrupt."

And as I spoke, I knew how Daniel must have felt when he fell off that chair. We had each made the decision to reach for something better, when the bottom fell out from under us.

"If I had been an actual innkeeper," I began, slowly, "I would have made sure you had proper chairs in your cabin. Instead of the dried-out ones that broke."

My lodger frowned as he listened to me.

After a pause, I said "Daniel, I owe you an apology. I feel responsible for your injuries. I'm sincerely sorry that you got hurt."

Daniel regarded me with a certain intensity, but didn't speak for a few minutes. When he did, it was as though he didn't hear the monumental confession I had just made.

"I think, Kay, you need to *decide* to run Kerby Lodge," Daniel said.

"Decide?" I asked. "But… I already run the lodge."

As I tried to comprehend Daniel's meaning, he became more emphatic.

"What I mean is, stop looking at the lodge as a thing that happened to you, that you can't control. Take ownership—of the problems and solutions, and the potential," he said, slightly exasperated. "You don't have to love a business to be good at running it. In fact, love can cloud your judgment. Trust me, I know."

I was sure he was referring to the ad agency that he was loyal to for many years. Daniel was likely so close to the day-to-day operations that he completely missed the broad strokes—the winds of change that blew him right out of there.

Was I guilty of the same tunnel vision?

Was I building walls instead of windmills?

One common thread I noticed in the makeover stories was that nearly all changes were made by new owners. Hardly any existing owners pulled the trigger on a renovation. It's as if they could not see the potential that was right in front of their faces.

"Make it yours. Make it profitable," Daniel continued, "and then make your decision about the lodge's future from a position of strength. Not from desperation or panic."

These thoughts stewed while I enjoyed the view of the lake—rising and falling in the gray, wintery wind—from the warmth and comfort of the great room. In time, I let my gaze fall on the room itself, while revisiting my sleepless revelations.

Would I want to vacation here, if I didn't have the memories and love associated with the lodge? Would I bring my small children to this room to ride out a rainy summer day playing board games and eating popcorn—as hundreds of children had done over the decades?

Or would today's young, health-conscious mothers "helicopter" their little ones away from the musty books and stained rugs? Would they, instead, make them wash their hands and then take them into town for an expensive ice cream cone, and then to Spondike's for overpriced toys?

It made me very sad that I allowed Kerby Lodge to become less inviting—less savory to families. They have been our bread and butter for years. And historically, kids have loved this place, where they could roam free, and enjoy adventures.

The Mayne brothers certainly did, but that was more than thirty years ago. And while Daniel had wanted to come back to Kerby Lodge—maybe his wife would not.

24

Happy 70th to me this week at the Kerby.
I'm still kicking, just not as high.
-KERBY LODGE GUEST BOOK-

"Ha! We did it again!" Jennifer threw her winning cards on the table, and shot her arms straight up in a victory pose. She and I had trounced Patrick and Daniel in three rounds of Euchre, following their earlier winning streak.

"Let's break for pizza," Patrick exclaimed. "My soul can't take losing any more."

"And after dessert, I demand a tie-breaker," Daniel chimed in. My lodger had his charming host face on for the evening, and seemed to be enjoying himself. It would make it hard to convince Jennifer that he was not always fun to be around.

But maybe, like me, he was happy to have the diversion of new faces and activities to take our minds off of the relentless snow and isolation, and our troubles. Between the November storm, the most recent snow, and the drifting snow, this was already an epic winter—with the big snowfalls still to come in January and February.

Our friends had brought fresh pizza from town, which was warming in the oven, and a big green salad that Patrick had assembled, since he had the day off from work. I baked a chocolate cake from supplies in my pantry, and brewed a fresh pot of my infamous coffee.

Earlier, with Christmas less than a week away, and our friends coming, I had brought in a small Frasier fir from the forest, and decorated it with ornaments and lights. Thankfully, the old string of white lights lit up when I plugged it in.

I also trudged through the woods in search of evergreen boughs to line the fireplace mantle, and boxwood sprigs to fashion into a wreath. After shaking the snow off, the deep greens were like a breath of fresh air. As they warmed to the indoor temperature, the scent of balsam filled the lodge.

The twinkling lights and tree sparkled in the firelight. When it came to Christmas decorations, I always preferred the beauty of nature when I had the chance to scavenge it. The melting icicles left a few puddles beneath the fresh mantle greenery but it didn't matter, we Kerby's never babied the lodge.

While Daniel sat on the sofa and thumbed through another issue of *My Home Looks Better Than Yours*, or whatever it was he was reading, I pulled out a box stored in Tad's old closet. Removing the lid, I carefully took out several large twig stars, and placed them on top of the mantle. I stepped back and admired my work.

"I like those," Daniel surprised me by saying.

A few years ago we had a somewhat dry December, and I was able to spend time in the forest searching for Christmas inspiration. At last, I took armfuls of straight, sturdy twigs of a certain length, and brought them back to my kitchen. When they warmed up, I glued the tips together to create rustic stars. Once the glue dried, I hit them all with a spray of gold metallic paint from an old can I found in the carriage house.

Now, sitting on the fragrant evergreen boughs, these gold stars reflected the fire light and tree lights. While we sat around the great room eating our pizza, Jennifer noticed them too.

"Ooh, pretty. I could sell those stars in my shop, Kay," she said. "Why don't you make more of them in your free time."

Jennifer had been searching for a location to open a storefront for the past year. The downtown spaces are outrageously expensive to rent for the peak season, and the remote locations are just too far off the beaten path to be profitable. In the meantime, she has a garage full of "treasures" that she and Patrick have been restoring and repurposing.

"Did you find a space?" I asked, genuinely interested.

"Not yet, but I'll see what opens up in the spring."

Jennifer always impressed me with her ambition and creativity—in addition to her expertise in emergencies. And while I wish Daniel had never taken that bad fall, I got to see Jennifer in action.

"If you do find a storefront," I ventured, "will you have the time to run it?"

Patrick overheard my question, and jumped in with the answer. "You must have missed the article in the *Shop and Save*. Funds were approved for two more EMT teams."

"Apparently," Jennifer jumped back in, "and sadly, there are enough people drinking while driving their boats, and wave runners, and snowmobiles…"

"…and falling off of chairs," Patrick chimed in playfully, as I winced.

"…to warrant additional resources," Jennifer finished.

We all laughed a little at the reference to Daniel and the lightbulb, which I doubted he'd ever live down. At least in our little circle of four.

"I'm glad for the new EMTs," I said. "But if I ever need to call 911 again, and I hope I don't, I'm asking for you both by name."

"Well you can try," Jennifer smiled, "but I hope to be selling adorable pieces at my little shop this summer—at least on Saturdays. It's relaxing to breathe new life into castoffs, and it takes my mind off of the emergencies we get called to."

The rest of us nodded in support. I could only imagine the stress of being a resort town EMT, and didn't want to think about the day-to-day tragedies and rescues that were a way of life for Jennifer and Patrick.

I mentioned to my friend that after the snow melted a bit, we could trudge to the carriage house to see if there were a few old tables or chairs she could repurpose and reuse. She was more than welcome to them as she prepared for a second career.

It was common for people around Lake Michigan to have second, and even third jobs and careers, by necessity. Mitch is a perfect example. He had income from his very successful peak season restaurant, as well as an off-season mail order pie business.

Locals are always struggling to keep up, it seems. When property price tags are high, like they were before the recession hit, everything is expensive: rent payments, taxes, and the costs of living. And only the wealthiest can afford to buy land and cottages.

Now, when property is cheap, most locals don't have any extra money. The tourists, who we all count on, have stopped spending. Businesses have shut down and jobs have gone away. A neighbor's foreclosed property may seem too cheap to pass up, but when it's hard enough just keeping dinner on the table, buying land is not an option.

Many locals are fortunate to have homes and land that their parents, or grandparents, bought long ago. But the newer generations, and those relocating to the area for jobs, have to scrimp and save and work like mad to have their own American dream.

"Kay," Jennifer asked, a bit cautiously, "have you considered taking a teaching job at one of the local schools—in addition to running the lodge? The schedule seems ideal."

I smiled and shrugged, and turned to look into the fire. It must have been a hard question to pose after all these years, but I'm surprised more people didn't ask me. I forced myself to turn back to her.

"I have thought of that, Jennifer." I heard the sadness in my own voice. "That extra income would be great."

Patrick and Daniel, who had been carrying on an animated conversation about the Chicago Bulls, became silent as they tuned in to my answer.

"But I'm afraid that I've waited too long," I said to the room.

"And, I think… I'm just afraid."

25

Loved our little cabin. Wanted to take it home.
But thought you might notice.
-KERBY LODGE GUEST BOOK-

"Yikes! He said that to you? In *class*?"

I had been talking to Luke Mayne more and more—and less and less about Daniel. I suppose it began when I asked Luke to tell me all about his students. Maybe I wanted to live vicariously through him, I don't know. Whatever got the ball rolling, I found I couldn't wait to hear the latest installment of his interesting world.

And happily, Luke seemed pretty eager to call and tell me.

Through his colorful stories, I realize just how much new teachers these days need to toughen up, and abandon romantic notions they have about kids and their behavior. There are many more complexities and influences than when Luke and I were students.

"He did say that, Kay!" Luke said. "I couldn't believe it myself, but I had to keep a straight face, and escort him to the office. I hope his suspension isn't too long, though—and that he comes back soon."

"You do? I would think you'd be glad to be rid of him," I said.

Luke laughed. "I'll be glad for the break, for sure. But he's a good kid. Smart kid. And those are the ones we do this for, right Kay?"

We?

I finally told Luke about my waylaid career in education, the career I considered to be beyond my reach now. Immediately, he started talking to me as if I were a colleague—a teacher. As if I understood his challenges and his motivation.

I felt like an imposter.

But I also felt included once again in the circle of professionals I had worked so hard to belong to—and hopeful that someday I could know the feeling of dedication and satisfaction Luke Mayne had in his work. No matter what I chose to do.

And though the Mayne brothers are different in their own jobs and approaches to life, it was through talking with them both that I was piecing together a few common threads.

First, I did need to take ownership of the inn, in every sense of the word. Owning Kerby Lodge did "happen" to me, as Daniel put it, but that was years ago. It was time for Kay Kerby to stop being just a name on a brochure. I would be the proprietor. It may be too late to save the inn, but I wanted to fight for it, and do all I could.

Also, Luke inspired me to find my motivation, "the ones we do it for," and work for them. Who are these families, the ones that aren't coming to Kerby Lodge anymore, or who have never been here? How can I draw them in, and make them want to come back?

With or without Daniel's help, I needed to figure things out, and move Kerby Lodge in a positive direction. I would be my own happy ending; my own *Christmas Eve Benefit*. I hadn't mentioned this to Daniel, but through our conversations some rusty gears had started to turn. So I'd begin there.

Before saying goodbye to Luke, I repeated my offer to have him come for Christmas, just two days away, but his answer was the same. His charter school had pretty short breaks in anticipation of an early spring release—and though it was hard, really hard this time of year, their classes would be done months sooner than other schools.

"I'll talk to you on Christmas, right?" Luke asked, sounding a bit lonely and vulnerable. "I'm not super excited about Christmas Day tapas, and chow mien, and the other foods on the pot luck signup sheet."

He added "I wish I could be at Kerby Lodge with you and Daniel—maybe even more than with our parents in Chicago. But please don't mention that to them!"

It was my turn to laugh. Luke had a nice demeanor, and I found myself looking forward to our next call. Just two days away.

On Christmas.

"I never thought to ask you, but do you celebrate Christmas?" I was still feeling happy from my talk with Luke when I walked into the great room. Daniel was putting his foot up for a rest. I worried that he had been trying to power through the healing process.

"Celebrate is a big word," Daniel replied, closing his eyes and leaning his head back in the wing chair.

I waited for him to continue.

While slightly humbled by his job loss experience, Daniel Mayne had retained the habit of thinking the world was waiting for what he had to say next. And at the moment, I was his world.

But honestly, there was no point in rushing him. Where else did I have to be?

"If you mean Santa Claus, and gifts under the tree, then sure. I celebrate Christmas," he said eventually, still with his eyes closed. "If you mean more than that—no."

I waited until curiosity would get the better of him, and he would open his eyes to see if I was still in the room.

When he turned his head to look at me, I was ready. "Every year, I go to church on Christmas Eve. The service is held in the morning, with a town lunch at the Community Center afterwards, and everybody goes," I said. "I'd like to go this year. I'm hoping you'll come with me. I think the roads will be clear enough for us to take the Jeep."

He rolled his head back to the center of the headrest, and closed his eyes again.

"Will the taxi driver and Gretel from the post office be at the lunch? And Doctor Petersen?" he asked, with a wry smile on his face.

Trying to picture that image, I said "we'll see the doctor on Christmas Eve morning. He said he can fit us in before church if the weather holds. As for the others—we can only hope."

"I suppose I can come," he said, now looking right at me, "with two conditions."

My goodness, this man was full of himself.

"One," he said, holding up his index finger, "do not tell my mother I went to church. She'll never let me off the hook in the future."

I agreed. My secrets were adding up. "And two?"

"Two," he said, "I don't want to hear any *It's a Christmas miracle!* jokes from you when I limp into church without my crutches."

26

Kerby Lodge without Fitz and Raya,
is like a day without sunshine! So sad.
-KERBY LODGE GUEST BOOK-

"That's so great! Can I help Kay?" As we enjoyed our Christmas Eve lunch at the Community Center Jennifer was excited to hear I wanted to give the great room of the lodge a little facelift, and she insisted on pitching in. Especially now that her reinforcements were being hired and trained, freeing up time for her creative endeavors.

"It would make this winter much less dreary," she said.

We decided to put our heads together at the lodge on the day after Christmas, weather permitting. Jennifer had a few well-deserved days off, and I would be glad for her input.

At the lunch, Daniel sat at the table next to mine, looking for all the world like a local. He was talking to Patrick, Mitch, Chip, and a few other guys from town.

While the two of us had our heads together, quietly plotting, the men's table was bursting with loud voices and laughter. Once or twice, I looked over to see Patrick or Chip clapping Daniel on the back, as if he'd said the funniest thing in the world.

Why on earth was he so charming to everyone except me? This man was a mystery.

He still hadn't acknowledged my apology about the broken chair, by the way. And while I felt a sense of relief at taking the high road, in spite of Tad's warning, I had no idea whether or not Daniel planned on suing me and taking the inn.

But I wasn't bringing it up.

I wondered, did Daniel think I was unmovable in my resolve to keep the inn the same? It was Jennifer I told my secret plans to, and not Daniel. He'd find out soon enough in a few days, when Jennifer and I got together.

I could hear Jennifer talking, and knew I should pay attention to what she was saying. Yet I couldn't stop my mind from wandering to Daniel Mayne.

What was his deal?

I've heard of people who "bring out the worst in each other," but I always thought that was just an excuse people made for their own bad behavior. Did I bring out the worst side of Daniel—the side I saw the most?

Did he bring out the worst in me? Possibly. It's not like I was brimming with jokes and good humor in his presence. And why would I be? I will own that the rickety chair was a mistake, but he's the one foolish enough to stand on it, and put my future in jeopardy.

He's the one who foisted himself on me that day in November, in a way that left me no alternative but to usher him into the lodge, and into my life. I'd be sure to tell the judge that little tidbit if his case against me ever came to trial. Which could get ugly, I realized, as I looked over at Daniel—making new friends and character witnesses.

"…and have you considered painting the paneling?" Jennifer was asking, but I was not doing a great job at hiding my distraction.

"Hmm maybe," I said, quickly trying to cover up my rudeness.

Jennifer was not convinced. I followed her as she abruptly got up to refill her plate from the long serving table, overflowing with a bounty of casseroles, carved meats, cold salads, and of course, Mitch's pies and other desserts. I did the same. Afterwards, however, she went to sit down with a group from the hospital, in the only available seat.

Crossing the room, I found my fellow inn owners.

It was a well-attended Christmas Eve lunch, and everyone from town was in good spirits. Collectively, I think we all hoped the worst years were behind us, as far as the recession. We had all been beaten down, humbled, and financially stretched to our limits, and were anxious to usher in even modest levels of prosperity.

We didn't need good times, necessarily. We'd settle for better times.

As two of the inn owners talked about their new websites, we could hear the tinkling of glass in the background. The town mayor, Peder Maki, was standing in the middle of the room, trying to get our attention by clinking on a serving platter with fork tines. He was wearing bright green snowmobile coveralls, and a red stocking cap with a white Nordic reindeer design, no doubt hand-knit by his wife, Marj.

Peder and Marj own a small yarn and knit shop downtown, the launching pad for Marj's handmade creations. But their real income came from Maki's Greenhouse and Nursery, five miles inland. They supply the vegetables, flowers, plants, and trees to both summer people and locals.

Every December, they end their season by selling live Christmas trees, boxwood wreaths, and fresh cedar roping. Then close up for a two-month vacation.

I wondered as I waited for everyone to settle down, if Peder realized just how much he looked like St. Nick on this Christmas Eve, with his white beard and festive ensemble. I decided that the look was deliberate for this third generation Swedish-American. And while I didn't see Marj, I could picture her at home baking almond coffee cakes, and waiting to light the Saint Lucia candle wreath again tonight for the grandchildren.

The Maki's were central to our town's community of Scandinavians, who were some of the earliest immigrants to the Great Lakes states. Many years ago, they brought with them a love of the winter weather, and a proficiency for mining, forestry, and fishing—the growing industries of the time.

"Everyone, everyone…" Peder said, "just a moment of your day!"

Eventually, we all quieted to hear what he had to say.

"Let's give a hand to this year's hosts, the men and women from the downtown storefront association—didn't they do a great job organizing our holiday lunch?"

Cheers and hoots as we recognized this group. Next year's hosts would be the lakefront inn association, of which I was a member. I wondered as I looked around at the other inn owners by my side, who of us would still be standing this time next year.

"Before you get back to your gabbing and gossip," the mayor tried to grab the wheel again from the excitable townsfolk, "and before you head home to your Christmas trees, and your shiny presents, and your stuffed turkeys… let's raise a glass together."

We all lifted our plastic cola cups and paper coffee cups, and waited for the toast.

"*God Jul,* Merry Christmas, friends and neighbors," Peder said, with warmth and sincerity. "May the good Lord and Santa bring us everything on our wish lists: Healthy families. Friends, new and old. Full inns, busy restaurants, and sold-out inventory. And wealthy tourists that multiply like loaves and…"

"And Swedish fishes!" someone shouted from the back of the room, causing an outbreak of laughter. A few men got up and clapped Peder on the back, good naturedly.

"Here, here!" Everyone said, and then exploded into chatter once again. Whether the mayor had more to say or not, he had lost the room.

Daniel and I began saying our goodbyes so that we could run a few errands in town before the stores closed, and before the snow started falling in earnest. We would need to stop at the post office, the grocery store, and the hardware store.

My lodger seemed to have more people pulling on his sleeve than I did, I was surprised to note, and it was hard to get out the door. Some were the old timers, happy to have a new face to tell their tall tales to. But other people seemed to genuinely enjoy Daniel Mayne's company.

"Well aren't you just mister congeniality," I said, as we walked through the light snowfall on the way to the Jeep. I was trying not to slip as I carried half a pie that Mitch had handed to me, in exchange for a kiss on the cheek, and a casserole dish filled with buffet leftovers that we could warm up later for Christmas Eve supper.

I had come to observe that the community feast leftovers were dished up for the widows, widowers, single mothers, and the *auld maids* such as myself—in that order.

"You seem surprised," he said. "But I like people, Kay. I like the people in this town."

"If only they knew what you said about their awnings," I said.

Daniel gave me a sideways glance, "You're the one who still doesn't like me."

"Well," I stammered as we drove, "I don't dislike you…"

"That's good, because you did ask me to stay through the winter—and according to the pharmacist at my table, this winter is just getting started," Daniel said. "And his bunion is never wrong."

With that statement, he was out of the Jeep, limping on his walking cast to the doors of the post office.

27

I've spent the past twelve Christmases completely by myself. Like an old woman from a long-ago fairy tale, one who lives in a gingerbread house in the forest. An old woman who has forgotten how to interact with real people. And whose quirks are suddenly exposed.

But were my Christmas traditions quirky? I had nothing to compare them to. They were simply a continuation of what Mum set in motion for me and Tad, years ago. Only this morning, it occurred to me that I was neither mother nor child. And not alone.

The first tradition, which Daniel already poked a hole in, was wearing my dad's favorite buffalo plaid flannel. It was his Christmas shirt, and now it's mine. Another is rising earlier than usual to pop a special breakfast casserole in the oven. This I assembled on Christmas Eve.

Afterwards, I pad to the great room to stoke the fire. I like to sit next to it and enjoy the twinkling lights of the tree, long before the sun comes up. Because the magic of Christmas morning is fleeting, and best in the wee hours.

From my chair, I can see what's under the tree—though for the past twelve years, there haven't been any surprises. One gift from Tad's family, and one from Zeke and June. Before opening them, I enjoy an orange-iced sweet roll, and sip coffee laced with peppermint cream. And wait for the casserole to bake.

I've kept these simple traditions alive for a party of one. This morning, I hoped to enjoy them in solitude—long before anyone would be up and about to make me feel silly or childish.

But the surprise was on me as Daniel entered the great room just as early as I did. Sounding as excited as I felt.

"Merry Christmas!" Daniel and I both exclaimed.

His sounded like a festive greeting. Mine, like the startled response it was.

I was startled. The genuine warmth in Daniel's voice threw me off kilter. Using the excuse of grabbing our mugs of coffee, I turned back towards the dining room to collect my composure.

Standing by the Methodist Church coffee urn, stirring creamer into the mugs that I save for this one day, I forced myself to take a few deep breaths and get ready to go back into the great room.

This was Christmas day, after all. My favorite day of the year.

Dad once told us about soldiers during the first world war, who declared a Christmas Day truce. When Tad called later today, I would remind him of that story, and tell him that I had a little taste of it this morning. He was still concerned about Daniel's intentions, and wished I would have dropped him at a hotel on our trip to town.

All of a sudden, I missed Tad, and the Christmas mornings we spent together as kids. Tiptoeing in to see if Santa had eaten our cookies. Amazed at the overflowing stockings hanging on the mantle—they had been flat and empty the night before. Gasping at the presents from Mum and Dad, Gram, folks from across the pond, and Santa.

We weren't allowed to wake our parents until six in the morning, but we could whisper excitedly and finish off the half-eaten cookies. Tad was older, and allowed to stoke the fire embers from Christmas Eve and add a few logs, while I huddled under a wool blanket and gazed in wonder at Christmas.

But this morning, as I handed a coffee mug to Daniel, the wonder of seeing new Christmas gifts wasn't just a memory—it was reality. Under the tree, there were several beautifully wrapped gifts that hadn't been there when I went to bed last night.

And even more amazing was the unfamiliar look on Daniels' face—it might have been happiness, but I couldn't be certain.

"It looks like Santa came," Daniel said, looking like a man with secrets.

I was a bit speechless, and could only nod and search his face for answers. There were numerous boxes waiting at the post office for Daniel yesterday, but I assumed they were more of his magazines. And since Doctor Petersen had given him the go-ahead to spend less time using his crutches, he carried the boxes without my help. At his insistence.

"Look," Daniel said, pointing under the tree, "there are gifts for you to open, and a few for me. Let's grab those orange sweet rolls and then we'll see what's what, shall we?" he said, limping towards the kitchen.

Who was this giddy person? Was this the same man who had a temper tantrum just six weeks ago in the hospital? Who had turned up his nose at my hospitality—after practically inflicting himself and his problems on me during a snowstorm?

I wordlessly followed Daniel into my own kitchen, where the savory breakfast casserole was filling the air with the aromas of sausage and herbs.

"Mmm," we both said simultaneously, and then laughed at ourselves.

I had to admit, this day was already more fun than I imagined it would be.

"To Kay," Daniel read, as he handed me a gift. "Thank you for being our good luck charm. From Nan and Sperry."

He was perched on an ottoman in front of the little tree, handing a gift to me, and opening a few himself.

I took the large package tentatively.

"Nan and Sperry Mayne are my parents," he said.

"Your parents got me a Christmas gift?"

Do they think we are a couple? What had Daniel told them, I wondered.

As if reading my thoughts, he said, "I told them you helped me after my accident. And that you were a very nice person."

I took this information in, feeling relieved.

"They're grateful to you. And probably thrilled that I'm staying here, and not living in their guest suite while I recover. I'm sure I'd be a wet blanket on their travels, and bridge club, and cocktail parties."

"Nan and Sperry have a guest suite? That sounds pretty fancy."

"You do too, Kay," Daniel reminded me.

I shrugged in agreement, thinking of the little paneled room with the pine dressers, handmade quilts, and heavy plaid curtains that my lodger had settled into. Technically, the tiny attached washroom made it a suite.

Then he said, "I can't lie, theirs is awesome, with Italian linens and a view of the Chicago skyline—but it comes with a steep price tag of expectations and obligations I'm not ready for."

I wish mine did too, I thought, remembering my plea for help at the diner.

Lingering over the beautiful wrapping paper, I ran my hand over the thick reflective foil with the embossed logo of a Chicago boutique. On the top, wide grosgrain ribbons and bows in gold, red, green, and a Scottish plaid, held a sprig of balsam. It was an upscale presentation, and told me a lot about the Mayne's of Chicago.

When I opened the big box, there was a smaller flat box on top of the tissue paper. There I found an elegant gold chain, with a gold and diamond horseshoe pendant dangling from the center.

"Ahh," I gasped at the beauty as it sparkled against the light of the tree and fire. "Daniel, this is lovely, but it's too expensive. I can't accept this!"

"You can. Nan has always wanted someone other than her boys to buy for, and I know shopping for you gave her great joy. You wouldn't take my mother's joy, would you Kay?" Daniel sounded concerned.

I held the weight of the heavy gold in my hands. Raya had left me a few pieces of fine gold that I had tucked away in a dusty box under my bed, so I recognized the quality. Finally, I unclasped the chain and refastened it around my neck. It felt like satin on my skin, and hit at the perfect spot.

I smiled at Daniel, and he nodded his approval.

When I peeled back the tissue paper, I discovered the softest, most luxurious cashmere sweater in a lovely Loden green that would complement the red tones in my hair. The size was perfect, even down to the extra length in the waist and sleeves to accommodate my height and willowy arms.

I suspected my lodger told his mother much more than he had let on.

"Daniel, your parents are very generous."

"I'm sure Nan had to practice restraint—especially when shopping for you."

While I was opening my gifts from Nan and Sperry, Daniel had also opened a few gifts from his parents—a soft leather jacket, shirts, and a very expensive looking automatic watch.

"Oh look," he said, "this watch is water resistant up to 1200 meters."

Nodding towards the churning, icy lake, I said "care to try it out?"

"Maybe tomorrow," he said, smiling at me.

I opened a large box from the Atlanta Kerby's, to find a beautiful pair of slim suede boots that would hug my calves and look great with everything. Including my new sweater and necklace. The note inside said:

Merry Christmas Kaker.
These aren't snowmobile boots!
Love, Tad, Selby, and the girls

I read the note out loud and Daniel said "Kaker?"

I shrugged. "Family name."

He didn't respond, but seemed to be filing that knowledge away.

There was a pretty box from Zeke and June, with a note saying they had liquidated several retirement accounts, and had to move funds around. Underneath the note was a check for a substantial amount of money—more than I'd seen in a long, long time.

"You'll know what to do with this," the note said.

I couldn't believe the generosity of their gift. I'd need to revisit this later today and give them a call. I shook my head in wonder and placed the lid back on the box.

Then Daniel picked up a small, beautifully wrapped package and laughed as he read the oversized gift tag. "To Kay. Thank you for all you've done, and for letting my clumsy brother stay at his favorite place in the world. Your friend, Luke."

My goodness. Weren't the Mayne's just special little elves, straight from the North Pole.

Inside, I found a delicate pair of earrings and matching bracelet. The stones were a pale blue sea glass, set in exquisite gold. I'd only seen glass stones like these at high end art galleries, but never set in such beautiful gold. Where did the Mayne's find this magical jewelry, anyway?

Daniel was watching my face, not knowing what emotion to expect from me. I hardly knew myself. I felt overwhelmed, and so loved by family and strangers alike. Here I'd let one new person into my life, though reluctantly, and that led to such overflowing abundance. Not of *things*, which I never cared about, but of thoughtfulness. A quality I valued, I was discovering.

At that moment, I felt determined to broaden my sheltered, isolated world, and seek out new people and new experiences in the coming year.

"I have to say," I said, "other than a secret Santa exchange in college, I've never received gifts from people I don't know. And such considerate presents," I swallowed hard.

Daniel watched me closely. His expression almost kind.

"Two gifts still under the tree," Daniel said, and I saw it was true. One was the gift I had wrapped for Daniel, and the other, I didn't recognize. "Let's take a break and eat that breakfast casserole. Then we can grab our coffee mugs and come back."

Obediently, I followed Jack Frost to my kitchen, enjoying the indulgent feel of the gold necklace as it swayed back and forth on my neck.

28

Nice find! We just took a
right at Lake Erie, and here we are!
-KERBY LODGE GUEST BOOK-

"And you've never travelled to share Christmas with your family in Florida, or Georgia, or even to Scotland? With all the down time you have each winter?" Daniel was astounded.

As we were taking delicious bites of our casserole and gazing at the fire, I tried to tell him how important it was for me to stay at Kerby Lodge through the winter, to troubleshoot any problems with the furnace, or the electricity. Or deal with wayward bear cubs. But the more I heard myself talk, the weaker my reasoning sounded. Especially since actual problems were few and far between.

Even after Tad and I had grown up and left the lodge, our parents chose to stay through the winter because they'd had their fill of world travels. But what was my excuse? There was no reason for me not to winterize the lodge and go be with family.

But what did it matter now? This could very well be my last winter here—so sayeth the unopened letter in my apartment.

Yesterday, when Daniel went into the post office to retrieve his packages, he picked up a large stack of lodge mail, accumulated over a few snowy weeks, and handed it to me. At home, sorting through the pile of Christmas cards and utility bills, the tax assessment fell onto the kitchen table—with all its weighty importance.

I picked it up to open it, but then changed my mind and set it aside. Why ruin the holidays? Instead, I'd mail it to Uncle Zeke—and we'd go from there.

Bad news can *ahlways wait a day, lass,* Mum had brogued to me.

110

Of course, her idea of bad news was a little rain on our day off, or the bakery not having the raisin bread we all liked. Not the squandering away of a multi-million-dollar real estate parcel. But I shoved my anxiety aside.

Nothing to be done about it on Christmas.

Sitting by the tree again with our fresh mugs of coffee, I reached down and handed Daniel a package that I had wrapped the day before in plain brown paper, stamped with fading gold metallic snowflakes.

I had made reams of this handmade giftwrap one winter, during a creative burst. Unfortunately, it was fading, and lasting a lot longer than I had expected. Especially with as few gifts as I sent each year. What I once thought looked clever and rustic, now looked sad.

Thinking of Nan Mayne, and the conclusions I had drawn from her fancy embossed foil, what did my mousey brown paper say about me, I wondered?

Merry frumpy Christmas.

"Merry Christmas, Daniel," I said, simply, handing him the package. I felt shy about my gift, in light of the ostentatious generosity shown by Daniel's family. "It's just a little something. A token of peace and goodwill."

Oh sheesh, did I just say that?

He smiled as he took it from my hands, and smiled even broader when he opened up the new sketch book and drawing pencils enclosed. He had a nice smile, I decided.

"I don't know anything about designers and artists, Daniel," I said, "but you might want a creative outlet while you're here, if you stay. Our winters can be a bit much," I laughed a little, stating the obvious.

"Thank you!" he said, as effusively as I sounded when I opened the diamond necklace.

He was raised with good manners, it was clear. I was sure he had that same polite enthusiasm as a child, opening a dollar store toy from his great aunt—under the watchful eye of Nan, no doubt.

I shrugged, chagrinned about the gift, and the presentation.

"No, I mean it, Kay. Thank you." And then he said "I'd forgotten how much I missed sketching, and will enjoy these charcoal pencils—they're top of the line!"

He looked at me and reached under the tree for the last gift.

"I'm a little nervous about this, to tell you the truth," he said. And I could see that he meant it. The great Daniel Mayne was nervous!

The gift was the size of a small book, and about as thin. Definitely not jewelry.

I took my time opening the wrapping paper, but couldn't prolong it. It was a handmade book, with a scripted KL on the cover, in a *fleur delis* circle. I realized it was meant to be a logo for Kerby Lodge.

The title read: *Kerby Lodge Marketing Plan.*

I caught my breath as a wave of adrenaline shot through my veins, followed by a euphoric sense of hope. I couldn't believe that Daniel Mayne, marketing guru, had actually agreed to help me save my inn after all. I hadn't expected this!

What solutions and steps had Daniel written out? I couldn't wait to see—my future would be determined by this marketing plan, after all.

I flipped to the first page, which had the header: *Contents.* It was followed by three categories, which read: *1. January, 2. February, 3. March.*

Wonderful.

I smiled up at Daniel, who remained still and quiet. His countenance didn't match my enthusiasm, which should have been my first clue that something was not right. It didn't take me long to discover what the problem was.

When I turned to January, the page was blank.

Then I turned to February and March—also completely blank.

But that couldn't be. I looked up at Daniel, and could barely speak at his cruelty—what elaborate lengths he had gone to, telling me that in his eyes, there was no future whatsoever for Kerby Lodge.

Ho Ho Ho.

29

Over the river, through the woods to Kerby Lodge we go.
Our van knows the way, been drivin' all day, yo ho ho.
-KERBY LODGE GUEST BOOK-

"Is this some kind of joke?" I asked when I could speak again.

"No," he said.

"So… you've given me a marketing plan. Without a plan?" I asked.

Daniel grimaced. "You seem upset."

"I seem upset? I seem upset?" I hardly knew how else to respond to this devastating *gift* and all that it meant to my future. Or to my lack of future.

"Kay, regardless of what you think of me, I would never pull a mean stunt—especially on Christmas. You must know that!"

He had to be right. Not even Daniel Mayne, at his worst, was capable of toying with my financial ruin in such a manner. On such a day. I needed to stand down and let him explain—although outwardly, it didn't look promising.

"Look," he said, "this is my clumsy way of telling you that I'm at your disposal for the next three months, for what that's worth." Daniel exhaled. "Full disclosure, I have never created a marketing plan before—at least, not on my own. But I'm willing to try. To work with you as a team, and devise our plan. We'll fill in these pages. Together."

Okay.

I was trying to focus on what he was saying. Before I could speak, Daniel jumped back in.

"I do have ideas." Daniel sounded both energetic and agitated. "But I'm going to need your complete buy-in to pull off what I think we can do."

He went on, "and they aren't small measures."

Not knowing what to do with my nervous energy, I flipped through the blank marketing plan by the lights of the Christmas tree, and let that sink in.

"If we're going to make your phones ring, we're both going to have to work hard, and stick our necks out, which terrifies me," he said. "For me, it means coming out of hiding, and being exposed again."

"That has to happen sometime, doesn't it?" I asked. I was genuinely confused about what one thing had to do with another.

"Yes, but helping *you* could be a career killer for *me*," he said, "if our ideas fail."

At this, I snapped my head up, and looked at Daniel—how could helping me come up with ideas jeopardize his career?

"I know this doesn't make any sense to you, Kay," Daniel said. "But perceptions stick. How people perceive me will determine my employability going forward—and how people perceive Kerby Lodge will determine your future success."

And then he made a comment that both insulted and angered me.

"We have to be smart," he said. "We can't print new paper placemats and call it a day."

I wanted to protest, but Daniel jumped back into his monologue.

"We need to develop authentic marketing. I'm talking about digital, viral, and relational," Daniel said. "*Real people* will say whether a product is good or not, not the other way around. I'll have to reach out and engage with people I know. People I've been… avoiding, I guess, in order to bring awareness to a new and improved Kerby Lodge."

I opened my mouth to speak, but didn't get the chance.

"Yes Kay, a *vastly* improved Kerby Lodge is essential. Because believe it or not," he said, "it's just as much work to market a bad product as a good one."

He held his hand up to stop me from interjecting. He was on a roll. Daniel went on to tell me that his name and reputation would be on the line, as much as the future of my inn.

"People are watching for me to resurface. As the owner of my own business, maybe. A film director with a production company," he said, "or, as the creative director of at least a mid-sized agency."

"*Not*," he continued, "a broken down—sorry, but it's true—family camp on a lake."

I nodded, though that last bit was painful.

"Your inn's future is at stake. But the future of my career is too," he said. "I don't have the money to retire—I'm only 44! Before long, I'll be making a dent in my savings. I made a good living for years, but do you know how expensive it is to live in Chicago?"

I shook my head, because I didn't.

"I'll have to give up my apartment soon because I can't afford it without an income. And the car? That's going away too—the lease is almost up. And health care! I have to pay for that now, since I no longer have an employer paying for it."

I knew that expense all too well.

"I have to jump back into my field in a strong way this spring, Kay Kerby, so don't for a minute think you're the only one with skin in this game," he said.

Daniel took a deep breath and then exhaled. I was silent, wondering if there might be one more final blow he wanted to land, and there was. "I know that you don't want to end up penniless, on your brother's doorstep," Daniel said, quietly, "well neither do I."

There were a few moments of silence following Daniel Mayne's speech when we both silently sized each other up. Could we work together? What were we getting ourselves into?

Never in my wildest dreams did I think that asking Daniel to help me save my lodge would lead to such a heated, emotion-packed discussion. But he was right—we both have a vested interest in this outcome. We have to want success for the other, as much as for ourselves.

"Kay," Daniel said, more quietly than before, but no less seriously, "it's going to be hard work, with risk involved, and enough pain to go around if we fill out this marketing plan together. And no turning back. I want your word on that."

I nodded but didn't dare speak.

"Because these next three months need to count. If we start," he said, "we finish."

30

We're on Lake Time, where it's always
"beer thirty" and "wine-o-clock"
-KERBY LODGE GUEST BOOK-

"Merry Christmas, Luke," I said, "the sea glass jewelry took my breath away!"

While my lodger was napping by the afternoon fire, I answered a phone call from his brother. Unlike my serious and draining talks with Daniel, my conversations with Luke were lighthearted and uplifting. How could two siblings be so unlike each other?

I had already called Nan and Sperry, thanking them for their beautiful gifts. They thanked me in return for helping their son recover from his "little tumble" at my inn.

In the background, I could hear the tinkling of glass, and laughter—and Nan explained that a few neighbors were over for Christmas cocktails, with "lots of frosted red cranberries and bright green limes!"

Judging by Nan's accent, she wasn't originally from the Midwest—my guess was Massachusetts, or Maine. The Mayne's from Maine, perhaps? If she knew my nickname, she would pronounce it "Kakah" and not "Kaker." If it weren't a family name I'd tell her, just to hear her say it.

"Oh, Nan, everybody calls me Kaker," I'd say.

"Kakah!" she'd answer, "how wonderful."

We kept our conversation short, but each promised to call again soon.

I remembered what Daniel told me, and realized with a smile that it was probably true. There was more social butterfly in his mother than nursemaid.

Luke replied, "Merry Christmas to you, Kay. I'm glad you liked my gift. Dan told me how much you were captivated by the water."

"Well I guess that's true," I said, looking out the window at the snow falling lightly on the deep swells of Lake Michigan. Wondering if the Mayne's of Chicago had expensive jewelry to go with all their hobbies and interests.

"It seems you're practically one of the family now," Luke went on, "and probably the favorite, if you ask me. Mother wants me to find out when your birthday is!" he said, laughing. "And if it's a milestone, she'll probably insist on a family cruise to celebrate."

We were both laughing at the absurdity at this point.

Although, wouldn't that be lovely?

31

Go jump in the lake?
Why, thank you. Don't mind if I do!
-KERBY LODGE GUEST BOOK-

Whatever delusions I had that turning my failing business around was as easy as creating a new website, radio commercial, or maybe an ad in a travel magazine, were quickly doused by a cold bucket of water named Daniel Mayne.

On a big new yellow pad of paper, he wrote down the costs for producing and airing even a short radio spot, and the numbers were astounding. The same was true for the smallest of ads in a glossy travel magazine.

"And you can't reach your audience unless you place a lot of ads, or buy a lot of radio air time—still, with no guarantees," Daniel said.

As for the website, he steered me away from this as an investment for the time being, but did convince me to spend ten dollars purchasing *kerbylodge.com* so that I would have it for future development.

Nope—my ideas of investing in advertising to attract new customers were not popular with Daniel. "If they do come to Kerby Lodge," he said, "will they like what they see?"

It was a rhetorical question and I knew better than to answer it.

And so it was that over early morning coffee, on the day after Christmas, my new marketing partner and I determined that we could either spend my limited budged drawing people to the same old musty resort, or spend it refreshing the resort. While I was still a bit doubtful, the second approach seemed to make more sense.

"But how will people find Kerby Lodge and know it's different and fresh, or whatever, if I don't have any money left to advertise?" I asked. It seemed like a classic "which came first, the chicken or the egg" puzzle. But Daniel simply nodded to indicate that he heard me.

"One step at a time," he said.

Later that morning after Jennifer arrived, the three of us talked about what could be accomplished in the month of January.

"Paint everything white," Jennifer said. "The great room and dining room, the walls and ceilings, the hallway to the guest suite, and all the bedrooms."

Her comment made me recall one of the magazine articles I read recently that had me laughing. A couple had purchased an abandoned ramshackle farmhouse to renovate, and decided that "if it didn't move," they'd paint it white. And if it did move—they'd "step on it, and then paint it white."

To Jennifer's point, we could leave the old carpets in place as drop cloths and then remove those last, revealing the original heart pine flooring. I'd already pulled the carpet back from one of the corners—and there they were, in all their pale golden glory!

"Where do we put all the furniture and books while we paint?" Jennifer asked.

"We can store them in the carriage house until we're ready to bring them back," I answered, and then noticed Daniel looking at me sideways.

"What?" I asked. He was looking at me like my clothes were inside out and I was the last to know.

"The books are musty and they shouldn't come back," he said. "All those humid summers have taken their toll—same with most of the furniture."

My jaw dropped in shock. Jennifer took that as her cue to leave the room and find another cup of bad coffee.

"Get rid of all my parents' books?"

Daniel just shrugged.

I knew that this process would be painful at times, but didn't expect Daniel would be scorching the earth quite so soon. I grudgingly admitted to myself that he was right.

"Take the ones that are special into your apartment, Kay," he said. "But be honest here. When was the last time you—or any guest—took a book off those shelves to read." I didn't want to admit that the last time I opened one it spawned a coughing fit. The dust mites jumped off the page and into my lungs.

"Okay they can go." Now it was my turn to shrug. I would need to choose my battles.

When Jennifer came back into the room, she told us about a great resale shop a few hours away that sold hardcover books by the bag, for next to nothing. "And they're practically new," she exclaimed.

We would plan a boondoggle after we got all our painting done.

She also told us about furniture consignment shops where I could find like-new pieces that were only four or five years old, and not 40- and 50-years old.

"When rich people redecorate," Jennifer said, "everybody wins."

"What about the cabinet from Scotland?" I asked my new team, pointing to the hand-carved open shelving. It was a gift from the *auld* country to Mum and Dad from her parents. It nearly filled an entire wall, and held a dusty array of carved wooden ducks, beer steins, photo collages, and other what-nots that had escaped my notice for decades. Yet, I couldn't imagine altering the piece itself in any way.

"I can't paint that," I said, waiting for someone to dare and challenge me.

"Merchandising!" Jennifer exclaimed. "All the great lodges—and believe me, we've gotten emergency calls to all of them—sell tee shirts and sweatshirts, and books by local authors, and local honey and pottery... that cabinet would make the perfect display."

Daniel and I looked at Jennifer appreciatively, nodding our approval.

Later, we were alone again, sitting by the fire with a plate of leftovers from Christmas dinner. Taking a printed calendar page of the month of January, we divided it up into a very aggressive painting schedule that allowed for just a few days to tackle each space. It would be a long, relentless month, with down time for sleeping and eating only.

We might as well get snowed in, because we weren't going anywhere until February.

I would have liked to focus on the cabins, which brought in more money than the guest rooms. But even if we could trudge out to them, it was too cold for painting.

"Besides, what we do with the lodge will set the tone for everything else," Daniel said, and that made a lot of sense.

And we would be ready to tackle the cabins by the end of February, or mid-March, weather and budget permitting. I had decided to use the money Zeke and June had given me for Christmas for the re-design of the lodge. And if I could make it stretch, the cabins too.

Not setting that money aside to subsidize the tax bill was a gamble. Though more and more, I realized the bigger gamble was to keep the inn the same while expecting different results.

Sitting in the great room after Daniel had hobbled off to bed, I took one last look around the lodge that I'd known as home my entire life. No one understood how much I relied on the sameness of these rooms to help me conjure up the warm but fading memories of my family. I could picture Mum taking a winter cat nap on the sofa, and Dad reading by the fire.

Tonight, this room was a stage for those precious images for one last time. Tomorrow it would completely change forever.

"*Och,* Mum and Dad," I whispered to the empty room, "I miss you so much."

32

Happiness is the sand between our toes.
And a little sunburn on our nose.
-KERBY LODGE GUEST BOOK-

"Too many whites!" I grumbled at Daniel the following morning. The paint clerk at the hardware store visibly shrank, and moved as far from us as possible.

We were perched on stools, looking at a great open book of colors. It was massive. The kind of book I imagined Santa had for his naughty or nice list.

Leaning on his crutches, Daniel held his face just inches from the paint chips—examining each one as if they were facets on cut diamonds. And here I always thought white was white. Apparently, there's a whole world of whites I never knew about.

For instance, there are cool whites and warm whites, Daniel told me—losing me immediately.

According to the paint chip names, there are meringues, and cottons, and snow whites. Whites I wanted to put in my coffee, like Clotted Cream, Sweet Froth, or Whipped Sugar.

There was Popcorn, White Chocolate, and Tortilla, which all made me hungry.

Others were locations, such as Nantucket White, Mackinac Island White, and Isle of White *White*. And architectural references, like Cottage White, Pillar White, and Rafter White.

Clearly, I was going to be no help at all. But Daniel, after closely examining each sample, pulled just one chip—then closed the big book with a definitive *slam* and shoved it aside dismissively. The paint clerk obediently took it away.

"This one," he said, putting one paint color chip in front of me.

"Irish Lace," I read out loud.

I felt an unexpected catch in my throat and had to turn away to see if I could swallow it, or if it would escape. Turns out it was the later, which made me glad the paint clerk was off helping another customer.

Every day of my life I have passed two photos from my parents' wedding, hanging on the wall of the apartment. In one, I see my mum's lovely image in her beautiful lilac linen dress. She's wearing a small veil of Irish lace. Dad is standing straight and tall next to her in his military dress uniform, looking handsome and pleased with the day.

A second photo shows the larger wedding party. A handful of the engineers who traveled with Dad are standing at attention in their uniforms. In contrast, Mum's sister Kay, my namesake, leans against her with familiarity and affection. As does another woman, a friend, who looks like she's about to tip over and topple them all like bowling pins.

Their ceremony was held at a wee country church. Afterwards, Mum and Dad and their handful of guests walked a *stretch o' the legs* across a meadow, and back to the inn for sandwiches, coffee, and cake. They traveled to Edinburgh three days later to enjoy a second luncheon with Mum's parents, who weren't in the habit of leaving their neighborhood.

Dad was expected at his assignment in London the following week.

Mum resigned, and packed up to join her new husband in his travels. And while they would miss her welcoming ways, the townsfolk were delighted that two people of such advanced years could find love, and wanted to give Raya a proper Scottish sendoff.

I have heard bits and pieces about the farewell *fete* thrown for "Raya and Himself," which was more robust than the sandwich and cake affair, I think. I would sometimes ask Mum about it, just to hear her say *Och, it was one for the ages, Kaker.*

"Irish Lace" was warm and crisp and perfect in every way, just like Mum. It felt like Raya's blessing on my plans for the lodge she loved so much.

"I adore it," I said, when I could speak again. Daniel was watching me as I swallowed hard, trying to regain my composure. Much like the many creative people who had cried in his office, after hearing his *iron sharpening iron* critique of their work.

But I had to admit that I was more than a bit impressed with Daniel Mayne, and his ability to make an informed design decision. This was his element, where I could see new confidence beginning to emerge.

And I found I was eager to call Luke later tonight, and tell him the story of Prince Daniel, slaying the many, many whites.

"Good," Daniel said, "because you're going to be seeing a lot of it." And then he was back to business. "Let's talk paint finishes—eggshell, flat, gloss, or semi-gloss—and then roller textures."

"Paint finishes? Roller textures?" I wished we were at the diner, eating meringues and popcorn.

"I can't believe how full my Jeep is," I told Daniel later, when we were actually eating lunch at the Village Diner. The cargo hold was stuffed with multiple cans of paint, brushes, rollers and roller covers, tarps, and work gloves.

We were in the same booth as before, looking out the window. The view was different from our last visit, though, as a few of the shops that had remained open through the Christmas shopping season were now closed until spring. And the sun was hidden behind deep dark clouds that hinted of inclement weather.

"We'd better make room for groceries, because I think we might be getting more snow soon," I said.

"I'm expecting a few boxes to be waiting at the post office," Daniel said.

I nodded, taking another bite of my delicious burger—one thing I never cooked for myself at home, but thoroughly enjoyed eating when I was out. Looking up, I saw Daniel was staring at me with a familiar frown on his face.

"Kay, are you ready for this level of change? Because once we start…" he asked in a decidedly kind voice. He was throwing me an "out" if I needed it.

I gazed out the window before answering, thinking about my lodge, and my town, and my family. I felt at peace with the changes we were going to make. Excited even, about finally trying something new. Excited about making decisions. Right or wrong, pass or fail, Kay Kerby, owner of Kerby Lodge, was making decisions.

I sat up a little taller in the booth, looked Daniel in the eye, and nodded.

"Be careful, don't hurt yourself," I said to the two guys who were carrying the large sofa to the carriage house later that day. Two more guys were behind them, trying to maneuver the heavy log coffee table on a furniture dolly.

I had arranged to pay a few of the local high school students, still on break, to help empty the rooms for painting. And not a moment too soon, as a new snow storm was predicted for early evening.

As soon as we returned from town, I got to work shoveling a path while Daniel hobbled in and out of the lodge with the paint supplies. Jennifer had agreed to meet us at the lodge and help me put red tape on the pieces we needed the boys to move—which was nearly every piece in the great room except the wing chairs, and the heavy hutch.

In the guest rooms, we thinned out all the clutter and detritus, deciding to keep just the beds, along with one dresser and chair in each room. And just like that, out went the little trunks, the wash stands, the dusty end tables, the stools, the clocks, the curio cabinets, the cases, the paintings, and the framed pictures that had filled these rooms for decades.

Using a few photo spreads I had earmarked for inspiration, we would pare down each room, and then bring back a few key pieces—perhaps after giving them a coat of paint—creating a clean and fresh décor for a new Kerby Lodge audience.

Sadly, all of the patchwork quilts had to go.

Daniel convinced me that while the Irish linens and sheets had stood the test of time, the more delicate quilts—many made by Gram Kerby and her friends—didn't give off the mildew-free vibe we were going for. I cringed at first, but agreed to put them into the cedar trunks for safe keeping in the carriage house.

To make the moving and storage of furniture easier for the boys, I reluctantly opened the large doors of the carriage house, which I hadn't done in a few years. I was immediately sorry. Because if anything stood as a visual representation of the state of my life, it was the carriage house in all its neglected disarray.

It felt like the world's biggest junk drawer, on display for all to see.

I stood in the driveway, staring at the jumble of rusty bikes and trikes and wagons, along with another layer of widowed wooden chairs and tables and benches and hutches. There were neglected beach chairs, umbrellas, and toys. And pieces that were so far back in the dark corners, that I couldn't tell what they even were.

Everything was mounded up and pushed aside, as more items from the lodge were stacked and stored. Turning my head, I saw that Jennifer was standing next to me, mouth open in what I assumed was shock and disappointment.

"I know, I know! It's a royal mess, isn't it?" I asked her, horrified and embarrassed.

"It's… the most beautiful thing I've ever seen," she answered.

33

Forecast for Lake Michigan:
mostly swimming with a chance of boating.
-KERBY LODGE GUEST BOOK-

I heard my alarm going off at 5:30 the morning. It screeched in an urgent crescendo, as I had programmed it to do. It was impossible to ignore, and yet, I did not move or open my eyes.

Two weeks ago, when we had first started painting, I practically leapt out of bed at the sound of my alarm. There were even a few days after we started our project when I woke up before the alarm went off—that's how eager I was to get to work.

Today, however, I listened to the relentless screeching—weighing and measuring which would be worse, the ear numbing sound, or the shooting pain I knew would feel as soon as I lifted my arm to turn it off.

I decided I could listen just a little longer.

Maybe I would grow to like the screeching. Maybe I just needed to give it a chance.

Kaker, yer'all skin and bones, Mum used to say. But she was wrong, I now knew. I discovered I also had muscles in my twig-like arms, because they were on fire from hours upon hours of sanding, brushing, priming, and painting—for days and days.

My feet and legs hurt from climbing up and down on the ladder. My neck and shoulders were sore and stiff from reaching and contorting. My back and shoulder blades ached from the rolling and more rolling of beautiful Irish Lace paint on the old brown paneling.

I had a new respect for all the before and after photos I had been looking at these past few weeks—the state of a "before" may have been dark and dated, but there was also a blissful ignorance attached to it. The ignorance of the high toll every renovation took.

"Coffee?" I asked Daniel, as I dragged myself into the great room. Thanks to muscle memory, I had already thrown on my painting jeans, my splattered flannel shirt, and the old tennis shoes from the back of my closet. I was dressed to get to work, anyway, even though my arms and legs were not enthused.

He barely looked up from his laptop, but indicated that he already had a mug.

"Pull your chair over," he said, in the echoing room. "I want to show you something."

Such a simple act, moving a chair a mere three feet. Yet I groaned with each nudge. Finally, Daniel looked up and grabbed the arm, pulling it towards him. I noticed, however, that he grimaced himself. *Good.* Daniel was working alongside me every day, but it was still gratifying to know he was sharing in the pain.

"Go grab your coffee and toast, then sit down and relax for a bit," he said, looking up at me from his chair. "We're ahead of schedule, and we can change gears for an hour or two. There's a few things I want you to see."

Toast with my coffee was my happy place, and Daniel knew this. He must have bad news to deliver, or maybe he wanted my approval on an idea we didn't agree on—I sincerely hoped he didn't want to paint the hutch after all.

I lumbered off to get my breakfast. As I waited for the toaster, I glanced up at the kitchen window and saw that it was still dark outside—it would be for another two hours. We'd been working such long days, that the already anemic winter sunrises and sunsets were blending together and barely noticed by either of us.

What I did notice was the brightness of the walls in the great room— even though it was only lit by the fire and a few lamps near our chairs. And the way our voices bounced around the room, in the absence of books and furniture.

I found that I could hardly wait to finish the infernal painting so we could begin pulling up the carpets. I knew that it would probably be a harder job than painting. But I was anxious to see the heart pine floors underneath, and the overall effect they would have on the lodge.

"I started a blog," he said when I returned. He had turned the screen on his laptop to show me. What I saw was a header that read *ReMayne*, and under that, a line that read: *Reimagined Designs of Daniel Mayne.*

What stood out most was an image I'd never seen of Kerby Lodge, taken from the shore. It looked rustic and complex, and very inviting. There was a shaft of sunlight shining through the birch trees that gave the lodge a happy glow, and the photo caught a slice of the beach and waves—showing the proximity of the lodge to Lake Michigan.

"I don't know what to comment on first, Daniel," I said, "but this photo of the lodge is beautiful. Where did you find it?"

"I took it myself at the height of the colors changing," he said. "Before I fell."

"Fall before the fall?" I said.

"Is that a joke?" he asked, looking up at me.

"Was it funny?" I asked in return.

"No," he said, "I don't think humor is your thing."

"What is my thing, Daniel?" I asked, wanting to know, all of a sudden.

Daniel looked at me for a minute before answering.

"It's six in the morning, Kay," he said, in a tone that bordered on dismissive. "Right now, toast is your thing. Then painting. But first, let's take a look at the blog, shall we?"

I nodded and took a bite of my breakfast. Toast was my thing.

As I scrolled through Daniel's blog, I saw that he had posted five entries—the first one documented the history of the lodge, complete with the sepia and faded photos that lined my walls. Another entry showed a montage of "before" photos of the great room, dining room, porch, and guest rooms. The lodge was already beginning to transform into something much fresher and lighter.

A third entry was titled *Which White is Right?* In it, Daniel talked about choosing the shade of white for any project, and specifically, how he came to choose Irish Lace for Kerby Lodge. A fourth entry was titled *Book Smart*, and talked about vintage versus new books, and when to use each in reimagined designs.

And if I wasn't already fully awake, the most recent entry was enough to make my eyes open wide. It was titled *Meet Kay Kerby, Lodge Owner*.

I remembered now that Daniel had asked me to smile for a picture a few weeks ago. I wore a clean flannel shirt, and posed with a fresh paint roller in my hand. In the photo I'm smiling—a sure tip-off that it was the onset of our adventure, before holding a roller had become painful. And before I began looking paint splattered and worn out every minute of the day, like I do now.

After the shock wore off of seeing my face on a website page of any kind, I felt pleasantly surprised at the photo Daniel took. I chalked it up to his eye for lighting and angles.

When was the last time anyone took my picture, anyway?

Dad and Mum were always snapping photos of us kids, and of each other, when they were alive. Somewhere, there are boxes and boxes of loose pictures that I should take the time to organize and put in albums.

In one of my desk drawers, I have pictures from college, taken by roommates and friends. But in the past twelve years, there hasn't been anyone in my life who felt the need to capture my image. My family was gone, I wasn't married, and I hadn't seriously dated in years.

Yet, there I was, on the computer screen. Looking older than I had looked in college, but also hopeful—like someone whose life was not yet over. Like someone with a future.

I couldn't imagine what Daniel had written, but was ridiculously pleased at being documented. Of having proof that I existed, I guess—proof that I wasn't just fading away with all the other old and useless things at Kerby Lodge.

I read this last entry more closely than the others.

Meet Kay Kerby, Lodge Owner

My client, Kay, was just a child when I was introduced to Kerby Lodge. She was staying close to her mother while my brother and I were running through the woods and climbing trees. She was sitting on the white shores with a bucket and shovel, while Luke and I swam with a vengeance through the waves of Lake Michigan, to the far away sand bars. Now, after inheriting Kerby Lodge, Kay is taking giant steps to make it her own—and it's no small task. Painting that first white swatch of Irish Lace (*link to: Irish Lace, satin finish*) over the beautiful wood finishes she's grown up with her entire life was a leap of faith. So was removing the artifacts and nostalgia that guests have loved over the years. But Kay has style, and sensibilities that are all her own, which are starting to shine through. Guests lucky enough to stay at Kerby Lodge this summer will find fresher, brighter spaces, and reimagined cabins and guest rooms that enhance the spectacular views of Lake Michigan. Kay has a natural instinct for warmth and hospitality. She's spending her winter making sure your summer will be amazing! Don't miss Kay Kerby, and the reimagined spaces of Kerby Lodge.

"This is… really, really cool, Daniel," I said. My coffee was going cold as I couldn't seem to take my eyes off of Daniel's blog. He was waiting for more from me, I was sure, but I was mesmerized. He seemed to capture the best of Kerby Lodge, as well as the hope that I had for its future and re-invention.

"Thoughts?" He asked.

"Thoughts… yes," I finally answered. "I had no idea you were doing this—when did you do this? *How* did you do this? How does this fit into our marketing plan? And how…?"

"Whoa," Daniel said, holding his hands up, "those are a lot of thoughts."

"First," he said, "I started before Christmas. I… don't always sleep through the night."

"Second," he continued, "it wasn't difficult. Every designer knows just enough computer programming to get themselves in trouble."

"And last," Daniel frowned, "it could very well be a complete waste of my time, because it could fall flat and do nothing for us at all."

I started to open my mouth and say "then why bother?" but didn't get the words out.

"Or," Daniel continued, "it could be our first legitimate marketing step, as soon as I take this site live and send it to a few key people. If there's interest, the site will be shared and viewed—continually. The more shares and views, the better."

"Take it live?" I said.

"It's not visible to anyone but us at the moment," he said. "But I'm ready to launch it if you are." And looking at me out of the corner of his eye, Daniel said "how about it? Are you ready to come out of hiding Kay Kerby?"

Maybe I am. According to Daniel's photo shoot, I was looking pretty good and rather confident a few weeks ago, before I stopped bothering to peel the paint flecks off my arms. And after seeing the inn through Daniel's photos, I could see with fresh eyes just how beautiful it was, and how much it deserved to have a second life, with new guests.

"Are you sure you're not overselling me, and the lodge?" I asked.

"I'm sure," he said, and he sounded sure.

"In that case, I'm ready," I said, looking back at the blog.

He nodded.

"But Daniel," I asked, looking back up at him, "are *you* ready to come out of hiding? Are you ready to let people know where you are?" By way of answer, Daniel didn't answer. Instead, he grimaced and turned away to stare into the fire.

"I think it's time," I persisted to a still frowning Daniel. "You absolutely should announce the big promotion you accepted—as creative genius for Kerby Lodge. After beating out all other candidates."

I was trying for the smallest of smiles.

"We can unveil your new theme line," I said.

He turned my way out of sheer curiosity.

"Kerby Lodge," I said, with a hint of theatrics, "a broken down family camp on a lake!"

Bingo.

Who said humor wasn't my thing?

"Wow," Luke said on the phone that night, "I'm pretty blown away by the projects you and Dan are taking on at your lodge this winter. No wonder you haven't answered or returned my calls lately."

I had the phone propped on my night table in order to avoid the pain I felt in my hands when holding just about anything. In fact, I was wondering if I could duct tape my toothbrush to my bathroom cabinet, and just move my teeth around it.

"Thanks—you must have seen Daniel's blog. Feel free to come by anytime and grab a roller," I said, only half-joking. "We are exhausted, let me tell you. With still so much to do."

"Hey, I'd pitch in," Luke laughed, "even with these nerd hands. Though I'm not used to lifting anything heavier than a pencil. But where did Dan get the guy skills to do all that work?"

I wanted to laugh at that, but knew that everything in my body would shake and hurt.

"He's not shirking from the hard things," I said, slightly surprised to be defending Daniel to anyone, especially his brother. "Which is impressive when you consider he has to balance on his walking cast, or his crutches."

"That blog, though, is amazing!" Luke said. "What a natural storyteller Dan is. I am impressed—once you strip away all the big ad agency budgets and teams of people, I can see just how talented he is."

"You know, Luke," I said, genuinely touched, "that's nice of you to say about your brother. I don't suppose you'd care to tell him that, would you?"

Luke laughed out loud. "Oh no! That would violate the Mayne family code—to repress all outward displays of vulnerability or affection," he said. "We have to sign an agreement as newborns, before they let us come home from the hospital."

I did laugh at that image. And it did hurt.

"I have to confess," Luke said, more seriously, "that my favorite blog entry was the article Dan wrote about you."

"That one took me by surprise," I said.

"And that photo, Kay! Dan said you were pretty, but *pretty* is an understatement." Luke spoke this last sentence very slowly.

"Oh?" I said, uncomfortable to think Daniel and Luke were discussing me in any way. Although I guess it was inevitable. "The blog is just an experiment," I said, trying to steer the conversation away from me, "to see if we can generate any interest."

"Well," Luke said, "consider interest to be generated."

I felt a slight shift between us that I couldn't put my finger on.

Were we still talking about me?

34

It's the end of an era, Kerby Lodge.
After so many shenanigans, we're moving on.
-KERBY LODGE GUEST BOOK-

"Daniel! Daniel!" I said in an urgent whisper. "Wake up!"

"Nnnn," was his reply. I couldn't tell if it was an actual word, or just a guttural sound in his sleep.

"*Wake up!*" I said, louder, "someone is breaking into the lodge!"

We were three weeks into January, now, and sleeping on the floor of the great room. High winds had knocked the power out after dinner, and there was nothing to do but put our tools away and call it an early night. I pulled out the sleeping bags and turned on the space heaters that were powered by the generator.

I felt bad for Daniel, trying to wrestle his walking cast into the tight-fitting sleep sack, and then curling up on the hard floor—especially after such a taxing day of sanding and painting. Thankfully, we still had the layer of carpet under us, though decades old and somewhat stained and disgusting. I opted not to mention the worm story to Daniel as we tried to get comfortable, and tried not to think of it myself.

We were exhausted and glad for an early bedtime, and both felt we could sleep through just about anything. I hadn't considered that a break-in would be one of those things.

Now, my thoughts were frantically racing as I heard the door being tampered with, and saw the vulnerable position we were in—just 15 feet from the lodge door, and coming out of a deep sleep. I was trying to, anyway.

My "fight or flight" instincts were kicking in big time, but there wouldn't be any flight while wrapped up like mummies, and there was nothing left in the great room to defend ourselves with, I realized. Not even any musty old books—which could be great projectiles.

Reaching for my phone to call for help, I remembered I had left it in the apartment. In fact, I had been so busy that I rarely checked for calls or messages anymore, and barely kept it charged.

Sitting up, I regretted that neglect.

Reaching over, I nudged Daniel hard in the shoulder, as I tried to orient myself to the dark room. The fire was almost out. There were a few embers but they didn't give off much light.

Maybe I had been dreaming! The winds were strong and I could hear tree branches scraping the siding and windows, but there—definitely there—I could make out the unmistakable sound of the door handle turning back and forth.

"Daniel! Grab a weapon. Anything! Quick!" I said urgently.

Now on high alert, he sat up and then tried to scramble to his feet, as did I. Unfortunately, we knocked heads in the pitch dark and then became tangled in each other's sleeping bags.

Daniel's long legs were like tree trunks wrapped around mine while I was trying to break free. In spite of his injury he was strong, and we were both dazed and clumsy in our efforts. Under other circumstances it would have been comical.

At last, we were both successful in standing—just as the lodge door flew open with a gust of wind and snow, and the electricity and lights came back on at the same moment.

Disoriented, both of us gave a loud yell of shock and surprise—as did our intruder.

"Don't shoot!" the voice yelled.

Blinking hard against the bright lights, I could see a man standing in the foyer.

He had pushed the big solid door closed on the swirls and whirls. The man was covered in snow and ice, staring at Daniel who was standing upright with the sleeping bag still hugging his torso—holding his crutch like a baseball bat.

Next to him, I had one foot in and another outside of my sleeping bag, menacingly aiming a paint roller... at my brother, Tad.

Forty minutes later, Tad and Daniel were sitting by the now blazing fire, staring at the flames, stealing wary glances at each other. I had brought them both mugs of hot tea, and then retreated back into the kitchen, without making eye contact with either.

Tad had traded his wet and cold clothes for his old high school sweatpants and one of the flannel shirts I kept from Dad's closet.

I had finally calmed down from the shock and joy of seeing Tad, and from the trauma I felt at his entry. While heating more water for my own tea, I washed my face and brushed out my hair, trying to appear somewhat composed.

It was midnight, I noticed, as I plugged my phone into the charger.

Stepping back into the great room, I passed Daniel, limping on his crutches and heading to his room. The furnace had kicked on and the lodge was beginning to warm up.

"Okay," Tad said, gaping as he looked all around him at the great room—now void of most furniture and all books, and painted Irish Lace white. "Please tell me what the *HECK* is going on here, Kaker?"

35

*Another summer of making waves
at the wonderful Kerby Lodge*
-KERBY LODGE GUEST BOOK-

Once I climbed into bed I slept soundly, knowing my brother was tucked away in the room next to mine. I woke up sporadically, and each time drifted back into a deep sleep.

When was Tad here last?

Apparently, he wrapped up a medical conference in Chicago and decided to make a detour on his way home. Of course, if I'd checked my phone, I would have known he was coming! It seems I had caused everyone in my family to worry about my whereabouts and well-being these past few weeks. I'd have to remember to call my aunt and uncle later.

Not wanting to get snowed in, Tad parked his rental car at the top of the hill by the closed-up house, and hiked down the driveway late last night—before making what will forever be known in our family as the world's most epic and historic entrance.

Neither one of us could sleep after the surge of surprise and emotion, at least for my part. So, we stayed up for hours and talked.

He was more than a little nervous, he confessed, walking down the dark and snowy road to the lodge—especially after seeing that all the lights were out—though we'd both made that walk more times than we could count during our school years.

Back then, the Kerby Lodge snow plow was old and small. It could barely touch the drifting snow that the fierce wind would pile onto the steep lodge driveway. But since most of our classmates lived closer to town and to civilized roads, school was almost always in session except during the worst blizzards—we had to make our way.

I know people love to exaggerate the hardships and travails of their childhood, but it did feel like we walked five miles to school in the winter— uphill both ways. After school, the bus driver would drop us off at the stone pillars that marked the entrance to Kerby Lodge. We'd hop down into the frigid air that would burn our nostrils, while the wind blew stinging snow or sleet onto our cheeks and into our eyes.

On the worst of days Tad and I were inclined to trudge a much shorter path through the deep snow to Gram's house, just across the driveway.

"I thought you'd be coming to see me," she'd say, with a happy smile on her face.

We'd trade our cold and wet layers for the flannel pajamas we kept in her guest closet, as Gram phoned the lodge to say we were staying at her base camp for a few days—until the storm died down.

We were always grateful to walk into her warm home, and for the cocoa powder that sat in two mugs on the table—ready for us to stir in hot water and marshmallows. And hungry for the stews and soups, which Gram always had simmering on the stovetop in winter—and which would be accompanied by crusty bread and soft butter.

And for a day or two, while our parents kept the fire burning in the lodge at the bottom of the hill, Tad and I were glad for a reprieve; for the extra trees and distance that provided a buffer between us and Lake Michigan in winter.

Our years together at Kerby Lodge seemed like they'd go on forever. But like all kids, we wanted to grow up fast and get to our *real* lives. And that worked out just fine for Tad.

My real life, on the other hand, has been marked with struggles and loneliness—maybe of my own making, since I'm the one who insisted on staying on and running the lodge.

I had no idea what time it was when I awoke, feeling more rested than I had in weeks. I could see light streaming in the window, which was highly unusual.

Noon!

I panicked when I saw the time, thinking I was late for our daily work schedule, which had the precision of a Swiss time piece. What must Daniel think?

And then I heard the voices of two men—low, but excited. Tad was here, I remembered! Was he arguing with Daniel? Tad certainly wasn't a fan of the "dude" who was going to get a slip-and-fall attorney and take my lodge away in a settlement.

The two were polite but distant when I introduced them last night, after a scenario I'm sure we all wanted to forget. There was Tad, frozen in an ice-covered parka. And Daniel, looking like a lanky caterpillar stuck inside a cocoon. And between the two, someone was wailing hysterically. I suspect that might have been me.

But no, I realized, the men weren't arguing—they were laughing. There were happy sounds coming from the great room. And when I opened my bedroom door, I breathed the aromas of fresh coffee, breakfast sausages, and pancakes with maple syrup.

This day was starting out much better than the last one ended.

"…then that kid, Benji, took the bike from your brother, remember?" I heard Tad say.

"*Remember?* I've never seen my dad so mad at a little kid before," Daniel laughed. "For a minute there, I thought he was going to let me slug him."

When I walked into the great room, Tad and Daniel were laughing and talking like long lost best friends. In the light of day, they remembered each other from the Mayne family vacation at Kerby Lodge. Tad remembered both Daniel and Luke for their spirited antics, and Nan and Sperry, for their generous tips.

"I think your parents put me through med school," Tad joked with Daniel.

In addition, they had discovered a shared friend—one of Daniel's fraternity brothers is a physician at the facility where Tad spends much of his time.

As they swapped stories, Tad sat on the stone hearth, examining Daniel's injured leg with professional ease. He had the walking cast off, and was rotating the ankle this way and that, looking for subtle nuances in flexibility.

Before they saw me and could check themselves, I could see they had the ridiculous grins on their faces of two carefree adolescent boys—before the sobering responsibilities of patients and clients, mortgages and leases, or relationships and careers. And my heart opened up a little more to both of them, right then, as I tried to memorize this moment in time.

"Well, it's all pretty impressive, Kaker," Tad said, his words echoing around the nearly empty great room. I hoped he was sincere.

I was sitting by the fire with both Tad and Daniel—Tad had carried in a third chair from the apartment. I was finishing my breakfast, and Tad was reading the *ReMayne* blog posts on my laptop, as Daniel was looking at his own. I noticed, looking over Tad's shoulder, that the blog had seen hundreds of visits already, and had just as many followers.

"Probably just nosy ex-coworkers," Daniel remarked, when I mentioned this.

I found that I trusted Daniel's written words to express what we were trying to accomplish at Kerby Lodge far better than I trusted my own. Because, although he made a great show of leaving the lodge behind after high school, I was sensitive to the fact that this was still Tad's childhood home, and home to his memories of our dear parents.

Maybe that's why I hadn't told him of my plans for the lodge—since I was on the verge of either losing it to unpaid taxes, or spending my last dollars completely altering it.

Probably both.

"Mum and Dad made running this lodge look easy," I said, trying not to sound emotional or defensive. "But it's much harder than I ever realized, Tad."

Tad nodded while Daniel, sensing a private conversation, excused himself and went to his room. I think it was understood that no painting was going to happen today, and I was relieved beyond measure for the break.

"Kaker," Tad said, choosing his words, "I hope your plans work out the way you want them to—but you know that I'll always take care of you, right? You will always have a home and family, wherever I live."

I nodded gratefully. I knew that I was more fortunate than most—I would never be homeless. I could show up at Zeke and June's Florida condo on the golf course, and be their third wheel for early-bird dinners, canasta tournaments, and trips to the urologist.

My aunt and uncle would treat me as their daughter, and fuss over me if I wasn't home each evening to watch Wheel of Fortune with them.

I could also show up on the porch, or veranda, I should say, of Tad's historic home near Atlanta. There, I could share bunk beds and fluffy pink pillows with my nieces, get manicures with Selby, and listen to her friends gush over what a big help I had been at their latest fundraising luncheon.

And while I was certain that warmth and love would await at each location, one place rivaling the other, it would be an extension of the last twelve years. It would be me, the little sister, the orphaned niece, finding a hiding place to ride out a storm—but not living my life. And as I looked at Tad in gratitude, I felt more resolve than ever to do just that.

"Tad," I said, hearing in my voice the authority I longed to possess. "It's been so good to see you, and I love you like crazy for checking in on me."

"But…" he said.

I smiled back at him as I got up to go change into my work clothes. "But… this lodge isn't going to paint itself."

36

*Thanks for the fun. We made memories to last
a lifetime—or at least through a cold winter.*
-KERBY LODGE GUEST BOOK-

The end of January is here at last. And along with it, the end of the painting.

Daniel and I are in the large dining room, finishing the last wall. We had kept pace with our aggressive painting schedule, more or less, and could now see the fruits of our efforts.

Every room, every wall, every piece of trim, was now crisp and clean and new.

The two of us had spent the past thirty days working side by side, from the dark of early morning until the dark of night, tackling what I once considered to be insurmountable.

Today, as with every other day, we talked occasionally, but allowed long periods of easy silence between us. Neither of us felt the need to fill the air with the sound of our own voices, thank goodness.

Being with my lodger was a lot like being in a room by myself, I realized. My mind was blessedly free to skip over different topics while I focused on the task in front of me—without being asked "penny for your thoughts?" or some such inane question.

Looking out the window at the snow, I imagined the spring thaw, and all the cleaning and renovation work waiting for me in the cabins.

I wondered if, in a few weeks, the groundhog in Punxsutawney would see his shadow, or if we'd have a shorter winter this year. It certainly started out early. So maybe it would also end early. I'll ask the pharmacist if his bunion has any insight.

My mind wandered to my extended family, and where Zeke and June might go on their retirement trip—they were leaning towards Spain and

Portugal. Tad and Selby might know. I tried to think about when I had last seen my two darling nieces in Atlanta. I should try to get down there in the spring, before welcoming my summer guests.

And then I thought about my summer guests. January was when I usually began getting emails for reservations, after everyone had recovered from the holidays. But so far, there were none. In all fairness, though, I had been preoccupied with the inn itself, and not with my email inbox.

Except to see if Luke had sent me any messages.

I let my mind wander to Luke, and our recent conversations. He only had another six weeks left in the term, and was considering job offers from around the country—and around the world. He was invited to teach English as a second language in both Beijing and Seoul.

Alaska schools wanted him, too, and bad. They had been dangling a hefty bonus if he'd sign on for two years.

Or he could come here, which seemed to be the least exciting of his possibilities. Nevertheless, Jennifer had mentioned to me again that there were openings at the local schools, and asked me to pass on the information to Luke—which I had.

What would it be like to have both Mayne brothers in my backyard? I couldn't imagine.

Lately Luke and I chatted about our interests and lives—we hardly ever talked about Daniel these days. Daniel was no longer the glue that held us together.

We talked about where we came from, and where we wanted to go. I told Luke about two boys, one from high school and another from college, who had been close friends of mine. Though neither relationship amounted to anything more.

Luke asked if either guy was the "one that got away," and I had to say no. Definitely not.

He wondered out loud whether either guy considered *me* to be the one who got away. I didn't know that answer. I guess it was possible.

I offered glimpses of my past, and shared how devastating it was to lose Raya and Fitz just after graduate school, and how guilty I still felt about not spending more time with them towards the end of their life.

I even confessed to him that, not so deep down, I doubted I could actually save Kerby Lodge, even with Daniel's help. And how at times I felt careless for allowing the inn's value to tarnish—things I had never admitted to anyone.

Finally, I told Luke how humbling it felt to have an advanced degree in education gathering dust in a frame—while I'd never set foot inside a classroom.

In turn, Luke said that I was being too hard on myself on all fronts. For one thing, the economic downturn was out of my control. He reminded me that the recession and had taken down more financially savvy people than me.

He told me it was never too late to put my feet inside a classroom.

And as far as my parents went, he said I should forgive myself.

"From what you've told me about Fitz and Raya," he said, "they would never have doubted your love. They must have been so proud of all your hard work and accomplishments, even in the darkest days of their illness. How comforting it must have been for them to know you would be self-sufficient, in a career you were passionate about."

I hadn't quite thought of that before.

"We can't go back Kay," Luke told me. "We can only keep searching for the right path that takes us forward."

I wondered what path Luke would be taking. Whether he was content to be single. Luke did tell me, in a recent conversation, about Lucy. The young woman he had been in love with during his first year of teaching.

"She broke my heart," he said. "When she wouldn't answer my phone calls, I trusted that she was just busy with her job. But she was busy falling in love with my roommate." And then he tried to make a joke of it. "Which is why I live alone now," he laughed.

I didn't laugh with him, I only told him how sorry I was.

And as I painted the dining room wall, I found myself wondering what it would be like to be in a relationship of my own. Luke Mayne certainly ticked off a lot of boxes—except the big one of living anywhere near me. Would Luke be the one who got away? It was impossible to say, since we'd never met.

Luke would be the one that *stayed* away, I decided, and chuckled to myself.

Daniel looked over at me, but I just shrugged and kept working.

No, sadly, Luke will always be my mysterious stranger. Any feelings he was stirring up in me were obviously one-sided—just my lonely heart desperately grasping at straws. Luke will finish his job in California, and no doubt jet off to Asia, or to Alaska. Our phone conversations will inevitably taper off, as he builds a new life for himself.

And what about Daniel Mayne—would he be the one that got away? Or would he always be the one I never wanted in the first place? The one I couldn't get rid of.

Or, should Daniel be the one I don't *let* get away, I wondered. After all, my animosity towards him had faded. I could barely work up a snarky attitude to throw his way.

Did we have anything in common? It did seem that two people who were interested in each other would talk more than we do, even about inconsequential topics. If we were dating, wouldn't we try harder to keep conversations flowing?

Penny for your thoughts?

I liked his family, that much was certain. It seemed as though his brother had been in my life forever—I felt as though I could tell Luke anything, and often did. And Nan was a dream. She was supportive without being controlling, and her shopping skills seemed unmatched.

However, there was a definite disconnect between Daniel and Kerby Lodge that I couldn't overlook, even though he was working hard to help me give it new life. He still saw it as a product, and not a passion, I was sure. But I could be wrong. My experience with relationships, and love, was minimal—it could be that he felt strongly about both the inn and its owner, but didn't know how to express either, as Luke had jokingly eluded to.

Or maybe his love had, as was common in my favorite movies, "grown so slowly, that he hardly recognized it." That seemed unlikely. And honestly, I couldn't say I would return the feeling of love if he did express it. I only knew I was more open to the possibility.

I'd gotten used to Daniel being at the inn, that much was true.

Maybe I was just feeling the excitement of being done with the painting—or the novelty of having a man under my roof for the winter. And not a bad looking one.

Glancing over, I could confirm that Daniel was definitely looking stronger and healthier—trimmer even, with more pronounced muscles in his arms and back. I knew this because as our work days wore on, he would sometimes remove his flannel shirt, and paint in a tee shirt. I found I didn't hate that.

The scratches on his face had healed and his complexion had improved. He looked good. As long as he wasn't scowling or sneering at me, which he did with less frequency.

Is it possible to be attracted to a work ethic? Because if so, Daniel had me at "can I clean your paintbrush for you?" He matched me minute for minute, day after day, on all of the painting and sanding. And then he stayed up long after I went to bed, writing his blog.

He had posted three more entries, titled *Lighter and Brighter*, *Edit your Rooms*, and *House Calls*, where he documented (with Tad's blessing) the unexpected visit from Doctor Kerby—complete with a group photo. We noticed a definite bump in activity after Tad's stay, most likely from Tad and Selby's network of friends and coworkers. "But that's okay," Daniel said, "because doctors make a lot of money." He's sure that more than one summer reservation will come from Tad's sphere of influence.

Daniel noted that another reason our follows surged was because people like a good story, "and that's what we're giving them with the renovation of Kerby Lodge." It's not just a blog about paint swatches, but about people. And real lives. And unexpected visitors, he said.

Each blog post now has a link to the new Kerby Lodge website landing page, which Daniel also developed in between painting. It looks amazing, and has a new email address for guests to contact me for availability. I won't have to rely on phone messages.

"I'm dragging your lodge kicking and screaming into the new millennium," Daniel had said. It took me a while to realize he was making a jab at my archaic communications.

"Touché," I acknowledged.

"I know a guy who owes me a favor," Daniel told me recently. "When the time is right, I'll ask him to build out an interactive reservation calendar. Then, people can see which cabins and rooms will be available for the weeks they want to travel in the summer."

They'll be able to see photos, and a site map of the lodge property, he said, and even pay online.

But first, Daniel wanted me to take time to do a "competitive analysis" on other lodges in the area, and what they were charging for their rooms and cabins. He thinks I've been undercharging. And while my initial response was fear—with such a sharp decline in the number of my guests, why on earth would I raise my rates?—Daniel insisted that with the renovations, my lodge would attract people who would pay more.

I was amazed. Truly amazed at all Daniel was doing for Kerby Lodge. Maybe inspiration was coming to him while he painted, or wrote, or stared into the fire—but gears were turning, and he was inspired. I understood now why the marketing plan was blank on Christmas day. Together, we were filling in the pages.

Maybe he wasn't such a bad guy after all.

I stole another glance at him—standing next to me with a paintbrush in his hands, filling in the details of the wainscoted walls. His muscles were flexing in his arm, and his eyes were dark and focused. There was just something about him that looked—good.

He caught me looking at him again.

I smiled and turned back to my work.

"Kay," he said. He stopped what he was doing and turned my way.

"Mmm?" I answered, doing the same.

"What's that thing you're doing with your face?" he asked.

"My face?" I asked. "You mean, smiling?"

"Yeah. You're smiling. At me." He levelled this as an accusation.

"You're not falling in love with me, are you?" he asked, and I stopped in my tracks.

I waited for the punchline, because certainly he was kidding.

I felt caught. Exposed. As though I needed to defend my own honor. I should know better than to let my guard down with Daniel Mayne. He will definitely not ever be the "one who got away." He will be the one who can't leave soon enough for me.

"Love you? I hardly *like* you," I said at last.

And as I stood speechless and dumbfounded, he did the worst thing possible—he smiled. But it wasn't a flirty or friendly smile. It was a *kind* smile of sympathy. Of pity.

It was a smile that made me want to throw something at him.

"Kay, this is Luke. I'm sorry I missed talking with you. I hope you'll have more time in February. Call when you can. Blog looks great. Can't wait to hear more about your brother's visit. Give my best to Daniel for me, okay? He's been hard to reach, too."

I deleted Luke's message and didn't return the call, even though it was only 8 p.m. California time. I just couldn't stomach hearing any Mayne voice right now.

"Kaker, Uncle Zeke here. We need to discuss your strategy for paying your taxes this spring. It's a good news, bad news scenario—so call me soon, but not tonight. I've got to get my rest for the canasta tournament. June sends her love, to both you and Daniel."

Nope, no love to Daniel, Aunt June.

I'd have to call Zeke back in a few days and find out what the damages are for my taxes, and how I'm going to pay them. And did he mention good news?

"Kay! Two things." It was Jennifer. "One, I need to talk about something exciting. I'll come by next week and catch you." She must have found her retail location. "Two, that new craft brewery in town, Moon Lake, is having a Valentine's Day dinner and tasting event—I made reservations for the four of us," she said. "We'll have fun."

Ugh. Say hello to Daniel.

Give my love to Daniel.

A Valentine dinner with Daniel.
Daniel, Daniel, Daniel.

37

Lake hair don't care
-KERBY LODGE GUEST BOOK-

"Red-eye or not, here we are," the man said when I opened the lodge door.

"Good morning, Red," I said to the man with his larger-than-life signature greeting. He sounded just like he did on the phone.

Red and his crew were at my door at 8 a.m., as promised. They came into the great room carrying boxes of tools, crowbars, and a case of heavy-duty trash bags. Most of the guys were holding a coffee cup from the drive-through restaurant in town, and paper bags filled with breakfast sandwiches—and nobody bothered to stomp the snow off their boots.

Honestly, it didn't matter today.

While the guys were looking in and around each room, Daniel came out of his bedroom on both crutches with his coat on, ready to go.

It had been four days since we wrapped up the painting, and we had been really great at avoiding each other since then. I concluded on my own that we'd had too much togetherness and too little sleep over the past month—which led to our awkward conversation.

But it was time to move on.

I made it a point of smiling right at Daniel, and making eye contact. I was determined to be the poster child for "smiling without ulterior motives" going forward.

Plus, I didn't want any weirdness between us—especially today.

"All right, Red," I said, with my own coat in my hands. "You have my number if you need me. Otherwise," I said, looking over and catching Daniel's eye once again, "we will get out of your way for now, and be back this evening."

A few days after Tad had gone back to Atlanta, Red had called my cell phone. After neglecting my phone for the month of January, and being in hot water with nearly every person I knew, I answered the unknown local number.

A very chipper man told me that he was in possession of a blank check from a Theodore Kerby, and he and his team were to come over—at my convenience—and remove all of the carpeting from the inn. They would haul away every bit of carpet and padding from the premises, leaving nothing behind but memories.

"And don'cha worry," Red said, "we'll move all the furniture as we go, and put it back where we found it." As he spoke, I pictured the oversized hutch in the great room. It would take a team of people to move that one piece alone.

Red went on to say that after all the fibers, nails, dirt, and petrified worm juice (he didn't actually say that bit, but I thought it) had been removed, his merry crew would bring industrial floor polishers inside, and "polish the snot" out of my vintage heart pine floors.

Daniel and I were both pretty excited about this generous gift from Tad. We had allotted the first week in February to do this ourselves. But by scheduling Red and his dream team to come to the lodge, we got a few days of much needed rest. And our schedule got a shot in the arm. Speaking of, we felt our own arms, legs, and backs had dodged a bullet—because pulling up the matted and heavy carpets from these massive rooms would be an achy-breaky job.

It hadn't occurred to me to polish the floors—but I couldn't wait to see the results.

We got another bonus. On the day we had scheduled Red and his team to come, a warm front was forecast to move in, and sure enough, it arrived.

Today would be dry and sunny, with unseasonably high temps—a lake effect anomaly, but a welcome one, for sure. We could take that all-day boondoggle to look at consignment furniture, buy bags of practically new books for the shelves, and eat, eat, and eat some more.

During the month of January I had been fixing partial meals, if I fixed any meals at all. Time was precious, and we often grabbed sandwiches or bowls of cereal for dinner, and skipped lunch with frightening regularity.

As a result, instead of putting on my usual "winter ten" pounds from cooking, napping, and watching movies, Daniel and I were sporting roller-toned muscles, clear complexions, and loose jeans and sweaters as we walked to the Jeep.

If I didn't know us, I'd swear we were a couple of outdoor adventure models.

Turning my face to the rising, already warm sun, it was impossible not to smile.

"Mister Mayne, this is a found day," I said, using one of Gram's favorite phrases from long ago. I put on my sunglasses with a dramatic flair, and dismissively threw my bulky coat into the back seat before getting in.

Daniel smiled and did the same. "A found day indeed, Miss Kerby," he volleyed back.

Everything was okay.

Our destination was Petoskey, a large town 80 miles from Kerby Lodge. Inspired by Red and team, we grabbed hot coffees and breakfast sandwiches at the Rusty Nail to devour as we made our way.

Originally, Jennifer was going to join us, but was called into work after a co-worker on her team came down with the flu. I'd miss her company, but this gave the two of us more time to talk business.

I had been trying my best to follow along as he explained the workings and purpose of his blog, beyond the obvious visibility it provided. But I had to ask Daniel, as we were driving and sipping our coffees, to repeat himself.

It was all *algorithms, blah blah blah,* and *keywords* and *analytics, blah blah blah.* But in a nutshell, the more visits the better, and if it got enough *traffic,* ads would begin to appear. Once people started clicking on the sponsored ads, things would get good. And money would be made.

"I have a… friend," he told me, "who makes her entire living off the income from her lifestyle blog. But this is rare," he went on, with obvious pride in his friend's achievement. "Only five percent of bloggers have this kind of success."

The way Daniel talked about his "friend" made me wonder if she was the rumored girlfriend Luke had mentioned in our first conversation. Looking over at him, there was a sweetness I'd never witnessed on his face before.

It made me wonder if, in my lifetime, I would ever be the subject of such a sweet expression.

38

Kerby Lodge,
I love you to the LAKE and back
-KERBY LODGE GUEST BOOK-

There are plenty of people along the coast of Lake Michigan who have money. Lots and lots of money. The recession that has meant complete and utter devastation for some, has only been a minor annoyance for others. Meaning maybe it hasn't been the time to buy a bigger boat, or build a new guest house.

With my distinction of being house-poor, I fall somewhere in between the people who have, and those who have not. Weathering the worst of the recession, I have been able to hang on to my once valuable property, but that's about it. I have very little after taxes for upkeep and improvement. And it's unsettling.

But whatever category people fall into around here, we are all "swimming in the same lake," as my dad used to say; we're part of the same ecosystem. While those who have money are watching the NASDAQ, they themselves are being watched—pretty closely, I might add—by those who are hurting financially.

The "haves" are our economic barometers. When they feel secure enough to buy the bigger boat, or build that addition, the rest of us exhale just a little bit.

Which makes Jennifer right. When the rich redecorate, everybody wins.

Today I feel especially grateful for the wealthy cottage owners with the financial confidence to buy housefuls of new furniture—consigning their gently used, still glorious pieces at a fraction of their original prices. All for me to snap up for the new Kerby Lodge.

While Daniel talked to Beth Wildberry, the owner of Wildberry Consignment Shop, I practically skipped from piece to piece. Touching the high-quality fabrics. Running my hand across the coordinating gussets and piping. Admiring the designs: the *fleurs*, the pineapples, the nautical, and the tartans.

Sitting on the down-stuffed cushions, I could smell wafts of perfumes—the Chanel's and the Lauren's. I could even detect the sweet shampoos of the fancy terriers and bichons; rich pups invited on the sofas of both town home and lake home.

A short month ago, I couldn't imagine these posh furnishings finding a new home in the worn brown rooms of Kerby Lodge. But my vision is much clearer now. The fresh white walls give my imagination free reign.

This morning, I appreciated that Daniel was giving me some space and time to form my own opinions. Eventually, he came and found me as I was sitting on a large horseshoe-shaped sectional sofa, upholstered in a weighty tone-on-tone burnt orange chambray.

"This is a great piece," he said. "Just imagine curling up on this in our sleeping bags next time the power goes out."

I smiled at that.

"Much nicer than the floor," I said, "plus, I think it would be amazing wrapped around the big log coffee table."

"With those navy and white throw pillows maybe?" he asked, pointing to a display nearby. And with my nod, he got up and brought them over to show me how great they looked.

"I like where you're going," said Beth, the store's owner. She came over to see if she could be of any help. "I have four upholstered easy chairs in the back that have a base color of sunny yellow, but they'd also pick up the orange and the navy."

She was right—they were perfect. And they were at their final marked-down price, which made them even prettier.

"Are you a decorator?" Daniel asked her.

"A dabbler," Beth replied with a smile. "But my twins, Jack and Stace, recently returned from Chicago with degrees in interior design. They're helping me with my store displays while they interview for jobs and look for clients."

"Have them call me," Daniel told Beth, and he handed her a card.

I looked over at him for an explanation, but none was forthcoming.

By the time we left, I had purchased the sofa, the chairs, and a large bolt of upholstery fabric, enough to re-cover the two wing chairs by the fireplace. Along with another bolt of a cheery yellow floral to re-cover the cushions on the sun porch—which would give that vintage rattan furniture a much-needed boost. Beth gave us the name of an upholsterer she trusted, who would "greatly appreciate the work" and give us a fair price.

Daniel and I picked out a dozen pictures and paintings that were bright depictions of wildlife, water, and shoreline. They would brighten up the great room and dining room far more than the faded hunting pictures— now tossed into the carriage house.

And lamps! I wanted to replace all the dingy burlap shades and the outdated bases they were sitting on.

I also waded through a tall stack of folded quilts and spreads—linens that would have been priced far out of my reach when new—to find fresh and colorful bedding for each of my six guestrooms, and the apartments.

Already deliriously happy with our finds, especially at the prices they were listed at, Beth gave us an additional high-volume discount, and for linking to her Wildberry website from the *ReMayne* blog.

We arranged for delivery, and left to find the used books.

"Have we not had anything to eat today?" Daniel asked at the end of our busy day, over dinner. "Because I'm ravenous!"

"I think you have a hollow leg hidden under your walking cast," I said, between bites.

He was holding a half-eaten, half-pound burger in both hands, and talking with his mouth full. Not to be outdone, I had to chew my own burger several times before I was able to continue.

"We had breakfast sandwiches in the car this morning," I said.

"That doesn't count as a meal," he responded, "it was in the car."

I nodded at his good sense and clear thinking.

"Cheese danishes while we waited for the consignment shop to open," I said.

"Again, we ate in the car. Car rules apply," he said. "Go on…"

"Let's see," I said. "Didn't we share a huge plate of nachos for lunch, along with our fish tacos and bowls of tortilla soup?"

"My stomach doesn't remember any of it," he said.

"You took a picture of the nachos—for your blog," I said.

"That sounds vaguely familiar," Daniel said. "Is that all we had?"

"What about the chocolate frappe lattes?" I asked.

"Beverages," he said.

"So, what you're saying is, it's no wonder we're famished," I said.

"Because we've hardly eaten all day," Daniel said, as if to finish my thought.

I smiled in between bites, and nodded.

Our day was so full of sensations, and exciting adventures, and *wins*, that we had forgotten about the transformation that was happening in our absence. It was dusk when we pulled into the circle drive with my Jeep packed with treasures.

Red and his team had disappeared like the shoemaker's elves. Thankfully, they left the great room lights on so we wouldn't have to find our way in the dark.

After opening the door to the lodge, Daniel and I stood speechless.

The pine floorboards that were hidden under well-worn carpet for decades were more beautiful than I could have imagined. Each wide plank featured rustic knots and deep grain patterns—now polished to a warm honey that complemented the Irish Lace walls.

"Red really did polish the snot out of these floors," I said in a daze.

The cavernous great room—this blank canvas—was now the most beautiful thing I had ever seen. As we walked into the dining room, I noticed, for the first time, that the wood grain of the antique tables and chairs no longer competed with the dark walls and floors. The pieces looked vibrant and inviting.

Each guestroom felt light and bright with the carpet gone, even in the moonlight. And the aroma of everything in the lodge spoke of newness and freshness. All the mustiness and dustiness were obliterated. Removed. Never to return.

Bring it on, helicopter moms. I would dare them to find anything but pure, clean loveliness now at Kay Kerby's lodge.

39

KEEP CALM,
and have a piece of cherry pie.
-KERBY LODGE GUEST BOOK-

"Sorry, there's no good news, Kaker," Uncle Zeke said on the phone. "I just didn't think you'd ever call me back if I said it was all bad news."

A few days after our all-day shopping trip, I screwed up the nerve to call my uncle to discuss the property tax bill, and felt my heart sinking at his words.

"I guess the good news is that you have just enough in the tax account to cover the bill this spring—but the bad news is that the taxes you owe seem to be going up, while the number of guests you take in is going down," he said. "And if you need any major repairs on the inn, you could be in a sticky situation."

I sighed deeply in response. It's the scenario I was expecting. Maybe it was foolish to spend the money Zeke and June gave me for Christmas on renovating the inn. But it was too late for that now. Besides, looking at the fresh new spaces, it was impossible to have regrets.

As soon as I hung up the phone, I could hear the lodge door opening, and a voice that sounded like Jennifer shouting "Hello, is anybody home?"

If I needed any validation as to how beautifully transformed the inn was, I found it on Jennifer's face as she stood in the lodge foyer, gazing open-mouthed at the great room. The furniture had been delivered the day before, and every piece fell into place like magic.

Daniel and I had already arranged the new books on the shelves. And though the inventory was a fraction of what my parents had acquired over the years, the new books were bright and colorful—with engaging spines that popped against the fresh white paint.

We used the empty shelving to display a few pieces of pottery and artifacts that had been invisible in the older, darker room, without allowing the shelves to become cluttered.

"There's power in the negative space," Daniel had said.

"Right," I said, pretending to understand what he was talking about. All I knew was, everything looked better than I ever dreamed it would. The furniture was perfect.

The paintings and prints we purchased were hanging on the walls, sitting on the bookcase, and perched on the mantle. Everything shone bright against the Irish Lace walls and polished pine floors.

After showing Jennifer the new linens on the beds in each of the guest rooms, I went to make us tea, leaving her to admire the freshness of the dining room.

"This dining room is massive, Kay," she said. "You can add a few smaller table-and-chair sets, and place stacks of board games on them for your guests."

"Great idea," I said, carrying a tray of tea and cake into the great room for the two of us. Daniel had gone into his room earlier to rest, but was likely crafting his newest blog post. He had been capturing photos of the rooms earlier in the day. But with the sun as bright as it was, I was sure he would be taking another round of photos as the sun was setting. The "sweet light," he had called it.

"Jenny, what do I owe this pleasure to?" I asked, as we settled in.

"Actually, it's business, Kay," she said.

"Oh?" I was curious, and gave her my full attention. I was ready to think about anything other than my tax bill.

"You know I've been scouring the county for the perfect storefront location, and I think I've found it," Jennifer said. Then she pulled out a postcard-sized drawing of a charming building that looked a little familiar, like a place I'd seen a thousand times but couldn't quite place. The quaint structure was sketched as a pen and ink drawing, with a sign that read:

Carriage House Treasures, at Kerby Lodge.

"Wait. Is this… my carriage house?" I said, inhaling a sharp breath. "Are you serious? But it's a jumbled mess."

"It's perfect, Kay. The carriage house is a hidden treasure—just like these pine floors. Buried for years and years, but now look!" Jennifer went on.

At this point, Daniel came out of his room, and was about to go back in when he saw we were talking—but I waved him over and gestured to him to pull up a chair and join us.

Once he was settled with a mug of tea, Jennifer went on to outline her business plan. First, we would all work together to host the first ever Kerby Lodge estate sale at the end of February, weather permitting, and swing the doors of the carriage house wide open to the public. This would be the perfect opportunity, she said, to clean house.

"We'll have a great turnout, I'm sure," Jennifer said. "People are dying for estate sales after long cold winters. Some will come out of curiosity, just to see the great Kerby Lodge. Others will love hunting for treasures in the carriage house. And trust me, they will buy."

"It could give us a cash infusion to keep working on the cottages," I said.

Both Jennifer and Daniel nodded in agreement.

"And once the great piles are gone," Jennifer said, "I can begin to turn the carriage house into my own storefront—to be open on weekends, or by appointment."

Jennifer planned to give me a percentage of her sales as rent. "And of course, I can continue to sell items that are from the lodge itself for you," she said.

I knew that Jennifer had been stockpiling repainted and repurposed pieces for years, and that she had a wonderful eye for taking forgotten items and giving them a second chance. It's no wonder she saw new life in the carriage house, where I had only seen rust and decay.

"Let's try it for a year, spring through fall," I said. "Shoulder season to shoulder season."

"Shoulder to shoulder," Jennifer agreed.

We sealed the deal with cake.

"*Alaska?*"

I shouted on the phone to Luke later that day. "You're seriously thinking about the assignment in Alaska? I guess I shouldn't be surprised, but it's so far away."

It was the second week of February, and Luke and I had been playing phone tag for a few weeks. Or more truthfully, he's called me—a lot—and I haven't called back. Honestly, I haven't had the time or energy. Now, though, I had a few minutes, and a million things I wanted to talk about with Luke.

I just assumed we would pick up where we left off. But right away, I could tell that we were out of sync. First, I wasn't even sure he was happy to hear from me. And there was none of Luke's usual ease, or light-hearted banter.

"I don't understand your reaction, Kay," Luke said in a distant tone, "after all, we can talk just as much while I'm in Alaska. Or just as little, if that's the way you want it."

Ouch, there it was.

"I owe you an apology Luke," I said. "I should have called you sooner."

But there was no thaw.

"I need to go," he continued, coolly. "My students are at the coffee shop for tutoring. I've got to meet them."

"*Oh yes,* how are they…" I start to say.

"Bye Kay." Luke had hung up.

40

May the waves hit your feet,
and the sand be your seat.
-KERBY LODGE GUEST BOOK-

"By the way," Daniel said as we were getting out of the Jeep, "you look very nice."

It was Valentine's Day, and we were at Moon Lake brewery, meeting Jennifer and Patrick for our special dinner. Of course, I would have preferred to be out with someone I loved, or even liked a lot, but this was much better than staying at home alone.

Again.

I was glad for the chance to wear my new cashmere sweater, sea glass jewelry, and suede boots. I even pulled out my hair dryer for the occasion, just to make sure I still knew how to use it. While I was at it, I dug through my drawers and found my long-lost make-up and a little bottle of perfume.

So yes, I suppose it was logical that I looked nice, compared to my usual functional, comfortable appearance that Daniel had seen every day now for three full months.

But it was sweet of him to say.

Daniel even stopped me before I got out of the car, and insisted that I wait while he hobbled his way around to open the door for me, and again at the entrance to the restaurant. Gestures I appreciated all the more since Daniel was still limping. He was using both his crutches and walking cast this evening, because of the light snow, but when we saw Doctor Petersen earlier in the day, he said it was just about time to be done with both.

"Thank you, Daniel," I said, both times. "And thank you for agreeing to come to a Valentine's Day dinner with me—I'm sure you'd rather be with anyone else, but I'll be honest. I'm glad to not be the third wheel with Jennifer and Patrick."

Our reserved table was ready, even though we were early. The brewery was packed with people, and we were pleased that they sat us close to the crackling fireplace, at a polished wooden high top cleverly crafted from crates. The mantle was draped with red and white twinkling lights, and red paper hearts.

We settled in, knowing the others wouldn't be arriving for another 15 minutes. I ordered hot tea, hoping the caffeine would do its job and help me feel less sleepy—I woke up often the night before, checking my phone for messages from Luke that never came.

"Are you kidding?" he said. "There's nowhere else I'd rather be tonight. In fact, we two are getting to be quite good at holidays."

I nodded in agreement, happy that Daniel was in good spirits and making the best of our forced date—just as I was.

"I'm just glad this isn't another community potluck," he went on to say. "Not that I wouldn't kill for the mayor's cashew chicken casserole!"

I had to laugh at that. This was probably one of the few holidays that wasn't celebrated by the entire community. Secretly, I was glad for those potlucks, because otherwise I'd be spending way too many special occasions on my own.

"Happy Valentine's Day, Daniel," I said, raising my hot mug. "Thank you for getting snowed in at Kerby Lodge, and for making this the most painful and exhausting winter of my life."

Daniel raised his drink. The firelight caught the twinkle in his eyes as he smiled back at me. "Happy Valentine's Day, Kay," he said.

"Wait!" I said, "what's that you're doing with your face? Is that a smile?"

"Okay, okay," Daniel said, holding up his hand as if to stop me from what I might say next. Which was probably, *are you falling in love with me?*

"I was about to thank you as well," he said. "for not leaving me in a snowbank, which you had every right to do. And for the most painful and exhausting winter of *my* life."

At that, we raised our drinks and took a sip.

For two exhausted people, we were both smiling a lot. It was nice to be away from the lodge, and out for an evening.

"What's this, have you started the party without us?" Patrick spoke as he and Jennifer arrived at the table and took their seats. After hugs, kisses, and handshakes, they gave their drink order to the waiter, and we picked up the conversation.

"Patrick, I don't think any party can start until you arrive," Daniel said. And we all raised our glasses to life, love, and to Saint Valentine. "Here, here," we all said in agreement.

Accompanying a flight of craft beer samples, dinner consisted of the most amazing platters of tapas and small plates, featuring bite sized empanadas, savory tarts, eggrolls, Asian salads, and Korean barbecue sliders, among other delicacies.

Enjoying each other's company tonight just as much as we had on that first impromptu Thanksgiving gathering, we all laughed and talked over each other, reaching across to sample this dish and that.

I noticed that Daniel was expert at eating the Asian salad with chopsticks—a skill I had not mastered during my sheltered life on Lake Michigan.

I tried to imagine what vacation the Mayne's might have taken that gave him this training. The rice paddies of Cambodia, maybe? I would have to ask Luke... but no, Luke still wasn't picking up the phone since our last uncomfortable conversation. Now, all the things I have been wanting to tell him are piling up—I'd never remember everything.

I wanted to tell him that I was sad he was moving to Alaska, especially before coming to Lake Michigan first. For some reason, I expected to meet Luke this spring, after his school term ended. Though I'm not sure why. I suppose I saw his trip to see his brother as unfinished business.

I wanted to tell him about the new furniture and the new books. And about our epic day of eating out—but he probably knew these things from the new blog entries. And yet, there were details from our adventures that weren't in the blog. And they could become stories, and laughter, and inside jokes—if only he'd pick up the phone, or call me back.

"Hmm?" I said, looking up and realizing that Daniel, Jennifer, and Patrick were all silently staring at me. "What?" I said.

"Kay, you were staring off into space again. Everything okay?" Jennifer asked.

"Oh, sorry," I said, trying to shake off the cobwebs and rejoin the group. "What were we talking about?"

"Daniel was telling us about the two decorators that are coming in a few days," Patrick said, slurring his words just a little bit, "Zack and Lace."

"No, no, no, it's Stack and Jace," Daniel responded, also a little slurry.

"It's Jack and Stace," I said, smiling at the two of them. I guess the girls were the designated drivers tonight.

Jack and Stace Wildberry were the young decorators whose mother, Beth, owned the consignment shop. Daniel's idea was to give these two a small budget to take on four of my most profitable cabins.

"Think refresh," Daniel had said, "not complete renovation."

They would be able to pull from their mother's vast treasure trove of furnishings, lamps, bedding, dishes, and décor, and breathe new life into these worn and tired spaces.

"Did you tell them to bring their snowshoes and boots?" I asked Daniel. "And I'm not even joking. The snow surrounding all the cabins is super deep."

As it is, Daniel and I would need to pack all our paint supplies on a toboggan, and pull it behind us to the cabins in order to give the kids—I mean the decorators—a clean palette to work with. We'll also have to first get a fire going in the cabin fireplaces, warming up the rooms to at least 55 degrees, in order to paint.

Still thinking about the logistics we'd be facing in the upcoming weeks, I realized that I'd be the one pulling all the supplies, since Daniel will be navigating the snow with his injured leg. And if we forget anything, guess who's trudging back to the lodge?

"They're not going to make a lot of money from this project," Daniel said to the group, "but they'll get great exposure."

"I think we'll all be getting exposure," I replied, shivering from just the thought of being snowy and cold—in spite of the warm fireplace near our lovely table at Moon Lake.

Later, after our farewells to Jennifer and Patrick, I returned the evening's earlier courtesies, holding the restaurant and car doors for Daniel. The few sips of sample beer had gone to his head slightly, as well as to his crutches.

"I rarely drink," he said.

The word "rarely" had sounding more like "rawhly."

As we drove down the dark winter roads, Daniel asked, "have you ever been in love, Valentine? For real?"

With the close proximity Daniel and I had been in these past few months, and the many topics we'd touched on, this hadn't been one of them, oddly enough.

"Nope," I said, still thinking about how much I missed talking with his brother.

"Have you ever been in love Daniel?" I asked.

"Yep," he said.

We were both silent for the rest of the ride home.

41

The sunset never changes on Lake Michigan.
It's timeless, just like the front porch at the Kerby.
-KERBY LODGE GUEST BOOK-

Jack and Stace Wildberry were young, but smart beyond their years. They arrived for our meeting at Kerby Lodge on time, with their design portfolios and snow shoes. And most importantly, with great attitudes—as if we were paying them a lot more than we could.

"Aw, this place is amazing," Jack said, while strapping on his snow shoes for the trek to the cabins. He was surveying the view of Lake Michigan from where we stood in the parking lot. Stace nodded her head in agreement, and began writing in her portable Field Notes notebook.

Though twins, they each had their own sense of style that broke from stereotypes, and from each other. Stace, it seemed, was more of a risk taker with her spiked hair, wild glasses, and a bright, responsibly sourced "fair trade" scarf tied around her neck. Jack's hair was shoulder length, with natural corkscrew curls that I would kill to have. He wore an eye-catching necktie with a conservative Windsor knot under his argyle sweater and anorak.

Daniel loved them both immediately upon introduction, and the three of them fell into a rapid-fire patter of design speak that left me behind.

"Did you say *elevated*? I was just thinking *elevated*..."

"Yes, I *did* see that documentary on Eames..."

"I'm on the fence when it comes to chevron, and here's why..."

As the three talked over each other, we trekked to each of the four cabins on our snow shoes. The outside temperatures were above freezing now, and the snow had begun to melt. It was slushy and it packed down easily.

Daniel had to take his time, and use ski poles for balance. Jack and Stace stopped frequently to take photos to post on their fledgling business' social media sites.

I had nothing to slow me down.

At each cabin, I stoked the fires I had started earlier in the morning to warm each space, as the three kindred spirits took measurements and photos—and talked some more. Daniel talked to them like a man starving for intellectual conversation, and I was more than a little put out by his over-the-top enthusiasm.

At one point, Daniel caught me rolling my eyes as they went on about "whimsical versus contrived" design.

"Is this a mistake?" I quietly asked myself. Then Stace looked over and told me their grandparents had a cottage on Lake Michigan, so they understood the "inevitable functionality" of tossing wet towels on the backs of chairs, napping on the sofas while wearing sandy shoes, and drinking out of jelly jar glasses from the cupboard.

"Yes, Kay," Jack chimed in, "our goal is to make these cabins fresh and inviting, without making them too *precious*."

"We'll sketch our ideas before we begin, and can design around our mother's current inventory, to optimize your budget," Stace added. "She's got some great new pieces."

The more they drew me out about the history and architecture of the cabins, and the experience my new guests would expect from Kerby Lodge, the more comfortable I felt with these two talented interior designers— who I resolved to stop thinking of as "the kids."

Back at the lodge, we all sat in the great room for a casual soup and salad lunch—vegan, just in case—and hot chai tea to warm our bones. Daniel and I had discussed giving Jack and Stace time to look in each of the rooms we had been renovating, to pick up on our design cues. Each cabin should have its own personality, but we were striving for overall cohesion.

As they did in the cabins, Jack and Stace documented the lodge with notes and photos. There was a great deal of excited murmuring between the two as they took in every detail.

"The deadline is tight," Daniel said to the pair as they sat down again. "We have to be ready for an event on March 16, just a little over three weeks away."

Jack and Stace nodded their wide-eyed consent, while I tried not to choke on a cracker. *What event did we have on March 16?* My eyes snapped to Daniel's, and he gave me a look that either promised to fill me in later, or wondered why cracker crumbs were rolling down my shirt.

By now, I understood that Daniel Mayne was always a few steps ahead of me in developing and executing our marketing plan. He would catch me up to speed when he was able to verbalize what he was trying to conceptualize—hopefully he wouldn't wait too long.

Until then, I would enjoy a quiet day at the lodge after the decorators said their farewells. All too soon, I would be extremely busy again, painting the main rooms of the four cottages—a task that would require every muscle in my body, and every ounce of energy to complete.

"I'd like to set things right," a contrite Luke said on the phone, the next day. We hadn't spoken in weeks, except for our last call, which was brief and cold.

"I'm miserable not talking to you Kay," he said.

I was elated that Luke called, but didn't think I could admit it. The coolness of his tone the last time we spoke had hurt me.

The era of the Mayne brothers was ending, I suspected, and it was just as well that I stop depending on them so much. February would be over soon, and Daniel's mysterious deadline of March 16 was fast approaching. He promised to reveal all in a day or two, as I was getting impatient. But I had the feeling it would be both a beginning—and an ending.

The Mayne brothers had changed my life, and I had learned so much from each of them. But while one was present in the flesh, he was emotionally unavailable to me in any meaningful way. The other? Well, the other was emotionally generous to a fault, but could never be in my life while staying so far away—in California, and soon Alaska.

I was lonely, but I'd waited too long to settle for just a part of anything or anyone.

Yet as I listened to Luke, I could actually feel his deep voice resonating through me, and warming me—thawing my resolve. "Luke," I said, "I can't see your face and I can't read your mind. So help me out here. What is it you want?"

There was a long pause before Luke spoke.

"Your friendship, I suppose," Luke said. "Being a nomadic teacher has made meaningful friendships a challenge—and wow, that sounded a lot better in my head. Did I really just say *nomadic teacher*?"

"You did Luke," I said, "and I can't unhear it."

Luke groaned dramatically. I knew he was trying to make me laugh. But I was not about to let him charm his way out of this difficult topic.

"Luke, you're a nomad by choice," I said, in a blunt tone. "And you'll continue to be if you keep taking short-term teaching gigs."

Before he could protest, I continued. "You don't have the market cornered on intimacy issues because you're on the move—I haven't gone anywhere in the past twelve years, and I only have a few true friends. But you were one of them."

"I am your friend, Kay, and maybe…"

I cut him off before he could say more. "Then you and I need to learn to trust. If you don't call me, I'll know it's because you're busy with tests, or packing for Alaska."

"That's fair," he said.

"If I don't call you back, it's because I'm pulling a sled full of paint to a cabin, which I will be for the next few weeks. It will be exhausting," I said. "And while my phone reception is unreliable, I'm not."

I stopped talking just in time, before reminding Luke that I wasn't Lucy—off falling in love with a roommate.

As we talked a little more my demeanor warmed, until slowly, I was sharing the anecdotes I'd been saving up. I told Luke about Daniel trying to snow shoe out to the cabins with the decorators, and nearly falling several times into the deep drifts. But except for a limp, which he'd have for a time, I said he was faring well.

I told him about the Kerby Lodge shirts and mugs that had shown up by the boxful, and were now displayed on the Scottish hutch.

I told Luke about Red and his team, who "polished the snot" out of my pine floors. I made Luke laugh by describing his signature "red-eye or not" phrase.

I tried to hold a little back, though—on both the stories and the warmth that had flowed so easily between us before. Trying to lessen the pain I would feel when Luke was no longer in my life.

42

Anyone remember the potluck dinners at Kerby?
I guess all the luck ran out.
-KERBY LODGE GUEST BOOK-

In the early years, my parents would serve breakfast in the big lodge dining room to all their guests. But then the health department paid my parents a visit, spelling out the laws that restrict food preparation to commercial kitchens. That was the end of that.

To replace the breakfasts, Mum and Dad began hosting a Friday night pot luck dinner on the circle driveway in front of the lodge. They'd push six or seven picnic tables together and cover them with various tablecloths, and all the families would take part in a "Clean the Fridge" night.

None of the families wanted to bring any food home. The next morning their cars would be overflowing with wet bathing suits, sandy towels, and a week's worth of dirty laundry. So guests would contribute partial casseroles, sweet corn from local farm stands, half-full bags of potato chips, and the last of the brownies, cookies, and other goodies from their stay.

My parents would fill a large galvanized tub with ice, and everyone would put the remainder of their pop cans in it to chill, to share with everyone. We'd start a bonfire to roast hotdogs—supplementing the leftovers and making sure no one went hungry. Even I came out of hiding for that night.

I ended that tradition the first summer without Mum and Dad. I was in deep mourning, which all the guests understood, of course.

But on this Saturday morning in early March, I am reminded of those happy picnics, seeing the row of tables set up on the circle driveway. They were perfect for displaying smaller items for today's estate sale shoppers.

We set up last night. I brought out the old coffee urn, running a long electrical cord to the house. The warmer weather was holding, but mornings were still very cold.

The free coffee and the cash box would be my job. Pricing all the various antiques in the carriage house would be up to Jennifer, Patrick, and the helpers they brought from town—Patrick's two younger brothers. It would be impossible for me to put a dollar amount on all these items from my family's past, I told them.

Other people struggle with making rational decisions after loved ones are gone, I discovered. When Gram passed away, I offered to help take her clothing to the donation boxes. The funeral was over and I would be heading back to school. But my dad declined my help.

"I'm not ready just yet," he said, near tears. I didn't understand what he was feeling then, but I learned soon enough.

In the absence of people, the stuff takes on greater significance. Stuff has your loved one's fragrance and warmth and life still attached—as if by invisible threads. Memories are associated with every trinket and keepsake. For nearly a year after Mum and Dad passed, I relied on the scents and the memories to help get me through each day.

But this winter, I've come to see that the things of the past have kept me stranded in the past—and just how much I want a future of my own. I don't want to be the caretaker of a "musty old museum," as Daniel once said. Every item I have pitched into the carriage house has set me free just a little bit, to move forward.

My life, I decided, won't simply be a continuation of my parents' lives.

"Good morning, Kay," Stace and Jack said simultaneously, in their charming twin-speak. They had been here for an hour already, hiking back and forth to the cabins, and conferring with Daniel, who sat in a camp chair between the carriage house and the sale tables.

Daniel was wearing his flannel-lined coat and a wool cap. His laptop was open, perched on top of the Pendleton blanket he had apparently come to think of as his own. He had his injured foot resting on another chair. It tired easily, I noticed, and we haven't had much down time.

I sniffed in the cold, stinging air, and waved a greeting to the decorators. Even though it was before breakfast I pointed out that lunch would be waiting for them in the lodge when they were hungry. I had lunch for the whole team, as a matter of fact, because I knew it would be a long, cold day. They nodded their thanks and began hiking back to their work.

The twins had been advised to come early if they wanted a parking space, which turned out to be good advice. Because in spite of the great numbers of fliers and invitations we handed out, none of us expected to see so many cars arriving so early.

Coming outside while it was not yet light, I found a dozen people standing in a rag-tag line. When Jennifer and crew arrived shortly after, they had to drive carefully around the walkers so as not to hit anybody.

"We'll be opening at 7:30 a.m., as promised," Jennifer told them. I took over a tray of coffee to the early birds as soon as the Methodist urn could percolate it.

This day would be hectic, but it would be a cake walk compared to the seemingly endless sanding, painting, and snow shoveling that had consumed January and February. But it could have been worse. The cabin walls, as it turned out, were mostly a light, unfinished wood, and didn't require the prep work and multiple coats that the lodge walls did. Daniel and I got into a groove and made quick work of it.

We turned the cabins over to Jack and Stace, and after approving their designs, we were able to agree on what would stay in the cabins, and what we could add to the estate sale. To my surprise, the decorators found a few treasures in the carriage house that they wanted to repurpose—namely, a few of the rusty vintage bikes.

The big reveals of the cabins would be a lot of fun. But first, we all needed to get through this busy day.

From the minute Jennifer shouted that we were open for business, the first Kerby Lodge estate sale was a blur of non-stop motion. Jennifer and Patrick would write a price on a sales ticket, and customers came to me to settle up. Many shoppers were making piles, which they guarded with their lives while shopping for more.

A few high school football players came, hoping to follow in Tad's footsteps and earn tips for loading heavy items into cars, or carrying pieces up the steep road for buyers. The boys were making quite a nice bundle, which would subsidize their prom expenses, they said.

Watching them work, I was glad I made extra sandwiches.

There was never a lull. Daniel took over the cash box a time or two just so I could go inside and grab a sandwich myself, or warm my hands by the fire. Everyone did the same throughout the day.

Jennifer and Patrick and their crew worked nonstop. As items went out the door, they would pull other antiques out of hiding and into the light for people to see. I was amazed at how much stuff we had amassed since my parents purchased Kerby Lodge.

How much of it was tucked in the dark corners from way before Fitz and Raya moved in? I would never know.

I was also shocked at how much money the dusty old junk was selling for, especially the vintage bikes, trikes, and wagons. "Oh, these are collectible," Jennifer said on one of the rare moments when we had a minute to talk. "People put them in their gardens, or by the entrances to their cottages," she said.

The old furniture was going too—to be repainted and repurposed, no doubt.

Before the day was over, the temperature dropped and a light snow started to fall. But that didn't scare anybody off. The last few shoppers picked through what was left by the light of the overhead bulbs in the carriage house, and made their final purchases.

"Should I take down the signs by the road?" One of the football players asked, and we all nodded that he should. I was cold and tired, and hungry for something warm and comforting. I wanted a hot bath, and my flannel pajamas.

I supposed everyone felt chilled to the bone.

Jack and Stace went home hours ago. Daniel helped to put away the coffee pot and the tables, then retreated inside. Hopefully to stoke the fire.

Jennifer and Patrick were talking in the carriage house, no doubt about next step plans for her shop. I caught them as they were closing the doors and locking it up.

"I never would have thought to do an estate sale, Jennifer," I said, giving her a hug before going inside. "You are brilliant, my friend."

"Was it hard to see all your family treasures leave Kerby Lodge, Kay?" she asked.

I nearly said *yes* without thinking. But honestly, it wasn't that hard. After all, if things are treasures, we don't let them collect dust for years, do we?

Daniel asked me this winter, shortly after my brother's eventful visit, how I would handle a real emergency—what would I save in a fire, for instance. And the two things that crossed my mind were my dad's favorite flannel shirt, that I happened to be wearing at the time, and my mum's wedding photo. Which I have since sent out to be copied, so I will never be without.

But family treasures?

And then it hit me.

"It was hard to see my *family* leave Kerby Lodge," I said. "They were my treasures."

43

We told our kids that there would be lots of other kids at Kerby Lodge—an off week, I guess.
-KERBY LODGE GUEST BOOK-

They say that March comes in like a lion, and goes out like a lamb— talking, of course, about the weather. But along Lake Michigan, it can just as easily be the opposite, due to lake effect winds, inversions, and other random weather systems that cannot be predicted from one year to the next.

I have been in my shirt sleeves in early March, enjoying the great outdoors as massive piles of snow melted in the unseasonable sun. And I have seen blizzards and ice storms in April.

But when Daniel told me what was going to take place on March 16, it felt as though the mother of all storm systems was about to slam into Kerby Lodge—and me.

"The influencers are coming," he said, in a matter-of-fact tone.

He went on to tell me that the two of us were going to host a group of hand-picked guests for a night at the lodge—all of whom he'd already been in touch with. Most everyone had agreed to come. "There are a few I'm still waiting to hear from," Daniel said, without elaborating.

As I listened, a slow and steady surge of adrenaline began coursing through my veins, much like the night of the break-in.

We could expect around twenty five people who would arrive the afternoon of March 16, and leave the next day. While they are here, we would "wine and dine" them, and treat them to the best of what Kerby Lodge has to offer.

"The Lake Michigan sunset will do its job, Kay," Daniel said, "and we will do the rest."

He told me that a few of the people were friends of his, a few were acquaintances and colleagues, and a few more were industry professionals who had been communicating with him through his blog—and who were highly interested in the lodge.

"We will have bloggers, travel writers, reporters, an author who's writing a book about Lake Michigan lodges, photographers, and even a young couple who have become authorities on family vacations," Daniel went on to say. "A field writer for a large Midwest magazine is also coming. And each guest is an influencer within their vast network of followers. Everyone will be posting on their social media sites and blogs, and writing articles— all linking to Kerby Lodge."

"If all goes well," he said, "and I believe it will, it could be viral marketing at its best."

"Daniel, that's just 10 days away," I said, my voice raspy from shock and panic.

"We have a lot to talk about," he said in response, seemingly not panicked at all.

"I think we should invite Jack and Stace to join us, at least for a meet and greet time," Daniel was saying, "and Jennifer, too. They are authorities on the area, and it will be good exposure for their endeavors, don't you agree?"

For the first time, Daniel looked up from his computer. I wondered if he noticed the blood draining from my face, and my waxy, crazed eyes—or if my reaction, like my panic, was all in my head.

I nodded without really knowing what I was agreeing to. My heart raced at the thought of the influential people who would be coming to the lodge—my lodge—all at the same time!

To expose my lodge for all the world to see.

I tried to speak, but my throat felt tight and constricted.

All my thoughts started racing and jumbling together—thoughts of towels, and coffee, and food, and firewood, and sheets, and pillows, and parking, and power outages, and wind storms, and questions, and the judgment of strangers who may not like the lodge at all.

Daniel was talking and talking, but I might as well have been submerged under water. I couldn't make out the words. And suddenly, without thought or reason, I found myself standing up and walking briskly towards the door.

Stepping into my boots, I ran out into the weakening late afternoon light as if I were being chased—grabbing my parka and hat as I went.

"Kay? Kay?" I could hear Daniel calling after me, but it didn't slow me down. I just had to be away from his voice, and away from Kerby Lodge.

My brisk walk became a light jog as I reached the resort road that led up towards the exit. I passed the swing set and shuffleboard court. Then I passed a few of the cottages that Stace and Jack had been decorating. Picking up speed, I passed the larger chalets.

My legs ached as I climbed the steep road, one step after another.

Before I knew it, I was parallel with the dark woods. The pond was on the right, and then I saw light again, as the woods faded.

At last, as I panted, out of breath, with cold air stinging my lungs, I saw the overgrown tennis court, and Gram's house—just across from the Kerby Lodge sign on the main road.

I could hear the cars going by as I pulled the key out from under the welcome mat, and jiggled it in the frozen door knob until it opened.

"I thought you'd be coming to see me," that's what I longed to hear Gram say just now—with her warm hugs, beef stew, and hot cocoa. But the house was ice cold and empty, colder even than the outside air, if that was possible. And as I looked around, I realized I was just as alone as always.

I looked down at my parka, which had wet streaks running down the front. Was it raining outside? I didn't even notice. Then I realized that the wet streaks were from tears. Rivulets of tears were falling down my face and onto my jacket.

I was shaking uncontrollably.

Somehow, I lowered myself onto the hearth, and put the logs that Uncle Zeke had stacked there into the fireplace. Reaching up, I took a matchbox from the mantle and, after a few attempts, lit the fire—thankfully I had the foresight to open the flue.

I don't remember when it was that I curled up on the sofa. I had no idea how long I'd been sleeping, or how a wool blanket had come to cover me up. As I started to come to, I could hear my breathing. It was as if my body was still sound asleep, while my mind was stirring.

Another sound caught my attention—the crackling of a fire. Did I light that fire? The warmth was comforting. I wasn't trembling anymore, I realized.

Just before I opened my eyes, a soft hand gently took the hair that had fallen onto my face and brushed it back behind my ear. It felt nice.

"Kay?" Daniel whispered. "Are you all right, Kay?"

I nodded, eyes still closed.

Sitting up a while later, the wool blanket still on my lap, I took a few sips of the hot, sweet coffee Daniel handed me. He had filled a thermos before setting out to find me, and poured it into two mugs from Gram's cupboard.

I looked at the green flowers on the china. It was a pattern I hadn't seen in years, since I stopped coming here long ago. I wished I'd come here more often to visit my sweet grandmother when she was alive.

Had I taken them all for granted—my grandmother, and also my parents? And my brother? My aunt and uncle?

I looked out the window and it was dark outside. What time was it?

My face felt flushed and tight. I noticed that Daniel had removed my wet boots from my feet; I saw they were warming up by the fire. He had my parka and hat drying on Gram's rocker.

I really must have been out of it.

"I've pushed you too hard these past few months," Daniel said, breaking the silence. "I should have consulted with you before inviting people to the lodge. That was a mistake."

I thought about that for a few minutes as I worked to pull my mind away from thoughts of Gram. I was staring at the green flowers on the mug without blinking—until they were almost floating off the white background. Somehow, I convinced myself to move my eyes away from the flowers to see the fire, and then to see Daniel. He looked serious and concerned.

Shaking my head ever so slightly, I searched for the right words to answer him.

"No. Not a mistake," I said at last, "because that's a chicken exit I would have taken."

Daniel held my gaze and gave me ample time to gather my thoughts.

"I'm just scared, plain and simple," I said. "What am I doing, Daniel? It's my *mum* who could have handled a gathering like the one you've planned, in her sleep. Not me."

"You've got the wrong person," I said. My voice sounded shaky.

Daniel remained silent, as my mind searched for the words I wanted to say.

"I've always been a…" I tried to continue.

"What?" Daniel asked.

"A shadow," I whispered.

I looked up and could tell he was having trouble hearing me.

"I've always been shadow of Raya," I spoke a little clearer. "A poor imitation. A strawberry blonde, and not a fiery redhead," I said, in a feeble attempt to lighten the mood.

Daniel did not smile at my joke. Instead, he was looking at me as if I were speaking a foreign language that he didn't comprehend—his face was screwed into a quizzical expression.

"Kay Kerby, you really don't see yourself for who you are, do you?" he asked.

I was silent at that.

"You have an incredible instinct for looking out for others. I wouldn't have invited people whose opinions I value so much if I didn't know what you were capable of," he said.

"My mum…" I began to say.

"You!" Daniel interrupted me.

"She could…" I tried again.

"No Kay, you," Daniel was adamant. "You are the one who has utterly amazed me from the moment I stumbled my way into your lodge. I don't remember your mother, I was just a kid. But I remember the warm blanket you offered me when I didn't deserve it—the soup you sat next to me when I was sick and injured—the thoughtful way you organized a room for me, and the extra quilts you put on my bed so I wouldn't be cold."

"I thought you hated that room and those quilts," I protested.

"I hated everything and everybody that day—but I was overcome by your kindness in the face of my rudeness," Daniel said.

I let that sink in.

"Kay, you have always had the perfect answer to every visitor, every holiday, every mundane weekday, and every situation we've been in together these past four months," Daniel said. "That's why I didn't give it a second thought that you would know how to welcome a handful of important guests—guests who will love Kerby Lodge, by the way, and love you."

I was wary still, as I looked at Daniel.

"But say the word Kay, and I will cancel with everyone," Daniel said.

I thought about what Daniel was saying, and gazed into the fire. He had said early on that this would be hard work, and painful at times.

And it was.

The sanding was hard. The painting was hard. And then painting even more was hard—because we had to pull our gear out to the cabins on sleds. Clearing out the books and the furniture from the lodge was back breaking.

Letting go of "safe spaces" and memories, and the things my family had accumulated and valued was physically exhausting and emotionally gut wrenching—as was spending what little money I had replacing everything.

But all of this was also very, very good.

And I did make a promise that what we started, we would need to finish. For both our sakes.

Pulling my eyes away from the fire, I gratefully took a few sips of my sweet coffee. How many mugs of coffee had I handed to Daniel over the past few months? And look at him now, taking care of me. No matter how afraid I was, I needed to get past my fears for his sake. He needed a success just as much as I did. I knew this, but this was the first time I'd felt it.

Finally strong enough to look up and hold his gaze, I saw no anger in his eyes. No recrimination. Only kindness, and true concern for me.

Daniel meant what he said; he would cancel the event he had planned if I gave the word. He would call his friends and respected associates—people who could put Kerby Lodge on the map—if I was too afraid to have them come.

And just then, I had a clear picture of his entire family, and their solid character. Nan and Sperry were undoubtedly good people, who had raised good people. Good people such as Daniel Mayne and Luke Mayne.

"I think…" I started to say, "that we should get a sampling of local wine and cider and cheese for an afternoon reception in the great room. "And you're right, this is where Jennifer, and Jack and Stace can help us meet and greet—and show guests to their rooms and cabins."

Daniel narrowed his eyes as he listened. His nod was almost imperceptible. As if I were made of glass, and a sudden movement would shatter me.

"They will be good ambassadors," I said, my voice getting stronger.

As Daniel watched me, a slow smile spread on his face.

"And while I can't cook for the guests from my kitchen, I know a great chef with a food truck—that would be a fun surprise, wouldn't it?" I asked. "Daniel, what do you think about cider-braised pork sliders and apple slaw?"

44

*Used to be impossible to book a cabin here,
now they're all empty. What's up, Kerby?*
-KERBY LODGE GUEST BOOK-

"Also, I've hired a local mixologist to come in the evening. He'll create specialty dessert coffees to go with the warm cherry pies that I'll source from my friend Mitch. He runs a popular restaurant, but bakes in the off season."

I was talking again to Luke, and telling him more about our plans for the guests. And if I had known it would be our last conversation for a long time, I wouldn't have been so quick to get off the phone. But I didn't see it coming.

We talked nearly every day now, and sometimes more than once a day. No matter how busy I had become with final efforts for Kerby Lodge, I made time to fill Luke in. And he had been doing the same for me.

"If the weather is mild we can sit around a bonfire outside, up on the bluff overlooking the lake and the sunset," I said. "Otherwise, we will be in the great room by the fireplace."

"I like dessert coffees," Luke said. "With Irish creams, and mint liqueurs."

"Well, enjoy those while you're still in California, Luke," I said. "I hear you can get beat up in Alaska just for saying the words *dessert coffee*."

"Is that so," Luke said, laughing. "Maybe I should reconsider."

"I wish you would," I said, before I remembered that I was trying to guard my heart.

"Hello Kaker. Hello Daniel. Zeke and I sure are proud of all your hard work renovating Kerby Lodge, and the pictures on the blog are just beautiful." I was video chatting with Aunt June on my laptop. Daniel was sitting next to me, at her request.

It was just four days before our guests were to arrive, and she insisted that we both stop and talk with her for a few minutes. After feeling such a sense of loss and regret in Gram's house, I was determined to respect her wishes. Even though time was precious, and my instinct was to put her off.

"But," she went on, "I spotted *two* very important things you missed! Things you need to address before the big unveiling."

I couldn't imagine what, and neither could Daniel, apparently.

"What two things still need renovating, June?" he asked, as we looked at June on the computer screen.

"I'm looking right at 'em," she said.

Daniel and I turned to look at each other, as June let that sink in.

We looked just as we always did—I had my hair pulled back, and was wearing my dad's shirt, on top of jeans and old tennis shoes. Daniel was wearing a baseball cap, and had his own flannel shirt on, as well as work boots and jeans.

Everything we were wearing flowed a little loosely—baggy, maybe—as we'd been working around the clock on most days.

"You two need to present yourselves as successful business owners—Kaker, honey, you're the sole owner and proprietor of a historic and viable resort," June said, with a business-like clip in her voice. "Daniel, sweetie, you're the owner of a startup design business—which I think will do very well."

In spite of the "sweetie" and the "honey" June was dripping, the tone of her voice let us know that we were to be quiet, because she was not through with us.

"But I wouldn't hire either of you to run a hot dog cart," she said.

We were speechless.

"I don't care how busy you are," June said, in no uncertain terms. "Tomorrow morning, you will drive forty miles to the salon where I have set up appointments for you both, and you will do as they say. It's all covered."

Daniel and I just stared at the screen, obediently listening to my aunt. Who, it was clear, would be tolerating no guff from us.

"Then, you will walk across the street to that big outfitters clothing and shoe store, where a personal shopper is expecting you both—again, it's all covered. And each of you are going to seriously up your game. *Capiche*?"

June asked if we understood, and we didn't dare cross her. This was a side of her I'd never seen—but I shouldn't be surprised. After all, she and Zeke had built and run a successful business of their own. One that was funding a comfortable retirement, worldwide travel and, it seemed, a couple of makeovers.

"Yes, Aunt June," Daniel and I said simultaneously, in twin-speak.

The next morning, I was up early, trying to check off a few of my to-do boxes before we had to leave for the salon appointment. I heard Daniel up and about in the great room, but when I went came out of the apartment with my coat and keys he was gone.

"I'll go warm up the Jeep and meet you outside," I called towards his door, which was closed. There was no answer. When I got outside I found out why.

There, in the circle drive in front of the lodge, stood a beautiful and shining silver BMW. Unlike the unmistakable rumble of my own vehicle, the BMW motor was humming.

It was purring, actually.

The passenger side door stood open, and Daniel was behind the wheel—looking at me with a grin that was bigger than his Christmas morning smile, if that was even possible.

"Aunt June said we should up our game," Daniel said as I got into the car.

"Yes, she did," I said.

Daniel guided the car up the lodge road and out into traffic. While he adjusted the volume on his smooth jazz playlist, I took my wool mittens off so I could touch and admire the soft leather seat—the one that was cradling my baggy jeans in perfect comfort.

"Can we drive by all my old boyfriends?" I asked, and Daniel laughed.

The trip to the salon passed like elegant time travel, and soon we were being shampooed, scrubbed, and massaged from head to toe. I couldn't look at Daniel during the his-and-her facials, or else I'd laugh the cucumber slices right off of my eyes.

We both had manicures, and in spite of Daniel's protest, pedicures. Afterwards, he had to admit that after months in a walking cast, the massage and sea salt scrub felt pretty nice.

"But don't tell Nan, right?" I joked, "or else she'll want you to get pedi's with her next time you're in town."

"Right after church," Daniel joked back.

Separating later to have our hair styled, I allowed my strawberry blonde hair to be cut considerably shorter, in order to frame my face. I even agreed to highlights.

While waiting for the foiled highlights to set, I was treated to a makeup tutorial. The stylist gave me a full bag of generous samples and great advice for staying *au naturel*, and not looking overdone.

"Throw out all your old stuff," she also said. And I told her I would—gladly.

I wondered what Daniel was agreeing to, but didn't have to wait long to find out.

As I was slipping my jacket on to walk over to the outfitters store, I saw an incredibly handsome man standing by the exit, waiting for someone. Then I realized it was Daniel, and he was waiting for me.

His face was clean-shaven and shining. His curly hair was cut short, with a few random spikes that were held in place by a wonderful aromatic product. I hoped that product was in the bag he was holding.

He looked and smelled like he was somebody's hero.

We stood by the door in silence for what seemed like minutes—painfully aware of many eyes on us both, including each other's.

Finally, Daniel broke the spell.

"Red-eye?" He asked, offering me his arm.

"Red-eye," I answered, as we walked with each other across the street.

45

The last days before our guests arrived flew by until it was the day before.

"Influencers Eve," I texted to Daniel and to Luke this morning before getting out of bed. Only Daniel responded.

I was learning to change my morning routine. Instead of what could be described as "rolling out and throwing on," I picked out one of the bright new fleece pullovers that accentuated my slimmer profile. Then, I pulled on the warm "action knit" pants that the personal shopper said would be perfect for hiking, yoga, or "adventuring"—a vague term that for me meant bathroom touch ups, firewood hauling, and window washing.

Nevertheless, I resisted the urge to throw on my old jeans and flannel shirts.

I took the time to apply my new makeup, and even picked out a few pieces from my mother's jewelry collection to supplement the diamond and gold horseshoe necklace I'd worn every day since Christmas. If I learned anything from the past few months, it was to use and enjoy the nice things I have, instead of letting them sit in the dark and collect dust.

To show off my pedicured toes, even though there was a chill in the spring air, I slipped on the new waterproof sandals—the ones with the all-terrain soles—and adjusted the colorful straps to my ankles.

Last, I scrunched my hair with the conditioner the salon had sent home with me, and defined a few curls with a finishing spray that smelled like a coconut and honey milkshake.

Before heading outside to meet the day, I tried to phone Luke once again, without success. These were his travel days, I knew, and he was making his way to his next destination.

"Your timing stinks, Luke," I said to the phone, when he didn't answer. I didn't see why he couldn't make a few minutes for me. But I told Luke I would trust him, so I tried to do just that.

Outside, Jennifer and Patrick were putting the finishing touches on Carriage House Treasures, in anticipation of this weekend. They had been working overtime, because the opportunity for exposure was too good to pass up.

They wouldn't be open to the public on March 16, but would be open for our guests—mainly to add to the experience and story of Kerby Lodge. I was grateful to them both!

Daniel was too. He had even "whipped up" a website for Jennifer, which she could later expand. For now, it featured a few photos, her hours, and contact information—as well as a clickable map. He had told both Jennifer and Patrick that he appreciated their care and friendship over the past few months, and he hoped they would always stay in touch.

I considered this gesture as I made my way across the parking lot to the carriage house.

Change was in the air, there was no doubt about that. And much of it felt good—like breathing the fresh scents of spring. And having the carriage house be a center of activity and filled with people again. But some of it felt sad. Like hearing Daniel say what sounded like farewell sentiments to our friends. And Luke distancing himself from me.

As I got closer to the carriage house, all sad thoughts flew away.

"Girl… Mm mm mm!" Jennifer said dramatically, as if we were in high school again. Patrick made a good-natured whistle between his teeth.

"What? What?" I teased as I stopped to perform a little twirl, because I knew *what*.

Aunt June had been right. I had neglected my hair and my clothing and just about everything for far too long. And the truth was this: I felt visible, and confident, and like a business owner.

Like a boss!

I would hang on to my dad's flannel shirts, maybe just to wear in the privacy of the apartment—or just in case my brother dropped in during a snowstorm. But never again for public-facing outings.

When Daniel and I went to the local vineyards and orchards to purchase bottles for our reception, and to talk about possible merchandising partnerships, there was a new level of mutual respect. They were taking me seriously. In turn, I felt a deeper appreciation of their hard work and their drive to succeed. Same with the cheese shops and bakeries.

Chef James Mauer, the food truck owner, greeted me as an old friend, but treated me as a business associate as we discussed our important event.

And I definitely had Jack and Stace's approval, I could tell, which made me ridiculously happy. I only had ten or twelve years on them, but had often felt like their spinster aunt, instead of their client.

They had my approval too! The cabins were amazing and colorful and inviting. I could hardly wait to get our guests' feedback.

One of the cabins was designed around two black and tan wing chairs from the Wildberry Consignment Shop. From there, the duo chose furnishings and elements in black, brown, and cream to complement the statement pieces.

Another cabin was designed around a buttercream yellow loveseat—and they set the tone by placing a rusty yellow bike by the front door, complete with white and yellow tulips hanging over the basket.

The third cabin was decked out in tasteful retro red and white gingham, with open kitchen shelving displaying vintage red and white dishes and cookware. And in a sunny little garden patch by the deck, I had to do a double take at what I saw. A small wooden cart, the *wee lass*, was now a newly painted planter, ready for buckets of fresh herbs and flowers. My decorators had meticulously repainted the hand lettering, over Raya's original sentiment.

And last, the cabin that was tucked deepest into the pines now felt like a tree house, complete with tree stump end tables, and Loden green accent pieces throughout.

I wanted to live in each of them!

I promised my decorators that we would be able to continue the renovations this summer as money allowed. In turn, they promised to always make time for Kerby Lodge—even though they were beginning to get calls on other projects, thanks to Daniel's blog, and their own diligent promotion on social media. Apparently, a photo they took of themselves moving furniture through the snowy woods on a sled "went viral," whatever that meant.

After making my way to each of the cabins through the melting snow, and making sure the wood supply would keep my guests warm for one night, I stopped back into the carriage house.

Jennifer had brought in her items by the truck load, and arranged her treasures in a way that would make everyone want to browse, and buy! Lights twinkled throughout the space, and bowls of scented pinecones made the old garage smell like vanilla and cinnamon.

A vintage bike leaned against one wall of the carriage house, with a photo mounted above it—a smiling picture of Tad putting air in the tires of a bike. Mum, no doubt, was the photographer. A little sign said that neither the bike nor the picture was for sale. On everything else, Jennifer's prices were written on hand-printed tags that she attached to her treasures with a rustic twine.

I felt great joy, looking around Carriage House Treasures—my good friend was realizing her dream. And just like the purple crocuses that were popping up all around the lodge, it was a sign of new life and hope for Kerby Lodge.

One last thing—there it was—I looked over by her cashier desk and saw the old Methodist Church coffee urn, all ready for tomorrow. After seeing a picture of the dining room in Daniel's blog, Nan Mayne had sent me a "lodge warming gift" of a beautiful and shining new stainless-steel coffee urn that looked sleek and modern. It was decades newer than the old one I had been using, which would now get a third life.

"Kay you simply *cahnt* serve bad coffee," Nan said on the phone, in her broad accent.

I knew I needed to tell this story to Luke, and checked my phone again, but he hadn't called me back.

I wondered if he had been in touch with Daniel, and went to ask him.

Making my way back inside, I nearly tripped over a large pile in the entryway—I recognized Daniel's duffel and computer bag from when I packed his belongings up back in November. There were boxes filled with magazines, and a few large bags of clothing—both from Christmas, and from our trip to the outfitters a few days ago.

Daniel was moving out.

My heart sank and I felt a jolt of panic shoot through me, seeing all these things about to leave—along with the person they belonged to. I couldn't believe how comfortable I had gotten with Daniel living in the lodge. *But where is he going today?*

I knew that my time with the Mayne brothers would be coming to an end before long, but seeing Daniel's packed suitcases, and not being able to get a hold of Luke, made it a very painful reality that I wasn't sure I was ready for.

Daniel came around the corner, and must have read my face.

"I'm not going far, I just thought I'd move back into the A-Frame for a while. You'll need my guest room—it is the nicest one," he said.

I opened my mouth, but couldn't find any words.

"Look," he said, placing his warm hands on my shoulders as if to keep me from falling over. "We have this weekend covered, and we're just making ourselves crazy by walking around and tweaking the same things, over and over. So, what do you say I take you to dinner at Mitch's later? We can relax a little, and celebrate our hard work."

Wordlessly, I nodded in agreement as he carried his luggage to his car. There wasn't anything more we could do to be ready for our guests, who would be arriving in less than 24 hours.

I really hoped I'd thought of everything, as Daniel believed I would.

Sitting down on the orange sofa, I looked outside at Lake Michigan, through the screened-in porch that now boasted vintage rattan seats with new yellow cushions. *What a sunny room.* It had been too cold to paint the wood porch floor in the winter, but I would get to it within the next few months. For now, it was rustic and inviting, and people would flock to it.

I had the French doors cracked just enough to smell the brisk air coming off the lake—which was juxtaposed with the crackling fire in the background. A perfect early spring day.

Jack and Stace had brought over a few lanterns that their mother acquired; they had painted them, and put in new candles for me. Now, the lanterns sat on the tables of the porch, ready to light in the twilight hours for tomorrow's special guests as they mingled.

They also found a large wicker basket in the Wildberry storage room, and placed it in the great room to hold my collection of vintage wool blankets.

"Your guests can use them on their laps while they sit outside by the fire, drinking their coffees," Stace had told me. She was a natural. And I believed she had become a friend.

Each bedroom, cabin, and apartment were clean and shining and ready for company, with new bedding, polished floors, and fresh paint. Our invited guests would find water bottles, snacks, and a gift bag filled with a Kerby Lodge mug and a long-sleeved tee shirt—as well as a business packet. In it we put a new lodge brochure with current rates, postcards for Daniel's ReMayne Design business, Wildberry Interiors, Carriage House Treasures, Wildberry Consignment Shop, Mitch's Pies, and brochures for all of the wineries, bakeries, and cheese shops that would be represented this weekend.

We included a glossy tourism magazine for the county, featuring the upcoming events and fairs for the summer season.

I closed my eyes and rested my head against one of the navy throw pillows, daydreaming about all that we'd accomplished, and all that I still wanted to do at Kerby Lodge. I might even ask Beth Wildberry to keep her eyes open for a few pieces to freshen up my apartment.

My arms flexed with a dull ache at the mere thought of picking up a paint roller again.

And what about Gram's house at the top of the hill? My mind began drifting as I imagined freshening up that space, and making that a year-round rental. Feasible, now that June and Zeke weren't coming back for the summer.

The breeze outside was picking up, causing the Lake Michigan waves to get louder as they crashed into the ice floes along the shoreline—breaking them into pieces that would soon dissolve and melt away until next winter.

The waves were lulling me. I closed my eyes and started to drift.

In my drowsy state I heard the doorbell ringing. Was someone here? *Ding ding.* But no, I didn't have a doorbell.

Was it a school bell? Was it the day after Labor Day? No. Wait—*I know that sound*, I realized, trying to swim up to the surface. And then I remembered. Daniel had programmed my phone so I would get Kerby Lodge email alerts—and that's the tone we chose.

I sat up, disoriented and excited to hear from Luke, and reached for my phone.

There, I found three separate emails from people—new people—who wanted to book cabins for this summer at Kerby Lodge.

46

"Maybe other brothers talk all the time, but Luke and me... well, we think we're doing good catching up every other month or so," Daniel was saying.

We were enjoying our meal in a quiet corner table of Mitch's restaurant. We ordered the French onion soup, which was delicious, and waited for our entrees of white fish and loaded hasselback potatoes—while sipping a local cider.

The sun was staying a little higher, a little longer, and even though I saw Lake Michigan nearly every day, the spring sunset was a treat to enjoy out of the restaurant window.

Daniel went on to say that he and Luke had talked more than usual this winter, following his fall and recovery.

"That incident jarred us both into a new appreciation of each other, I think," Daniel said. "But no, I haven't heard from him either in the past few days."

Daniel must have come to the same conclusion, that Luke was on his way to Anchorage. "I know he was wrapping up his final exams," he said, "and then on to his next job location. He must be under water with the details of moving. We'll hear from him soon."

"I'm sure you're right," I said.

There was little comfort in Daniel's words, which must have been apparent.

"Don't tell me that the Mayne family has gotten under your skin," Daniel said, smiling over the rim of his glass. "Did we all grow on you?"

Like a rash, was what I thought to say but didn't.

"Mostly Nan," I recovered. "I don't know what I'll do without her."

"You don't have to *do* without any of us Kay," Daniel said, "what with email and video chatting. We all know you don't answer your phone," he teased, "but there are other modes of communication. And you should use them all."

"I know, I know," I said, smiling, and taking a sip of the fruity cider. *But it will never be the same after tomorrow*, is what I couldn't bring myself to say.

Once our main courses arrived, we talked a little about the details of the day to come. With the help of our decorators and Jennifer, we would be an unflappable welcoming committee. We all agreed to be helpful but not intrusive, allowing our guests to relax, explore, and enjoy as they saw fit. All their needs would be taken care of, with treats and surprises planned—but the heart and soul of Kerby Lodge as a haven would remain intact.

"Did you hear back from all the guests?" I asked Daniel.

"Everyone but two people—I'm hoping they'll show up, though," he said.

I wondered who they could be as I flaked off a lemony bite of my fish.

"Do I know them?" I asked, "is it a surprise—is it Nan and Sperry? Zeke and June? The taxi driver and Doc Petersen?"

Daniel almost choked on his potato laughing at my guesses, and that made me happy. Usually he was pretty self-controlled—a little too much, if you asked me.

"You don't know them," he said, still smiling. But his smile waned as he stared out the window at the water.

As we finished our dinner, my own smile disappeared, thinking about how bittersweet the next step of this journey would be, because I would be on my own again. Starting tomorrow, Daniel wouldn't be waiting for me by the fire when I got up. I wouldn't be cooking dinner for him, or bringing him mugs of soup or coffee.

He had injected himself into my life like an unwanted virus, but now I was hard pressed to imagine my life without him.

I wanted to find the words to thank him for all he'd done, and for helping me find the *me* I needed to be, and the Kerby Lodge that was hidden under the sadness, and the darkness, and the past. But I didn't know where to start.

That's when I looked over and noticed that Daniel was still looking out the window, but his hands were trembling as they rested on top of the table. On impulse, I reached over and placed both of my hands on top of his to warm and steady them.

"Talk to me," I whispered.

He left his hands where they were, under my own, and slowly turned away from the window and back to me. He shook his head, as if to indicate that nothing was wrong, but neither of us believed that.

"I'm just nervous… really nervous about tomorrow. For the people I'm going to see. People I've been hiding from," he said, quietly. "A handful of them knew me as the boss—and I'm not that anymore. I don't want to be pitied, or seem foolish for the way I've been spending my time."

Once again, I felt such an anger well up inside of me towards that agency. For crushing the self-worth of such a good and decent man. A respectable and loyal man. I was angry at them for causing him pain, and doubt.

I wanted to see Daniel stop chaining himself to his past, and stop measuring his value against this… *place*, that had been nonexistent in their management of his career, and had long ago stopped considering him.

"You know," I said, at last, "someone very wise changed my life with their advice."

Daniel barely acknowledged me, but I kept talking.

"He told me to stop living as if running Kerby Lodge was something that just happened to me, and take ownership. Well, back at you, Daniel Mayne. Your independence happened to you—you didn't want it, but you can own it."

Daniel dropped his head in his hands.

"If I had to guess, I'd say that agency is sorry they let you go. I'm sure you left a Daniel Mayne-sized void that hasn't been as easy to fill as they imagined," I said, realizing I would be experiencing that void myself.

"Even if that's not true, that agency is your past. Make your career yours again, and make it amazing," I went on.

He nodded a little in agreement.

And as I heard the passion in my voice, I realized just how much I sounded like Mum.

"*Och*," I said, "I wish Raya were here right now. She always knew what to say."

I had to turn away.

"What would she say?" Daniel looked up and asked.

I shrugged.

"Come on, what's your best guess?" he asked, gently coaxing me. I could hear in his voice that he was genuinely interested.

I pictured my darling mother, full of life and wisdom, and wonder. I was fortunate—blessed—to have so much of her time and love before we parted ways. Raya Kerby didn't allow a single ounce of life to spill from her cup; it brimmed with abundance.

And while I resented her attention to the lodge during the summer, wasn't she always there to have breakfast with me every morning, and supper with me every night in the apartment, away from the guests, where we could talk freely—and didn't she keep a bead on me during every summer day, no matter how many people came and went.

Mum always knew exactly where I was. And wouldn't she stop whatever she was doing each bedtime to sing me a lullaby and talk me to sleep—telling me tales of the *auld* country, and stories of the many lands she and Dad traveled to, until my eyes were heavy.

Her hands were soft and sweet, but her hugs and kisses were hard and protective.

Sweet dreams, sweet Kakes, she would whisper. And every night as I drifted off, she would say in her poetic Scottish tones: *ye' are the most loved, highly esteemed dahhter of Fitz and Raya Kerby, and dunna forget it, wee lass.*

I had forgotten! But I wouldn't forget again. And at that moment I knew exactly what she would say, and it was just what Daniel needed to hear. It was up to me now.

I turned towards him and when I had his full attention, I burst forth with my best fiery Raya brogue: "*Och, Daniel, dunna cast ye' pearls before swine, lad!*"

Daniel smiled broadly and said "translate please?"

"You gave them your best, and they trampled you. Don't give them a second thought."

"Thank you Kaker," Daniel whispered.

And as he held my gaze he said, "You and your mum are very wise."

47

The good 'ol Kerby Lodge, just like I remember.
Some things never change, eh?
-KERBY LODGE GUEST BOOK-

If I had tried to sleep late on Influencer Day at the lodge, I would have been out of luck. The phone alerts that I had set for text messages and emails began *ding-dinging* before the sun had even come up. But by that time, I was already out of the shower and standing at the mirror, getting ready. I wanted to take extra time today, because I knew that I would be photographed for articles, blogs, and social media posts—whether I wanted to be or not.

I rubbed the fog off my phone screen with the sleeve of my flannel shirt robe, and began scrolling through my messages.

There was a long text from Tad, saying he and Selby wished us well. There were also separate messages from the girls, featuring little video clips of dancing kittens.

June and Zeke sent an email, saying how proud and excited they were.

There were confirmation emails from all of my vendors, per my request, including one from Chef Mauer. Should he bring gluten free buns in the food truck, as well as regular?

"Yes," I answered him. "Thanks for being one step ahead, James."

The mixologist sent his itinerary for the evening.

Mitch sent a text letting me know what time he would be delivering the warm pies—which would be fresh out of his commercial ovens, and served with hand-churned ice cream.

Daniel sent me a text from the A-Frame, saying "I missed this cabin."

I texted him back: "Just don't stand on the chairs."

There were two more emails from people who wanted to rent a cabin for a week in the summer—one of them mentioned Daniel's blog, and the other was a friend of Tad and Selby.

A good luck email from Nan and Sperry was short, but very sweet.

And finally, there was a text message from Luke.

When I saw his name on my phone, I felt lightheaded, and reached out to grab the edge of the sink. I took a deep breath, and went over to sit on my bed. My legs felt shaky and I didn't trust myself to stand. What could he possibly have to say to me this morning, and why did I feel nervous?

Tapping his name on my phone screen, I could see that his message was brief: "It's cold in Anchorage today. Only 34 degrees."

And that was it. I read the message five times to see if there was more, and each time there was not.

It's cold in Anchorage today. Only 34 degrees.

I held my finger on the Reply button, but no. I had nothing at all to say to him. What could I say? What had I expected to hear Luke say? But I knew that answer already.

"So that's that," I said out loud, "he really went." I exhaled a long, slow breath, forcing the knot in my stomach muscles to relax. I hadn't realized how tense I was.

"Let it go," I spoke out loud to myself.

Let him go, was what I thought.

Ding-ding! More vendor texts, and more questions.

Before standing up from the bed, which I desperately wanted to crawl back into all of a sudden, wet hair and all, I stopped to think about the day ahead, and what it could mean for Kerby Lodge and for Daniel Mayne. And for each vendor, and for Carriage House Treasures, and for Wildberry Design. We had all been working tirelessly towards this one big day, and I could not—could *not*—let anybody down. No matter how hard it was going to be, I had to push Luke Mayne to the back of my mind.

The past few years have been hard enough for little Midwest towns, and small businesses such as ours. This day was our shot. Our chance to keep the roof over our heads for a little longer, and hang on a little tighter to our own small dreams.

It was Daniel's chance to show that he wasn't playing by the agency rules anymore. They could no longer define who he was in the world.

It was our fighting chance.

I steeled myself to get through the day. But as it turned out, it was amazing.

The sun was shining. The sky was blue. And the air was crisp and clean. Right on time, lovely clean cars began pulling into the parking lot, and the spring birdsong competed with the sounds of doors closing, and boisterous, happy greetings.

Our guests were all in good spirits—not hard-to-please clients, or jaded and weary world travelers, as I had feared.

Every single person expressed their delight in Kerby Lodge and our Lake Michigan shoreline. They expressed their gratitude at being invited as guests. They sat outside in the Adirondack chairs and soaked up the sun. They lingered inside by the crackling fire, and helped themselves to coffee from the new urn, served in brand new lodge mugs. They browsed the book shelves, and pulled a few titles to take back to their rooms.

Every person was highly interested in me, and the inn, and Daniel, and each other.

There was so much warmth, and happiness, and these moods were contagious. I lost myself in all the goodwill, I really did!

Between Daniel and Jennifer and the twins, and myself, we all gave enthusiastic tours of the lodge and the cabins. We showed each guest to their accommodations, and basked in new waves of appreciation. We pointed out the gift bags, and the printed itinerary for the afternoon and evening. And left our guests to walk the grounds, relax in their rooms, and get ready for our mid-day reception.

"Be sure to stop in Carriage House Treasures to look around," we said. "We have a gift for you there." Jennifer had commissioned salt glaze pottery dishes with an image of the carriage house on them from a local artist. She wanted everyone to take one home.

Many of our guests had known Daniel in Chicago, or had met him online through the blog, and were anxious to speak in person. He greeted everyone warmly, as I knew he would.

A few people from his agency days greeted him like a long-lost friend or brother—exclaiming how good he looked, and how his new lifestyle *agreed* with him.

New lifestyle?

I managed to catch Daniel's eye for a shared conspiratorial glance. As if losing your job was a lifestyle choice. But he went along with it, good naturedly. I even heard him laughing pretty loud with a group of former colleagues. Daniel told me the story later, of how the creative guru the agency hired from the UK had already left for another position in Chicago—leaving the agency high and dry. *Brilliant!*

Throughout the day, I had time to sit down and talk with several guests. They all wanted to hear more about the history of the lodge, and how Daniel and I had decided to combine forces this winter for the renovations. He and I had agreed ahead of time on a rewrite to our storyline, one that would be kind to us both.

In our new story, there were no half-broken chairs in the cabins for any guest to sit on, let alone stand on, to change a lightbulb. Also in our story, Daniel didn't show up on my doorstep in a snowstorm looking like a sad and lost pup, as he had looked that day.

In our conversations, we made sure to mention Jennifer, as well as Jack and Stace. And just about everyone wanted directions to the Wildberry Consignment Shop so they could pay a visit to Beth on their way out of town tomorrow. I'd have to make sure to let her know that the cavalry was coming.

And the photos!

In addition to the countless selfies our guests were taking, there were posed pictures of Daniel, and of me, and of me and Daniel. The two of us in front of the fireplace. The two of us in front of the lake. The two of us, along with Jennifer, in front of the carriage house. The two of us with Jack and Stace by the cabins.

There were tripods, and monopods, and selfie sticks.

Daniel and I stood next to each other for so many photos throughout the day, that I knew what it must be like to be the bride and groom at a wedding.

And like clockwork, the welcome reception gave way to the arrival of the food truck. I'm sure Chef Mauer felt like a rock star, with the greeting and rave reviews he received! And if he felt special, that was nothing compared to Mitch's arrival with the warm cherry pies. Or the greeting the mixologist got when he showed up to make the dessert coffees for everyone—complete with a powdered cocoa *fleur delis* KL on the foam, for Kerby Lodge.

It was all going according to plan, and better than expected. And as the sun started to set on Influencer Day, I realized that all we needed to do now was to get out of our own way, and allow our guests to enjoy the sunset, the bonfire, the great room, and each other.

Tomorrow would be easy—I had fresh bakery items and cheeses arriving in the morning along with fruit, for a continental brunch.

I could relax, though Daniel seemed to be having a harder time with that.

As I watched him throughout the day, then into the early evening, he seemed to have one eye trained on the front door. He was still expecting someone, I thought, though I knew that all the guests had arrived. At least, the ones we had expected.

And then at last, while I was lighting the lantern candles on the sun porch, the front door opened and she walked in.

Her name was Francine, I found out later, and she was indeed a lifestyle blogger, and most likely the person Daniel had spoken about in such glowing terms many weeks ago. Unlike the other guests, who had come to Kerby Lodge for the lodge itself, Francine had eyes for one thing only: Daniel Mayne.

As for Daniel, the group he had been talking with might as well have been a grove of trees in the woods, for he had stopped listening to them. His eyes were fixed on the latecomer with the long jet-black hair, striking in a raspberry wool sweater and leather boots.

His group went on talking, oblivious to his disengagement to the point of closing their circle—pushing him outside their bubble.

But she saw him.

From where I stood in a darkening corner of the porch, I could watch them undetected. Neither ran to each other, or even made a move that was noticeable. But there was no doubt that they were inching closer, by the sheer force of their locked eyes, it seemed. As if they were gliding.

I found I couldn't look away, or even blink.

When they were within arm's reach of each other at last, Daniel tentatively lifted a hand to lightly touch her sleeve. And just like that, whatever Daniel had been for me this winter, he no longer was. That barely perceptible touch on Francine's sleeve was like the loud slamming of a door, and I was on the outside.

That touch, that movement, felt so tender and so personal, that I became aware of my own awkward presence in their reunion. I felt a flood of shame and embarrassment to be intruding on their private moment.

Introducing myself to her, as I had with every guest, was not an option. In fact, everything within me wanted to flee in the opposite direction. And so I did.

Unlike my blind run to Gram's house, however, the exit I made from the lodge was measured. I slowed and steadied my breathing as much as I could. Though my hand was shaking, I lit the last lantern, then I walked down the stairs from the sun porch—past the bonfire where guests were enjoying their cherry pie and coffee.

The sun was dropping fast, as it does this time of year, and I doubted that anyone could clearly see the distress on my face. In fact, most everyone had their eyes glued to the bright pink sunset sky on the horizon.

Nevertheless, I forced myself to keep smiling before walking, not running, out into the dusk, towards the road. To find a place where I could breathe again.

I stumbled across the parking pad and began walking up, away from the lodge, and all its windows. It would not do to have all these influencers see the resort owner breaking down.

It wasn't good for my *brand*.

A few guests walking from the cabins called out "hey there, Kay." I gave them a quick wave, which I hoped would look friendly and not dismissive. But there was no turning back, and nothing to do but take my impending floodgate of tears away from the guests.

Why my heart was breaking when I've never loved Daniel Mayne, I do not know. I don't have all the answers. I only know this: where there was Daniel Mayne, there was hope.

From the first time he drove past my window, I thought Daniel could be my happy ending. "People love a good story," he had said, and while ours started out a little shaky, it got better. And kept getting better. It practically wrote itself: *The tall, dark, brooding man falls in love with the innkeeper who nurses him back to health, and together they save the inn.*

Now that's a movie I would watch.

But some things can make sense on paper and not to the heart, I discovered today. True emotion isn't always scripted. If it were, Daniel would be telling Francine that his heart now belonged to this inn, and perhaps even to me. He'd realize I was missing from the crowd and come searching—hoping against hope that it wasn't too late for our love story. And as I saw him coming towards me, I'd realize that we were meant to be together. It would be a perfect storybook ending.

Instead, Daniel and Francine are sharing their storybook ending. And me? I'm walking on a cold dark road.

Daniel Mayne wasn't always the best of company, but for a season, we had each other. And I was sorry it was over. This weekend marks a new beginning, leading in two separate directions. Only he will have someone to share his new direction with, while I will be, once again, completely alone.

I'm not sure when the tears started falling. I brushed them from my eyes, but they wouldn't stop.

Tears on tears. Snow on snow.

When I'd walked halfway up the road towards the top of the hill, I stopped, and turned to look into the woods. There I saw a large boulder, tucked away under an apron of pine trees.

Stepping off the road, I walked across the cold leaves and twigs before sitting down. I grabbed the hem of my shirt to dab at my tears, but it was useless. Why wasn't I wearing one of my dad's old flannels? This new tailored blouse had no long hem for crying into.

Besides, wearing Dad's shirts made me feel like he was hugging me, and that would be great right about now. I was kidding myself, I knew. But what did it matter?

Swiping at tears with my cold, wet hands, I gazed down the road to the lodge, and to all the cars parked in front of it. I had not seen so many cars in front of Kerby Lodge in a long, long time. There were twinkling lights coming from the carriage house—they looked like starbursts through my teary eyes. I could smell the smoke from the bonfire. A sweet mix of cherry wood and pine.

The sound of voices, laughter, and the tinkling of glasses carried up the hill and into the woods as my guests sat outside with their wool throws, enjoying a clear spring evening on Lake Michigan. One guest had brought an acoustic guitar, and was playing a tune I didn't recognize.

Through the filter of trees, I could see warm light shining from each of the lodge windows, and the word *inviting* played over and over in my mind. Tonight, more than ever, the Cape Cod truly looked picture perfect and magical.

I wondered how it looked when Fitz and Raya saw it for the first time.

And I thought about their love story; how it must have been when they set eyes on each other—after wondering if love had passed them by.

Has love passed me by? I hoped not, but where was he? Where was my Fitzwilliam? Seeing Daniel and Francine together made me realize how much I longed to be someone's "Raya sunshine."

My dad always told me that if I got lost, to just stay put. I would be found. But that hasn't been the case. Would anyone search for me? *Ever?* I am not a moving target. I'm right here where I've always been, my entire life.

Fresh tears fell through soft sobs as I bent my head down into my hands. It was cold sitting on that rock. I was beginning to shiver. It was getting dark, though, and if I waited a few more minutes I'd be able to go back to the lodge, and slip unseen into the apartment.

Just as I was about to stand up, I heard footsteps and I froze. They were far away, but moving at a steady pace and getting closer. As was common with water and woods nearby, sounds bounced and echoed. It was impossible to tell where the footfalls were. However, it made sense that one of the guests was taking a walk.

Maybe they won't see me hiding here in the inky woods, I hoped, as I tried to sniffle in silence. The footsteps were definitely getting closer as they came towards the bend in the road where I had ducked into the trees.

In the deepening dusk, I could see an outline... and it *was* Daniel. I was sure of it! And he was coming my way. Only... could this be right? He was

197

coming from the wrong direction. Daniel was walking *down* the road, from the entrance. When he should be walking up the road, from the lodge. Which I didn't understand.

How could that be? He couldn't have possibly passed me.

I looked again.

It was nearly dark now, but this was definitely Daniel. In silhouette, he looked taller and leaner, and maybe younger—but it was him.

But wait, he didn't have his limp. Was I imagining this?

As he got closer to where I was hiding, he stopped and looked directly into the woods—to where I was perched on the icy boulder. I held my breath. When he spoke, his voice was so soft I could barely hear.

"Kay?"

I knew that voice. I knew that voice! And with a rush of emotion I felt overcome by a deep sense of safety and hope, and yes, love. I didn't need to stifle my sobs.

I cried out. As one who had been lost for a very long time.

"Kay, is that you? My God—what's wrong?" He sounded urgent as he ran through the darkness to the rock; to throw down his bag so he could lean down and put his arms around me. And as he found me, and pulled me into his arms, my heart knew exactly who he was. Of course.

"Luke. It's you."

48

Tuesday, the day after Labor Day

"The baby is due any day now?" Luke asked. He had his back to me, but I could see his crisp Oxford shirt and tie. I could smell the clean scent of the bar soap that he used in the shower. He was sliding eggs from the fry pan onto our breakfast plates, and buttering the toast that had just popped up.

"Hmm," I answered, noncommittally, as I packed our lunches for the day.

I was distracted.

First, by the lights of the school bus that drove down the main road, past the window in Gram's house where Luke and I now lived. The sun hadn't fully come up yet and it was still twilight outside.

I was also nervous and distracted thinking about what was ahead for me. I only hoped I was up for the challenge.

My biggest distraction, however, was the way my shining new diamond wedding band caught the light from the chandelier as I set our steaming coffee mugs onto the dining table. There were many facets, and they were all mesmerizing.

As it turned out, the Chicago Mayne's did have jewelry to go with all of their interests. And happily, Luke Mayne was interested in me—in marrying me! When he arrived in March, he had the ring tucked away in his duffel bag. It didn't stay there for long.

Nan and Sperry had helped him pick it out from the jewelry store they own in Chicago, and Daniel weighed in as well, they all told me afterwards.

Tad had given his blessing on the phone when Luke called him from California. And Luke even spoke with Zeke and June.

It seems that everybody knew Luke's heart and Luke's intentions, before I did.

"But… you let me think you were in Alaska!" I declared shortly after he proposed. "You sent me the weather forecast."

Luke had just smiled, running his thumb along my jawline, then caressing the side of my neck. "I did, didn't I?" And then he said, "but didn't you think 34 degrees was a bit cold for spring? I did, and I chose warmth. I chose love. I chose *us*."

Breaking with local convention, I married Luke during the peak season. It was a simple ceremony at the courthouse, at the beginning of August. Just four weeks ago! At the ages of 35 and 40, we certainly knew our minds and our hearts—we were ready to begin our lives together.

Daniel and Jennifer stood as our witnesses. Patrick and Francine were our guests. Later, the six of us had dinner in a private room at Mitch's, overlooking Lake Michigan.

We opted to defer our reception until the end of September, when we will host an outdoor dinner at the lodge for our family and friends. The area's hottest BBQ restaurant will cater so that Chef James Mauer can come as a guest. Marj Maki will arrange the flowers. And Mitch said he will bake our wedding cake in exchange for a dance with the bride. I happily accepted those terms!

My brother and family are coming, of course. My nieces have never seen Lake Michigan, and I am eager for them to know their heritage. Zeke and June will be back from their trip and plan on being here. I can hardly wait for them to see all that we have done to the inn.

And Daniel and Francine will be here, along with Nan and Sperry Mayne.

I blocked all the rooms and cabins for that weekend. And thanks to Daniel's connections, there will be a writer and photographer attending from a Midwest magazine. They'll be taking exclusive photos for their *Destination Wedding* issue.

After the courthouse ceremony, I moved my clothes out of the lodge apartment, and Luke moved his suitcase out of the guestroom where he'd been staying all summer—the one Daniel had spent the winter in. Together, we settled into the house by the road so that Luke Mayne, the town's new middle school vice principal, will have no problems getting to his job during the long, snowy winter.

It will also be better for me to live closer to the main road, as I have places to go now too. And not on the back of a snowmobile.

As for the future of Kerby Lodge as a resort, my brother-in-law, along with Francine, has agreed to remain in the apartment for the already booked fall color season, and act as hosts. She wants to write about the innkeeper lifestyle for her blog.

And Daniel promised he'd be friendly to guests—at least as friendly as I was, he said.

He has been enjoying the positive press he's received ever since the Kerby Lodge refresh, and is fielding his options. In addition to a few branding projects he's working on with Jack and Stace Wildberry, several former business contacts have asked him to creative direct and consult on various assignments.

He is starting to catch a vision for a different kind of future, one where he has more control. I enjoy seeing a wiser and more confident Daniel emerging. He's taking on the world of design once again, and looking at work and life through a more thoughtful lens.

My relationship with Daniel has changed, obviously. I love him like a brother, which he has become. And he comes and goes in between projects, which is perfect. I once told Jennifer that he is really great in small doses, and that's still true to some extent. But there will always be a place for Daniel at Kerby Lodge—whenever he can make it home.

On one of Daniel's return visits this summer, we had a rare moment together in the great room, on a chilly morning. Just the two of us. He was sitting in the wing chair by the fire, and I brought him a steaming cup of coffee.

"Just like old times," he said, smiling.

"Daniel," I ventured after a few minutes of comfortable silence, "when was it, exactly, that you decided to help me save Kerby Lodge?"

He looked at me for a long time before answering.

"When you said that you were sorry for leaving a rickety chair in the A-Frame," he said.

"I didn't think you even heard me," I said, surprised.

"Oh I heard you," he said.

And after clearing his throat a time or two, he went on to say that nobody had ever apologized to him before, for anything. And that there was so much power in that simple declaration, that he decided to try it on for size. And just then, Francine had walked in with her own coffee, and took his hand as she smiled at me.

At October's end, Luke and I plan on enlisting Red and his team of "Red-eye" professionals. Together, we'll properly winterize the lodge, which will then remain unoccupied until spring. It will be a first for Kerby Lodge. Just one more first of many.

Luke and I will run the inn together for at least one more summer, before deciding whether or not to sell the property—which is slowly increasing in value again. While Daniel and I had gotten the phones to ring this past peak season, I know that there are expensive repairs on the horizon that threaten to offset my additional earnings. But my husband and I will discuss the pros and cons at length over the winter, and then decide what is best for our family.

In the meantime, we have a lot to look forward to—Luke's new job, a wedding party, and two weeks in Savannah and Atlanta with my brother's family over Christmas break.

Luke came around the table and gave me a kiss on the forehead as he placed my breakfast in front of me. "A million miles away?"

I smiled. "You were asking about the baby—yes, due any day now."

Luke nodded, sipping his coffee and dunking his toast.

"And Rhonda Ellis is hoping she has a girl this time," I said, as I ate. "She is officially starting her maternity leave today. I will be subbing in her fourth-grade class for twelve weeks or longer—maybe even until the December break," I continued. "I just hope I'm up to it!"

I was happy that the town schools were adjacent to each other, and that the two of us would be riding together to and from work.

"You'll be great, Kaker Mayne," Luke grinned. "Now let's get going. I just love the first day of school, don't you?"

Kaker Mayne. That has a nice ring to it, I realized, looking once again at my left hand.

As Luke gathered up his sunglasses, backpack, and car keys, I turned off the lights and threw my new leather tote over my arm. Before heading through the door, I stopped at the coat hooks—grabbing my buttery soft sweater, and my husband's jacket.

"Shoulder season," I whispered to myself, and pulled the door closed behind me.

The End

Return to Kerby Lodge
in this preview of **Water Dance**
the sequel to **Shoulder Season**

Lake Michigan Lodge Story #2

Water Dance

A Lake Michigan Lodge Story

1

"Merci beaucoup, *Señor*," I said to Luke.

Luke set a warm cup of Swiss chocolate on the desk in our hotel room where I was sitting, then went to lie down on the bed. I heard him plumping the downy pillows to lean against, and pictured his long, tanned legs stretched out on the luxury linens.

He said, "that's *Monsieur* to you *Madame*, Danke Schön."

I smiled.

One of the many things I had come to love about my husband was his sense of humor. He may not always laugh at my jokes (though mostly he did) but I didn't have to explain myself. It was such a relief.

I knew he wanted the two of us to share the setting sun one last time, as it sank behind the spectacular Matterhorn. We'd be leaving for home in the morning.

After an exhilarating day of hiking along alpine lakes and wildflowers, I fell into our cool room late this afternoon and let the deep bathtub soak away all the aches in my muscles. Luke called the dining room and asked for our dinner to be sent up.

Now, I was so relaxed, I could barely lift a pen to achieve my last task of the day—of the trip—writing a promised postcard to Aunt June in Florida.

For three glorious July weeks, we had been touring the northern region of Spain, France, and now Switzerland, by way of Austria. Several countries, and many languages. This deferred honeymoon had been one magical day after the next, and well worth the eleven month wait.

"Spain was lovely," I said, reading out loud as I wrote. "The Bay of Biscay had islands that resembled castles. Luke and I explored caves, and medieval Spanish villages."

"You're missing the sunset," Luke said.

"We got lucky in the Provence region of France," I continued, "the lavender fields were in full bloom, filling the air with a delightful *parfumé.*"

"How big is that postcard?"

I smiled.

"You know," Luke said, "you'll be back in a few days and you can call your aunt."

"I'll do that too," I countered, and continued writing.

"Luke and I walked the cobbled streets of Old Town in Saint-Tropez," I said as I wrote, "and found a delicious patisserie."

"It's just a little card, not a journal," he said.

I nodded.

I had tried to write a journal of our trip. But it was too much repetition.

> *Breakfast in France, croissants and marmalade.*
> *Breakfast in Spain, churros and chocolate.*
> *Breakfast in Switzerland, muesli and hard cheese.*

Eventually, I decided this particular history need not be recorded—my snug waistband was document enough. I was a walking exhibition, titled: *American Devours Europe.*

That's the trouble with historical records—if you have time to do it, you record the mundane. And when something exciting is happening, there's no time.

I always wished my parents kept a journal, so I could have some insight and historical reference as I tried to fill their larger-than-life shoes, running their beloved Kerby Lodge on Lake Michigan. But they would have been too busy during the peak seasons and there was nothing to write about during the shoulder seasons and frigid winters.

Still, I longed to see their handwriting, and hear about their guests.

I was a hypocrite. I couldn't be faithful to a diary, even while on vacation. I had wanted to stay in the moment with Luke, instead. I've spent too many years living in the past. Mourning the loss of my parents.

But at least I could keep my word, and write one little postcard, couldn't I?

As I gazed out the window at the tiny Swiss village of Zermatt, I smiled to see lights coming on, twinkling throughout the town and dotting the hillside. The ancient cities and ruins of the towns we visited were unlike anything I'd ever experienced—Luke and I were small specks in the timeline of the world.

Yet here we were. Looking out at the highest mountains in Europe, church spires rising between us and the hills.

"Here, let me help you with that," Luke said, coming over behind me where I sat at the desk. He first kissed my neck, and then the side of my face—which was warmed by the desk lamp. When he turned the little lamp off, the setting sun cast us both in a golden glow.

"Having a wonderful time. Wish you were here," he said, softly into my ear.

"You wish they were here?" I turned to smile up at Luke, who was no longer looking at the Matterhorn, but at me. As if I were infinitely more mesmerizing than this cathedral-like glacier, frosted with snow and now deep in shadows.

"No," Luke said, gently setting the pen down and taking my hand, which he then used to pull me towards the deep bank of pillows.

"I wish *you* were *here*."

A day later, sleeping against the cold airplane window, I dreamed of those thick downy pillows. Like a puppet on a string, my head now lolled over onto an anemic travel ring propped around my neck.

It could barely support my head and cloud of unruly red waves. But at least it absorbed the thin stream of drool traveling from my open mouth.

After landing, I'd pop this pillow in the nearest bin, I decided.

It had served bravely overseas—during several flights, countless train rides, and one tour of duty on an Alpen bus that piped in the *Sound of Music*, while taking us to the gazebo where Liesl and Rolf had danced to *I am Sixteen Going on Seventeen*.

Removing my eye mask, I could see that Luke was putting his seat upright, and gathering his headphones and newspaper into his backpack. We were getting ready to land in the U.S., I realized, and forced myself to wake up.

It was late here at home—the middle of the night. As we descended, I opened the window shade and looked at the barren roads and sleepy neighborhoods.

Minutes later, taxiing to a gate, I could hear the *ding dinging* of phones throughout the cabin as they reconnected with the network—my own included. People around me began calling loved ones to say they had arrived. Others opened their phones and sent texts. Still others scrolled through their email, and checked the weather.

In my own backpack, my phone was *dinging* as it loaded three weeks' worth of unread messages. On the first night of our trip, Luke had shoved both our phones to the bottom of our mesh laundry bag. We only fished them out as we packed to come home.

Before we left I gave our itinerary to our college intern, Hollis Fanning, and my trusted friend Jennifer, who regularly came to the lodge to manage her repurposed furniture store located in the lodge's former carriage house.

"Call our hotel for any reason," I said, and they agreed.

Since I hadn't heard a peep, I assumed all was well at Kerby Lodge. But the dinging texts from Hollis now told a different, alarming story. My gasps cut through the white noise of the idling airplane, and Luke looked over at me as I stared at my phone.

"What is it?" he said, "is everyone okay?"

"I think so," I managed to say.

"Is it the lodge? What's going on?" he asked.

I couldn't speak for a moment. Finally, I looked over at Luke.

"There was a fire…" I said.

"A fire!" he said in alarm.

"And a flood…" I continued, looking up at his shocked face.

Luke was mute, staring at me with his mouth open.

"And an accident," I said.

Luke held his hand out for my phone, so he could read the messages himself.

Now trembling, I was glad to have a husband by my side who would be strong and comforting, and help me through the tragedies that had befallen my lodge while I was away.

"All that's missing is the plague of locusts," Luke said.

Look for Water Dance in late 2019

From the Author:

Thank you for reading *Shoulder Season*

I hope you enjoyed reading about the renovation and redemption of Kerby Lodge, Kay, Daniel and Luke as much as I enjoyed writing it. As I'm sure you know, reviews are the life blood of any author, so if you're inclined, I'd appreciate it if you could take a few minutes and leave a review.

More adventures at Kerby Lodge are coming soon!

Are you ready to dip your toe into the cool waters of a Lake Michigan summer? For Kay and Kerby Lodge, peak season is just around the corner—and so is the sequel to *Shoulder Season*. The next Lake Michigan Lodge Story will be out in late 2019. In the meantime, reach out to me at kathy@kathyfawcett.com and visit kathyfawcett.com for updates, and to read my thoughts on writing, life and renovation.

Now available – official Kerby Lodge gear!

Now you can take home a souvenir of your time at Kerby Lodge, just like Kay's guests in *Shoulder Season*. Tee shirts, long sleeved tees, sweat shirts, hoodies and more. Check them out at <u>kathyfawcett.com</u>.

About Kathy Fawcett, author of *Shoulder Season*

My characters are flawed optimists who approach life with energy and wit. Like me, they believe it's never too late to live an amazing life, in spite of life's bumps and challenges. With stories set in the surf, sand and snow of charming Lake Michigan towns, I hope you will cheer for these true life underdogs and smile warmly at the observations and inner dialogue of characters who should never be underestimated. Some background: I've lived and worked in Michigan most of my life as an advertising writer. I met and married my husband Steve while students at Northern Michigan University, and together with our quirky cat Sam we now reside in Western Michigan.

CPSIA information can be obtained
at www.ICGtesting.com
Printed in the USA
LVHW101328030521
686339LV00005B/31